# Other Titles by Susie Bright

*Three Kinds of Asking for It (editor)*

*Three the Hard Way (editor)*

*Mommy's Little Girl: Susie Bright on Sex, Motherhood, Porn, and Cherry Pie*

*The Best American Erotica, 1993–2006 (editor)*

*How to Write a Dirty Story*

*Full Exposure*

*The Sexual State of the Union*

*Nothing but the Girl (with Jill Posener)*

*Herotica, 1, 2, and 3 (editor)*

*Sexwise*

*Susie Bright's Sexual Reality: A Virtual Sex World Reader*

*Susie Sexpert's Lesbian Sex World*

http://www.susiebright.com

# The Best American Erotica 2006

edited by

## Susie Bright

A Touchstone Book
Published by Simon & Schuster
New York   London   Toronto   Sydney

TOUCHSTONE
Rockefeller Center
1230 Avenue of the Americas
New York, NY 10020

TOUCHSTONE and colophon are registered trademarks
of Simon & Schuster, Inc.

For information regarding special discounts for bulk purchases,
please contact Simon & Schuster Special Sales at 1-800-456-6798
or business@simonandschuster.com

Designed by Carla Jayne Little

Manufactured in the United States of America

1   3   5   7   9   10   8   6   4   2

ISBN-13: 978-0-7432-5852-4
ISBN-10:      0-7432-5852-5

# Contents

# Introduction
## After Andrea

The week I put this edition of *The Best American Erotica 2006* to bed, Andrea Dworkin died.

There was a time—when I started editing and encouraging erotica writers—that Andrea Dworkin's name would have inevitably been brought up in the first ten minutes of any conversation. Nowadays, I realize that I might have to explain who she was, due to the speed of American historical amnesia.

Andrea Dworkin was an influential political activist and writer, and was so charismatic that she molded a generation of attitudes toward sexual expression. She particularly dissected the image of women in literature, media, and pornography, where she saw it as evidence that our culture thrived on violence toward women as a gender, and humiliation of them. She didn't think sexism was naughty-cute—she found it deadly, and culpable.

As far as she was concerned, "erotica" could go fuck itself. It was just a prettied-up word for pernicious and patriarchal pornography. Yes, she was that blunt. One of the great whammies of Dworkin's antiporn rhetoric was that she used the most visceral pornographic language to describe and condemn her nemeses. Like Pandora, she invited every woman she encountered to open the lid of sexual magazines, books, and movies, and take a hard look at what came out.

The problem was, we did—and many of us came to different, or at least more nuanced, conclusions than Andrea. The day after she died, I wrote in my blog:

> Dworkin used her considerable intellectual powers to analyze pornography, which was something that no one had done before. No one. The men who made porn didn't. Porn was like a low-culture joke before the feminist revolution kicked its ass. It was beneath discussion.
>
> Here's the irony . . . every single woman who *pioneered* the sexual revolution, every erotic-feminist-bad-girl-and-proud-of-it-stiletto-shitkicker, was once a fan of Andrea Dworkin. Until 1984, we all were. She was the one who got us looking at porn with a critical eye; she made you feel like you could just stomp into the adult bookstore and seize everything for inspection and a bonfire.
>
> The funny thing that happened on the way to the X-Rated Sex Palace was that some of us came to different conclusions than Ms. Dworkin. We saw the sexism of the porn business . . . but we also saw some intriguing possibilities and amazing maverick spirit. We said, "What if we made something that reflected our politics and values, but was just as sexually bold?"

I remember walking into an old-fashioned "Adults Only" store in 1977 when I was nineteen years old. I was there (with an older female friend holding my trembling hand) on assignment from my college women's studies class, where we had been told to take a firsthand look at some "pornography," and write an analysis.

I thought I was going to throw up. First of all, the store smelled like stale smoke and chlorine. There was a surreal display of fishing and hunting magazines up front, which I later learned was part of a local zoning requirement to keep the business open as a "legitimate" retailer. Next to the glossy covers of giant salmon, there was a title called "Lactating Lesbians."

I was horrified. I was fascinated. I *had* to open that magazine, the way kids have to stick beans up their nose.

It was so easy to feel guilty, like an outsider, like a pervert of the first water. I realized right away that I had deeper reactions than what Dworkin had prescribed. I was ashamed to be seen as interested in sex. I was shocked to realize I'd never seen a woman express milk, even in wholesome circumstances. I felt concern for the models of the magazine, who I imagined must be desperate to pose for such pathetic photos. I was paranoid, wondering how many men came into this enclave, and whether this was what every man was thinking about—morning, noon, and night. Then I came back to the same bit about how much I privately thought about sex myself. I couldn't get out of that store fast enough, and I'm sure my resultant essay was something along the lines of: "This is sick, sick, sick."

Driving home, I thought about the "classier" erotic literature I had seen on my parents' bookshelves. They had elegant photo albums of the Khajuraho temples, formerly banned copies of *Lady Chatterley's Lover*, and volumes by Henry Miller. I remember his passages in *The Tropic of Capricorn* about "The Land of Cunt." Miller was so prejudiced in every aspect you had to wonder if he was a misanthrope. But he was also transcendent and lyrical on this subject of cunt, and his absolute submission to it. His words were poetic and a turn-on, and I wondered, Is this erotica? If I was a "lactating lesbian," could I write something about my breasts and my sexual feelings that would be authentic, that would inspire as much integrity as arousal?

I wasn't the only one wondering. So many women, and men, at the time, were determined to make sexual liberation their own, rather than a marketing device or a punch line at someone else's expense. That was the mainstream media's portrayal, certainly, but they were clearly out of the loop. It was already quite in vogue to laugh at women for going braless or taking birth control pills, as if the joke was on them—that they could only be exploited for their trampy ways, never in charge of their sexual destiny.

I resented that depiction; it played right into the hands of Dworkin's steadfast acolytes, who wanted every pornographer in a pine box or behind bars. In their view, the sexually outspoken woman was a dupe, a tragic victim, or a Judas. They thrived on these black-and-white distinctions, much like religious fundamentalists. If erotic creativity was doomed in a sexist world, if equality in the bedroom was impossible until "after the revolution," it didn't give you much room to breathe. They treated sexuality like a decadent, soul-sucking luxury that could be deconstructed with abstention.

But what if we start with the premise that sexuality is an integral part of human nature? Let's compare sex with another appetite: eating. There's no doubt that our food and water supply is compromised, and causes us no end of health problems, as well as screwed-up notions of what's good or bad for us.

Do we begin fasting; do we reject the planting season? Of course not. Many of us eat, shop, and cook as judiciously as we can. Many of us influence public life to promote sound practices in producing, consuming, and enjoying our food. The organics movement, for one, wouldn't exist without this change in consciousness.

Erotic artists and innovators have refused to treat sexual relations as expendable, or desire as a hopeless ruin. In our efforts, we have turned a lot of stereotypical conventions of pornography upside down.

The first revolution was self-definition. When I began writing and editing erotica, it was shocking for women to write about their sexual lives. We were delighted to kick the door down. The Lactating Lesbian pushed her phony proxy into a ditch and wrote her own damn manifesto.

Men also were anxious to break through the *har-de-har-har* routine of standard male conquest. They wanted to talk about sexual desires that had more substance than braggadocio.

Another sea change was the notion of "Who can be sexy?" Dworkin and her peers claimed that if you were old, fat, hairy, disabled, or nonsymmetrical in any way, you were eliminated from the porno casting call. Ironically, this had never really been the case with hard-core porn, for which producers were not that picky—but it is certainly true in Hollywood and high fashion.

The 1980s erotic renaissance changed that picture for good. Just looking at the material in this collection of *BAE*, I'm aware that there are characters of every age and appearance, every circumstance, who are the heroes of their erotic story lines. They are desirable and they desire; even when they aren't fulfilled, they are not pathetic. Erotic writing has been the cutting edge of positive body self-image; I've grown accustomed to it. The conformist appearances promoted by celebrity media are the ones that seem strange and out of touch.

Looking back on it, re-creating sexy bodies was the easy part. The more complicated flavor of the sexual revolution is how we advanced the discussion of power, dominance, and submission in our erotic imagination.

Once again, the public conversation evolved because of our personal observations. We started to confess our questions to ourselves, and then to our intimates. It seemed odd that an individual could be a paragon of social justice and equality during the day, but at night dream of pirates and wenches, tops and bottoms, hellcats and quivering flowers. We didn't want to be hypocrites; we didn't want to be closet cases. We wanted to let the erotic fur fly, but we didn't want to damage anyone: was it possible? We craved some psychological depth, not just wonky literal translation: "You want to be spanked because you are brainwashed by the patriarchy to think you are evil and must deserve abuse—Beep."

To accept the Dworkin orthodoxy, all fantasy, all dreaming, all whimsy, all wishing was wicked. But she forgot that she had let Hope out of the box, too, and no one else has been willing to let go of that.

When S/M activists began to use the terms "safe/sane/consensual," it didn't make a lot of sense to Dworkin's followers, who saw the whole scene as straight out of the *Inferno*. However, it was just the ticket for people who said, "Look, I'm not crazy or dangerous, but I am a lover who thrives on risk, sensation, and taboo."

Naturally, the themes of erotic power and conflict make for great drama and theater—that's why you see more S/M in fiction than you do in real life. It is all of our comedy and tragedy writ large. Even people who will never give up their vanilla tastes can still be aroused by explosive erotic stories, where our most anxious taboos are steadily squeezed into erotic juice.

That's the nature of sexual creativity: it just won't sit at the beach and watch a sunset without a reverie, without complicated feelings coloring the sky. To quote the Dude, "There's a lot of in's, a lot of out's, a lot of what-have-you's."

Dworkin's rebels, my compatriots, reminded me of the Ban-the-Bomb movement. The men who coined that term were the very scientists who had helped *build* the nuclear bomb. Yet when they saw how it was used, in Hiroshima and Nagasaki, they spent the rest of their lives in pursuit of nonviolence.

The erotic rebels were similar—we thought we had an effective way to abolish sexism forever, we thought that if you eliminated the

XXX, you eliminated a root cause. But once we deployed our theories, we were dismayed, to say the least. It wasn't liberating; it was disastrous. Who was going to be demolished next? There had to be a more positive way to address the sexual battlefield. Our army of lovers came into play.

We thought that sex itself had great possibilities, and that the creative erotic mind was a terrible thing to waste. There was no reason why we couldn't invent sexual speech on our own terms, turn the gender game upside down, and give the status quo a run for its money. We needed only the nerve, and the means, to distribute our courage.

Nowadays, there are still anti-erotic critics who sneer, "And what did your 'leatherette revolution' come to? Bimbos in bikinis selling cars with a sexual come-on, appended with the declaration that they're 'empowered'? Give me a break!"

That kind of advertising is the unfortunate marketing result of every counterculture movement. My stomach turns when I hear my favorite rock 'n' roll riff used to sell that same car, but I'm not going to say that the sixties music revolution was for naught. Madison Avenue is parasitical, and it will gravitate toward anything that might appeal to the zeitgeist. They are *not* the originators, and they are not the last word.

I wonder how many of the authors in this collection would say they were directly influenced by Andrea Dworkin. How many were inspired to roll their own after sampling her wares? I look at their names and see at least half of them who would say, "Oh yes, I remember the days." Some of us remember rather vividly being on the wrong end of the firing squad when we first defied her.

One young woman who wrote to my blog after I posted my eulogy thought I was exaggerating the bad old days for glorious effect: "That bit about staunch radical feminists later finding their Happy Hooker side strikes me as PR fluff."

Public relations? For whom? To defy the Dworkin/MacKinnon

feminist theology in the late 1970s and '80s was to become a pariah—and to wonder if you had given up your entire community to make a point about sex that you weren't even quite sure of. . . .

We knew only that to say nothing was to become a hypocrite and abuser like the very ones we were determined to overcome. To foreswear the positive power of sexuality, to put erotic creation up on the shelf, was unhealthy. It self-destructs. That's why the very phrase "sex-positive" came into the vocabulary—such a strange hyphenated word, and one easy to make fun of. But sex-positive artists speak to the attitude that without lifting a finger, sexuality will inevitably be portrayed in a shameful, prudish, and vindictive fashion, a place where lust and desire will always point to harm, will always do you in. Dworkin's agenda took her from the poetry and incandescence of erotic possibility and became entrenched in a view as fundamentally sex-negative as that of any of her patriarchal enemies.

I'm sorry Andrea Dworkin started a sexual revolution that she ended up repudiating. She never came to understand people like me and the rest of her protégées, who were inspired by her to question authority, to fly to a new dimension. I read the stories in this volume by authors who reveal sexual intention in every aspect, who voice what is felt but so often hidden, and I know my appetite is going to grow only wiser.

Susie Bright
Valentine's Day, 2006

# The Best
# American
# **Erotica**
## 2006

# Coyote Woman Discovers Email

## Gaea Yudron

One day Coyote Woman discovered email.
Nobody knows exactly how it happened,
her making the bridge from the old times to now,
or even figuring out how to turn the computer on
but suddenly there she was
with her nose pressed to the screen.

As fortune had it,
one of the first emails that she read said
Hypnotize women to your bed!
Hypnotize women to your bed!
And the next one said
Add 3–4 inches overnight—
It's guaranteed!
All you need and MORE

You'll be rock hard all night long!
You will exceed
all known records AND
Your dick will drag on the floor!
Your dick will drag on the floor!
Your dick will truly drag
all along the floor. . . .

First Coyote Woman blinked her eyes
then she rolled her eyes
all around in her head
and then she took her eyes out
and juggled them
the way some people bite their nails
or shake their legs
or shed their skin
when something makes them nervous.

Finally, Coyote Woman put her eyes back in her head
and she just howled and howled. She howled so hard
That she changed into Coyote Man.

Coyote Man laughed so hard
that his immense interminable,
unconfined and mythic member
snaked out into the universe.

He howled and laughed,
and his thang made a path up high in the sky,
snaking way out over the West Coast
and plunging deep into the waters of the Pacific
where he had various adventures
with voluptuous undersea maidens.

Whew, he had a great time,
but that is another story entirely.

The first thing that Coyote Man did when he returned
was to turn off the computer.
"This technology stuff is definitely overrated,"
he thought to himself. And after resting
for a while on the beach in the sun
he just naturally changed back into Coyote Woman.

Now things are back to so-called normal.
Coyote Woman is wandering
as she always has between the worlds
real imaginary interplanetary
vibrational situational metamolecular frissonary
electronic polyphonic and also places that
have not yet been charted in plain language.

You might never see her in your lifetime,
but then again it's possible that
she's juggling her mythic marbles
somewhere nearby. So watch out, people!
She might be disguised as a bird on the fly.
You never know with her.

And I'll never believe she gave up email.
In fact, she could be emailing you right now.
When she takes a liking to you,
it would be just like her
to feed your computer strangely delicious cookies,
play gypsy music and tango with your broadband,
invite your hard drive to relax,
saying, you won't lose anything if you take a break,

you won't lose anything. She will tell you that.
She will write email poetry that changes your software,
appear in your dreams wearing a yellow polka dot dress
with a tray of fruit and flowers on her head.

If she has her way, you will turn off your computer and howl a bit.
That much being said, good luck, amigo.
And in your mess rejoice. Toast this good bread.
Let down your hair. Give voice to el hombre mítico.

# Every Good Boy Deserves Favors

## L. Elise Bland

When I learned to read music notation, two phrases were drilled into my head: "Every Good Boy Deserves Favors" (E, G, B, D, F) and "Good Boys Deserve Fudge Always" (G, B, D, F, A). I understood the mnemonic devices with the letters and notes, but I wanted to know the rest of the story; if good boys deserved favors and fudge with their piano lessons, then what did bad boys deserve? Later in life, I learned that bad boys deserved spankings—and that being bad was not always a bad thing.

Once I became a piano teacher, I amassed my own entourage of "boy" students. Most were good, but some were decidedly bad. My favorite naughty student, Vito, was a New Jersey Italian-American living in the Deep South. His foreign looks and Yankee street talk made him an oddity in our parts, but he managed to find his niche in the local music scene.

Vito had been playing bass guitar for years, but he didn't

know a lick of written music. He signed up for piano lessons to learn to read and compose, and also to get a feel for the classics. Unfortunately, the only classics he wanted to learn were classic rock anthems. For his sight-reading piece, he picked my all-time least favorite song, "Stairway to Heaven." To make matters worse, Vito always botched the song. His rendition dragged on and on, peppered with painful mistakes and awkward pauses. Had it not been for the mischievous look in his eye, his crazy accent, and his pouty Italian lips, I would have dropped him after the first week.

One Saturday afternoon, Vito plunked away at my old upright, his sinewy guitar muscles rippling under the skin of his tan arms as he fumbled through his version of "Stairway to Heaven." His body was fine-tuned, but his piano technique was all wrong.

"This sounds more like a dog food commercial than 'Stairway to Heaven,'" I scolded. "You didn't practice at all this week, did you? I thought you said you wanted to learn."

"I do. I do," he said in his deep voice. "I just get sidetracked sometimes."

I wanted to reprimand him like I did my other students, but I felt silly since he was practically my age. Besides, it wasn't his parents' money he was wasting; it was his own. Vito was one of those students who liked the idea of piano lessons more than the actual work. He never practiced; he never paid attention; and he had the worst habit of staring and flirting during our lessons. I was partly to blame, too.

Since I had taken Vito on as a student, I found myself worrying more about my teaching outfit than my lesson plan. In fact, I spent all week deciding what I would wear for him. Something sexy? Casual? Or even severe? I didn't want to look like I was trying too hard, but somehow I always ended up in a push-up bra and a miniskirt with no panties on the day of Vito's lesson.

"Okay, let's get back to basics then," I told Vito. "Name the notes for the lines of the treble clef. I'll give you a hint. There are five of them."

"A, B, C, D, E," he spouted out immediately.

"You aren't even trying. Don't you remember what I told you last week? E, G, B, D, F—Every Good Boy Deserves Favors. Repeat after me." I got up in his face and mouthed the words. His soft lips mirrored mine. For a second, I thought he might kiss me. He was so close, I could smell his fresh shampoo and his toothpaste.

"And what are the lines of the bass clef?" I asked quickly, avoiding an awkward moment.

"E, G, B, D, F?"

*Wrong again!*

"G, B, D, F, A—Good Boys Deserve Fudge Always."

"I like favors more than fudge," he told me, staring blatantly at my chest and chuckling. "Got any for me?"

"You're starting to bother me with your juvenile nonsense," I said, trying my best to stay in teacher mode. "I come from a family of both musicians and disciplinarians. You are a lucky boy. Back when I had lessons, my teacher would sit next to me at the piano. Whenever I missed a note, she took a ruler to my knuckles."

Vito laughed nervously.

"It's not funny. I got a whupping during my lessons and there's no reason you shouldn't have the same. Except knuckles are no fun to hit. I think the fleshier parts of the body take punishment the best."

He shifted around on the cushy bench as I moved my hand towards his lower back. "Why don't we play a game," I said, toying with his belt. "Next time you make a mistake on 'Stairway to Heaven,' I'll give you a swat, but not on your knuckles—on your ass!"

He looked back at me over his shoulder and grinned, as if it were all a joke, but it wasn't. He didn't know that I was quite well

versed in the corporal arts. Over the years, I had developed a
mean spanking hand and a sharp cane stroke. I didn't make a habit
of punishing my students—just my boyfriends—but Vito was an
exception.

"You can't spank me if I'm sitting down," he told me.

Did he really think that such a minor detail would stop me?

"Don't worry," I said. "You aren't going to be sitting down.
Stand right here behind the bench and lean over so you can touch
the keys." He obeyed. I reached around his waist and unbuckled
his belt. Vito always pretended to be laid-back, but this time he
was really scared. I could feel his body trembling under mine.
Still, he wasn't too nervous to be excited. By the time his pants
and Jockeys hit the floor, his cock was already hard.

"Play," I ordered, ignoring his obvious erection.

With his hands reaching awkwardly over the keyboard, he
started the song. In no time, he missed a note. I swung my arm
back and gave him a loud, stinging slap on the ass. A bright red
handprint emerged on his butt cheek.

"Hey, that hurt!" he said.

"If it hurt so bad, then why do you have a hard-on?" I reached
around him and stroked what I had pretended not to notice before. It felt slender, firm, and smooth. He had such a nice cock,
but he played the worst piano I had ever heard. He couldn't go
one measure without faltering, and he had to be punished. For his
many errors, Vito received an entire symphony's worth of
smacks—fast, slow, loud, soft, dolce, andante, allegro, fortissimo,
and, of course, con brio. He rushed through the piece to escape
my spankings, but his haste only created more mistakes and more
spanking.

Finally, his torturous recital was over. "Maybe I'll take you for a
little ride now," I said. Vito's cock, which had relaxed some during
the heavy spanking, sprang right back into place. "No, not that
kind of ride," I said. "Lie down on the bench, on your stomach.

I'm not done with your spanking yet." I climbed on top of him in the "backwards horseback" position—my favorite for double-handed spanking. Two hands meant twice the spanking, twice the intensity, and twice the pain. As soon as the first slaps rang out, Vito began to wiggle and jump in between my legs, and I'll have to say, I enjoyed it. I rode Vito like a mechanical bull with my legs clamped around his sides and my pussy pressed into his back. The more I spanked, the more he bounced, and the more he bounced, the wetter I got. I thought I was going to come all over his back just from the grinding alone. I didn't slow down until I was out of breath.

"Can I please go home now?" he joked, reaching around to survey the heat on his skin. "I need to practice my 'Stairway to Heaven.' "

It was easy to forget about lessons when I was having so much fun spanking, but the very mention of that dreaded song hurled me right back into music teacher mode. I got off and towered over him. "Do you really think I'm going to let you butcher that song again today?" I asked. "How can you sight-read if you're musically illiterate? You're not touching that piano again until you know your basic theory."

Vito liked to push the envelope, but I had a solution for his sass. Back in college, I had taken a class in conducting and had a small collection of conductor's batons next to the piano. Most were short, with cork nubs on one end to steady the grip, but I had one that was longer—over a foot long—with a black rubber handle and a thin, sturdy plastic shaft. I held it in my right hand and swatted my left to test it out. A sharp, stinging sensation blossomed in my palm.

*Perfect*, I thought, eyeing my student, who was still draped over the piano bench. I sliced the baton through the air a couple of times to let him know I meant business. With each loud woosh, his butt cheeks clenched up in fear and anticipation.

"Calm down, silly," I told him, patting his still warm bottom with my hand. "I haven't even started with this implement yet. Now, let's review. Do you remember the line of the treble clef?"

"Sure, teach," he said. "E, G, B, D, F—Every Gay Boy Dresses Funny."

"Oh, how clever. So I have a little smart-ass on my bench? In the South, we don't put up with backtalk like that. You're in for it now, boy. Repeat after me—E." I reared back with the baton and gave him my best stinging cane stroke.

"Ow!"

"No, not ow. E. And what does E stand for?"

"Every," he mumbled. By that time, a delicious red welt had formed at the top of his buttocks. I traced the firm, hot band of flesh with my baton.

"And what comes after E? Let me give you a hint. It's not 'Gay.' "

"G—Good." At least he was finally cooperating. Another blow of the baton blazed across his skin.

"And B is for?"

"Boy," he answered. And what a fine boy he was. He definitely had a submissive side.

"And every good boy . . . ? Come on now. Finish the sentence. I won't hurt you too bad, I promise."

"Deserves favors," he panted. With the final words, I administered two wicked strokes of the baton—one right at the curve of his butt, and the other smack dab in the middle of the infamous sweet spot.

"Much better. If boys want favors, they have to do things my way. Stand up so I can see."

I stepped back to admire my work. My student now had five perfect red lines across his skin that mirrored a clef. I squatted down on the floor and ran my hands over the ridges on his roasted bottom. "Now can you tell me what these lines stand for one more time?" I whispered, as I grazed his hot cheeks with my palms, my face resting on his thigh. I was inches away from his crotch. I looked over and there was his hard-on hovering right before my eyes. I knew, as a teacher, I was supposed to be in control of my desire, but I was suddenly mesmerized by his cock.

"E—Every, G—Good." As my student recited for me, I did a very un-teacherly thing. I clutched the shaft of his cock and took the glistening head into my mouth. It was smooth and steady, unlike his piano playing. Vito was so surprised that he stopped mid-sentence and looked down. I reached around and smacked his sore butt until he finished reciting.

"B—Boy, D—Deserves, F—Favors," he said, inhaling deeply with each of my strokes.

Vito's flesh bloomed inside my mouth as he guided his cock in and out of my lips. I clutched his cheeks in my hands and worked him over with my tongue, always making sure that a little pain accompanied his pleasure. With one hand on his shaft and the other on his ass, I pumped him, teased him, squeezed him, and sucked him until my eyes watered.

Suddenly, Vito tore off his shirt and began to moan even louder than he had during the spanking. I looked up at him. He was beautiful, with his luscious lips, olive skin, and lean body. He even had a cute little bass clef tattoo that encircled his belly button. He was hotter than I had ever imagined. It was all too much excitement for one day—spanking my new piano student and then sucking him off. Had I lost my mind? I didn't care. I closed my eyes and tightened my lips until he came in jolts in my mouth.

Sucking cock made me unbelievably wet, and spanking made me even hornier. I wanted more. After Vito recovered, I made myself comfortable on the bench and pulled him in for a kiss. I leaned back on the keyboard with my legs slightly parted to show him that I was wearing no panties. "I want to see how talented you really are with your hands," I said. He knelt down low to the floor and caressed my feet, his reddened bottom high in the air. With a determined touch, he made his way slowly up my calves, my knees, thighs, and then into the darkness of my skirt.

"May I?" he asked, looking up at me. His floppy brown hair covered one of his eyes.

"No need to ask permission," I said. "It's an order. Fuck me or else I'll spank you twice as hard next time." I poised myself for action. My lips opened under his hand and soon I felt a firmness welling up inside of me. His fingers were practically as long as the cock I had just had in my mouth, and even more agile. I held on to the frame of the piano while he pressed his hand deep into me.

For some reason, I expected him to be timid after his ass-whooping, but he surprised me with his wild, rhythmic digits. He rocked me back and forth on the cushion of the bench, sometimes nearly lifting me with his fist. I felt like he was pulling an orgasm right out of my body. Just when I thought I couldn't take any more, he lowered his mouth onto my clit. His fingers and tongue battled for my attention until I felt a warmth rushing from my sadistic hands all the way into the depths of my aching pussy. I fell backwards into the keyboard, causing a crash reminiscent of a dissonant Shostakovich piece.

Afterwards we lay on the rug next to the piano. I traced the bass clef tattoo with my finger. "So Vito," I asked him, "If you don't read music, why do you have a bass clef tattoo? I mean, how did you even know what that was before you met me?"

He looked at me, shrugged and smiled.

"It just doesn't make sense that you would know music symbols if you don't read music, much less go get a tattoo of one." Suddenly I realized what he had done. "Do you mean to tell me you were bluffing? All that 'Every Good Boy' stuff? You knew it already?"

Vito turned away from me and rolled onto his stomach laughing, foolishly exposing his bare red behind. I gave him one more big slap for good measure and sent him scooting across the floor.

It turned out Vito didn't need music theory lessons after all, but he sure did need a spanking for tricking me like that. Vito was a bad, bad boy. But he was oh so good, too, and he deserved every favor he got that day.

# The End

## James Williams

They say these are like opinions because everybody has one, but Stevie's was so eloquent as to be a point of fact. More than that, it was the art he built his life around, at least as far as I was concerned. He used to get dressed up every now and then for any and every reason, but he almost always went out on a limb on Friday afternoons, so when I came home from work he'd greet me like some barefoot Chippendale in tuxedo pants and bowtie collar, or a bristly, pneumatic hunk out of Tom of Finland; now and then he'd show up at the door in hot pink deep-cleavage spandex tanktop tights, with or without a crinoline tutu. But whatever seriously grandiose sort of costume Stevie did on any particular day, he never liked to hide his chest.

Stevie's chest was sculpted like a young god's, curved in graceful planetary arches that rose, embracing bridges, crossing mountains, milk-white arabesques of blue-veined marble set between shoulders of monumental granite, tapered to a waist I could easily have held if I had had three hands, rippling like a school of fish in a tidal wave or like a dozen quivering cakes of fresh-baked pudding. His slim hips seemed to fade away from there, which made no sense at all atop his tree-trunk legs, yet there he was: cool and hot, chiseled and cuddly, firm and gentle, sweet and severe, perfectly proportioned like a 1940s cartoon of a he-man: he was my yab-yum, my juicy Lucy, my holy heavenly hunk-o'-honey, and I was the man he loved.

Not to say I didn't love him back, I did, and not just for his physical magnificence; but we always had different agendas. In between those dawn redwood lower limbs he tucked not just a dick as big—to borrow part of Lenny Bruce's famous *mot*—as a baby's arm, but also, right behind, a pair of cheeks like boneless fresh-dressed roasting turkeys. Oh, my: first I think of him as art, then elements of Earth, then in the original noir humorist's imagery, then in metaphors of food. . . . And even if he was never quite simply human to me, food was certainly one of his advertised delights. Those evenings he greeted me in the least elementary drag he also set before me the greatest alimentary delights, which he had prepared, I came to think, in order to watch with fascinated horror the gustatory pleasures I expressed. He brought forth from the kitchen large roasts studded with rare fruits and spices, pungent birds and fish and cutlets grilled crisp on the outside and soft on the in, toothsome grains and roots paired up as if for marriage with amendments made from their own juices, exotic pastel custards, sculpted vegetables intertwined with the opposites they attracted, buttered sauces savory and sweet, pastries puffed and tarts tatin'd; and while I ate he sat before me with his great, bare chest exposed, both massive, muscled breasts tripling the space they occupied whenever he raised his thigh-like arms to sip the steaming bowls of unadulterated, filtered, re-evaporated water he held to his face cupped in his pair of plate-sized hands, watching me through the fog he turned into a misty curtain every time he exhaled.

Food was a stratagem for Stevie, as costume was another, and as his magnificent physique may have even been a third. I'd put nothing past him. And why would anyone as sumptuous as he go to all these troubles for a live-in boyfriend when the troubles themselves would warrant their own worth? Because, I think, of what he really cared for.

Dinner over—or my dinner, anyway, since it has always been hard for me to believe he actually survived on the hot water which was all I ever saw him consume—and the food preparations somehow miraculously dispensed with even before I had come home, Stevie left the dishes for some hour when I was asleep or away, and came to sit in my lap. "Came to sit in my lap" is all the truth of it, but wholly apart from the disparity in our sizes—Stevie towered over me when we both stood, was broad enough to shield me altogether from the sun, and weighed nearly twice what I did—the phrase doesn't begin to convey the dimensions of the fable. When Stevie saw or decided I had finished with my meal he had a slow, salacious way of taking his steam bowl in a single hand and lowering it toward the table surface as if it were a Stanley Kubrick spaceship moving with balletic precision toward its orbiting satellite port: the cream-white cup of buffalo china, or the near-translucent bone of Royal Dalton, or the painted and filigreed low-fired clay of some contemporary artist whose name would be traded for Picasso's in a quick year's time, would start to dance in the embrace of his palm-sized fingers, and the plants along the highboy, decanters in the china cabinet, the glittering crystal chandelier, the dust motes its light shone upon, and the very air itself became the background against which the piece of pottery moved hypnotic. But as I started to imagine I could even hear its music, the cup would softly come to rest on the jacquard tablecloth, and only then might I become aware that I had watched its whole descent, entranced, transfixed, mesmerized, while Stevie watched my captive eyes.

Eyes to eyes Stevie then stood up, transported as if in a single fluid motion from his chair. Considering his size, I found his composure and grace such marvels to behold, there was never a moment in all the time I knew Stevie when I did not think he was well aware of the impression he could not help but make on me. The music I had thought so recently belonged to the floating, dancing, landing spacecraft of his bowl now seemed to occupy his own very specific movements. If he was wearing anything at all above his waist—the bowtie collar, the plunging tanktop, a delicately gaudy rhinestone choker—he next removed that, leading the length of one sinuous arm with a few more rapidly sinuous fingers all waving like leaves on a lengthy stalk of kelp in a languid Pacific lagoon; then he brought the isolated item down to the tabletop as if to land through water, where, effectively, it died. Whatever the piece of costume was it shone on him; and then, apart from Stevie, became just another discarded trifle no one had ever needed. His hands commanded everything as he seemed to let them rove across the landscape of his chest, or fluff his feathered hair, or pluck a nonexistent nothing from before my vacant vision, but they never roved without a destination known and plotted to its last coordinate, and then they moved with just that same sort of certainty to whatever belt or thread of elastic held his bottom clothing up.

I never saw a pair of pants descend as slowly as Stevie's pants descended. It didn't matter if he was letting the crisp black slacks from his tuxedo slide so their bold satin stripe crinkled as it caught the sun- or candlelight, or losing tights he had to peel away like Beulah skinning a summer grape, or pushing his legs free from tattered jeans with holes he could have stepped through, or dropping his drawers like a nighttime bathing suit in the moonshine. First those huge hands and every finger on them would begin to wander as if they were blind and hungry and searching for his waist. Like his hands, of course, his fingers were on a highly coordinated mission from which no force on God's green Earth could make them stray; yet always they seemed to have to seek that lean line out; always they seemed to have to make their ways from some far distant, civilized place across the mountains of his abs, down past the sultry valleys of his folded flesh, over his rivers and through his woods to the vast potential of his hot, humid, cloth-covered wilderness, where, by necessity and by design, they always managed to just stop short.

Some pants have belts and some have not; some have buttons and others do not; some zip and snap, some fold and tie, and some, even if they appear tight to the inexperienced eye, roll down easily as stockings off a close-shaved leg. Stevie let his fingers learn the nature of his pants each time, even if he had taken off the same pair every hour for a month. One finger might examine how the pants stayed up, while another began investigating how the closures worked this time; a third and fourth went off to learn how great was the expanse of pants, while a fifth remained aloof in case there was some call, unlikely as it seemed, to leave the pants in place a little longer.

"A little longer" is a phrase like "came to sit in my lap." A thousand simple words like these could never convey the story any better than a picture could. For Stevie "a little longer" lasted for whatever period of time felt right or otherwise served his purpose to the moment, and the length of a moment itself in which his purpose was served changed like any other chronological demarcation: now a moment was fast as a fleeing drop of mercury skittering away forever down the floorboards of a declined hall, *now* it moved as slowly as a glacier melting at 33°F in a permanently frozen ice field.

As long as Stevie thought he still held my attention: that was how long "a little longer" lasted, and the nature of the pants had less to do with how time moved for him than with what he perceived of my desire. In that way I suppose I might conclude that I was the one who controlled the flow of time, I was the one who determined the length of *now*, I was the one who could decide exactly what "a little longer" meant. But that conclusion would be no more true than it would be true for a person in a car, scouring the densest section of a major metropolis for a single vacant, legal parking space where he could leave his car before a bus prevented him from reaching it, or some delivery van claimed it out from under him, or a utility truck usurped it with a ring of orange cones, or another driver, spinning on a dime, made a sideshow U-turn in front of a dozen Keystone Kops all falling all over their feet to get to lunch, jammed the bumpers fore and aft, and slammed his Hummer into the forlorn formerly compact spot—it would be no more true for me to claim that I decided the length of Stevie's *now* than it would be for that driver to believe that when, after a helpless hour of frustration, tears, and curses, his car skidded and stammered and stopped hopelessly jammed into a pothole from which it could not maybe ever be withdrawn and that happened to be right in front of his destination and that also happened to have a working meter waiting for his coin, he was actually responsible for the miracle: to just such a degree was I the captain of my fate with Stevie.

But like the hapless driver whose reward comes only from the virtue of apparent accident, so in the genuine fullness of time, each time the time would come when Stevie's fingers, for whatever reason, found the switch, popped the button, opened the snap, untied the knot, flipped the zipper, and !! just like that his pants were gone, and in their place there stood revealed to all its splendid sculpted glory the ithyphallic member men and women the wide world over would have fallen to their knees to praise and worship if they only knew they could. Was it like a baby's arm? It was like the cartoon spout of a cartoon sperm whale, rising from the sea floor, sending forth into the world the single source of the nexus lexis plexus of creation. If I had never raised my eyes from what was then displayed I could have been excused. If I had sat still gibbering to my chair no reasonable man could have possibly found my fault. If I had been struck deaf dumb crippled and blind, fallen off my rocker, fallen head over heels, flown to the moon and back, flown on the wings of song, flown with the wings of angels, died and risen from the dead, heard the voice of God and sung duets with Him, no one could have possibly imagined I did anything he would not have done as well. Stevie had a beautiful dick. But he did not care about that at all.

Nor did he care about the Herculean balls he lugged about between those Douglas Fervent thighs he bared when all his pants fell down, though all the blessings, honor, glory, and power that belonged unto his dick most certainly belonged to them as well. But no: for Stevie all his costumes, all his cooking, all the stratagems of his musical, mystical body, all his hypnotizing actions and behaviors, all, all, all for him were nothing more than pre-foreplay, lead-ins to the final final act of finale, the moment when climax changed to dénouement. All of everything he did was meant to lead us to the moment he desired, and wanted to remember.

Sure of my attention and certain I would go nowhere, holding my eyes with his until the entire weight of his turning head had to be precisely balanced on the single soft strand of his twisted spinal cord, slowly, slowly, like a liner out at sea, Stevie turned his monolithic body around in front of me. His skin changed colors to every plane, each plane changed colors to every light, each light illuminated another carefully delineated muscle group and made him seem a holographic poster for the International Child. From his disappearing face in shadow deep below his sinewed neck, from his brawny football shoulders down his curling back and curving hips, from his wide, long thighs to his narrow, exquisite ankles, Stevie turned. He turned his side to me, he turned his back on me, he let me see the ripely rounded melons of his ass and then, only then, he peeked back at me across an abyss that seemed to grow from miles to years as, hopeful, shy, too eager not to let excitement show, he drew his hands back and took a pair of gracious grips on both his high, hard cheeks, bent just slightly at the waist, and millimeter by silly millimeter, spread himself apart.

I slipped off my chair as smooth as ice cream melting down a cone in hot July and threw myself across the scanty space that separated him from me. Kneeling, then, between the columns of his legs, looking up at the beachball he had split apart, gazing through the blood-gauze curtain of his wondrous ball-filled sac to the living room beyond, I was, for these few minutes, king of all I beheld. This was why he'd buffed the body, made the food, worn the drag, studied me so carefully that he could hold me by the eyes while he took it off: so that if I were not yet smitten I would still be made to feel beholden to my fleshy icon, and give him in exchange this one thing he most desired. He thought that he had bought my love, and he felt he'd made a perfect bargain: he amused himself and me, and I rewarded him.

But I—I did not feel that I had paid when he performed his arts for me: instead I felt like a maestro's courted guest. I did not think that I had bought my Stevie's love or that mine had been bought by him, nor did I feel that I rewarded him when I heaved up on his legs and threw him facedown upon the fainting couch and plundered his hot hole with my hungry tongue. Instead I felt I had seduced an idol, taken, for the price of feasting eyes and belly lavishly, what other men would give their hearts to have. I did think we had made a bargain, but I thought the bargain went to me, especially since Stevie never for a single moment did not think the world resembled the precious image he had made of it.

# From *Brass*

## Helen Walsh

## Millie

We turn onto Upper Duke Street and the view sucks the breath from my lungs.

The whole of the city is aglow and the Liver buildings, brightly drenched by the rising moon, reign magnificently in a cloudless sky. I snatch a quick glance to see if she too has been seduced by the vista but the eyes are paralyzed by some chemical excess. She's at least three or four years younger than me—a child in the eyes of the law. Yet she wears the spent constitution of a woman who has lived, breathed and spat these streets out all her life. There's mixed blood in her face too, the dark complexion suggesting the Mediterranean while her narrowed eyes hint of the East. It's a good face—awkwardly composed but pretty nonetheless. It doesn't belong to these streets.

We head down towards the Cathedral which pierces the night like some majestic foreboding, and she lopes off ahead, creating enough distance between us to show we're not together. At the graveyard gates, she swings round and instructs me with the flat of a palm to hold back. I watch her elfin silhouette slide down some steps and, without warning, dissolve into the petrol blue night. I doubt she'll return and I'm pricked with a mild spur of relief. The effects of the beak and the booze are fast ebbing away now and there's elements of the old me lurking in my subconscious, urging me to turn on my heels and flee.

The night spits her back into focus and she's standing before me again. Skinny legs and fat breasts. Coal black hair pulled fiercely into a high pony. I swoon.

She swings an arm in a beckoning arc and I follow, down a flight of uneven steps, through a dark stubby tunnel and out into a sprawling graveyard. For one lucid moment, a spasm of terror jolts my heart as I anticipate what looms ahead; but as we veer down towards the right of the Cathedral which now towers high above us, the brilliance of the moon finds us and all danger is neutralized in the serum of desire. Randomly, she selects a grave, which is located at the remotest corner of the plot. It's flat, wide and practical. She removes her clothes with a routine agility. She's serviced a hundred other punters on this very slab of timeworn concrete though I guess I'm her first female punter.

"I don't do fish," she said in a coarse Toxteth accent. "Norra done 'ting round 'ere girl."

And she was right. I'd scoured these streets, this city, relentlessly in pursuit of brass on many a drug-fueled bender and only twice had I struck lucky. However, once I assured her that *she* didn't actually have to do anything, just remove her clothes, *all* of them, and let me indulge myself, she began to crumble. I produced a fifty and she surrendered.

She lies back and the shock of the slab juts her nipples out and arches her slender back. Her breasts are large and intrusive. At odds with her pubescent framework. She has the hips of a twelve-

year-old. I run a hand across the width of her navel which is hard
and sticky and gleams in the moonlight as if lightly smeared in
Vaseline and lower my mouth to her breasts, sucking hard at her
dark nipples, manipulating them to solid black bullets. Her skin
tastes of stale, salty sweat. Cheap body lotion and spent chemicals.
Pungent and almost unpleasant. It drives me on.

"Look at your tits," I whisper. "Touch them."

She does so, reluctant at first but wanting to be urged on. I slip
an arm around her small back and flick my tongue across her flat
young tummy.

"Do you like that?"

She doesn't answer. I raise my head to find her eyes roaming in
their orbits. Her mouth is slack, lopsided. A stream of spittle trails
her chin. I prod her hard in the navel and she protests with a dila-
tory flinch.

Impatient now, I part her legs which are colored with fresh
bruises. I slide a finger inside. She's dry and stiffens at my touch.
For an instant, I feel I should stop, I should turn on my heels and
run. But as my mouth falls upon her cunt and the smell of rubber
smacks me in the face, I resume my role. Guiltlessly. As a punter.
With a stiff tongue I press down hard on her clit, and with short
purposeful strokes I slowly massage her to life. I feed in another
then another finger, and her resistance gives way to minimal yet
compliant thrusts. My movements become more forceful and her
juices gush freely onto my face. The body arcs upwards and out-
wards and holds up there as she strains against this pleasure.

I slide a hand in my trousers and seek my cunt.

The beak seems to have temporarily robbed its walls of all sensation but my clit swells beneath the clammy nest of my palm. I
manipulate myself hard and selfishly, the whore becoming nothing
but a body. A cunt in a magazine. My climax is powerful but as
soon as those crackling shortwaves subside I'm overwhelmed by
the impulse to abscond. I feel sober and awkward. I remove my

hands from her body; they are lathered in our sweat, and I wipe them on my hips. She props herself up, fuck-faced and shining with the stench of her latest trick, and stares into me. The face is no longer drug dead but wide open with questions. Her eyes stare out, large and frightened, giving me a glimpse of the girl behind the whore. She makes to speak but the words evaporate on her lips. Half of me wants to take her in my arms, the other despises her. Once more I take in the child's eyes, the woman's breasts. I force a valedictory smile and sprint off across the graveyard, spurred on by that unique tingling and euphoria that follows orgasm.

# Under the House

## Lynn Freed

Twice a year, the Sharpener arrived at the top gate, whistled for them to lock up the dogs, and then made his way around the back of the house to the kitchen lawn. Usually, the girl was there first. She squatted like him to see the files and stones laid out in a silent circle, the carving knife taken up, the flash of the blade as he curved his wrist left and right, never missing. And then the gleaming thing laid down on the tray, where she longed to touch it.

If the nanny saw the girl out there, she called her in. The Sharpener was a wild man, she said; he drank cheap brandy and lived under a piece of tin. He could be a Coloured, said her mother, or just dark from working in the sun, and from lawn mower grease, and from not washing properly.

But whenever the girl heard his whistle, she ran out anyway. He never looked up at her. He wasn't the sort of man to notice a child growing year by year, or to care. He seemed to consider only the knives, always choosing the carver first, holding it up to the light, running its edge along the pad of his thumb. When all the

knives were sharpened and he walked around to the front verandah, she followed him there. She waited next to his satchel while
he opened the little door and climbed down under the house to
fetch the lawn mower.

And then one day she asked, "What do you do under the
house?"

And he stopped on the top step and turned to look at her with
his dirty green eyes. He didn't smile, he never smiled. But he
tossed his head for her to follow him, and so she did, down into
the cool, dim light.

She knew the place well. It was deep and wide, running the
length of the verandah, and high enough to stand up in. Bicycles
were kept down there, and the old doll's pram, pushed now behind the garden rakes and hoes and clippers. There were sacks of
seed, and bulbs, manure, and cans of oil. Through an opening in
the wall, deeper in, were rooms and rooms of raw red earth, with
walls and passages between them, like the house above. In the
middle was a place no light could reach. She had crawled back
there once, and crouched, and listened to rats scraping and darting, footsteps above, the dogs off somewhere. It smelled sour back
there, and damp, and wonderful.

The Sharpener stood just out of a beam of light that came in
through one of the vents. He tossed his head at her again and
moved deeper into the shadow.

She knew rude things. She had done rude things with cousins
and friends. There was a frenzy to them—the giggling and hush-
ing and urging on. But now she stood solemn and still as the
Sharpener came to crouch before her. He lifted her skirt and
found her bloomers, pulled them down to her knees.

"We can lie down," he said.

But she shook her head, and he stood up again. He unbuttoned his trousers, pulled his thing through the slit and held it out
on the palm of his hand. She knew he was offering it to her, asking

for something too, his eyes never leaving her face. But she clasped her hands behind her back and looked down at the floor.

He pushed himself closer, pushed his thing up under her skirt, against her stomach, breathing his smell all over her, sweat and liquor and dirt. He turned her around and crouched behind her to push it between her legs. When she lifted her skirt, she saw it sticking through as if it were her own, and she giggled.

There was a man who sat at the bus stop outside school sometimes. He sat there smiling, teeth missing everywhere. Often his trousers were open, and there was a pool of his mess under the bench. The headmistress warned them in prayers about men like that, never to talk to them, never to take lifts from them either. Some had cars without door handles on the inside, she said; you could never get out.

The Sharpener laughed in a whisper behind her. He turned her to face him again, loosened her gym girdle and pulled the whole uniform over her head, the blouse too. Then she stamped off the bloomers herself.

"Big lady," he said. He touched the swelling of her breasts, the hair starting between her legs, ran a finger down the middle of it, under and in.

Once she had seen a boy at the edge of the hockey field. He was holding his thing while he watched them practice. "Ugh!" she had said with the others. But that boy had become a habit of longing for her, a habit of dreaming, too.

She watched the Sharpener undo his belt and let his trousers fall. She looked at his skinny thing between his skinny legs. "Big lady," he said, pulling her to one of the sacks and bending her over it. "Big lady, big lady," he whispered, fiddling at her with his fingers, stroking, separating, urging himself into her a little at a time so that she gasped, not with pain but with the fear of pain. And then, after the pain, with the beginning, with the surprise of pleasure, a wild and rude sort of pleasure, wilder and ruder than anything, anything. Even the tea tray rattling out onto the verandah couldn't stop it, even the nanny calling her name. He was grunting and heaving over her now. She wanted to tell him they wouldn't come down here; they wouldn't. But he jerked himself free anyway, he clutched and cried against her like a baby, crybaby bunting.

She wanted to cry, too. She wanted him to say "Big lady" again, and go on, but he wouldn't. He got up and went for his trousers, pushed his skinny legs into them and buckled his belt.

The back of her leg was damp and cold. She felt it with her hand, it was slimy with his mess. "Ugh!" she said, wiping it off on the sack.

But he didn't look up. He was over at the lawn mower now, pulling it free. He hawked and spat into the darkness. She wanted to spit, too. She wanted to tell on him, to tell anyone she liked about the dirty stinking Coloured who put his thing into her without asking.

And then she heard the dogs. She could have heard them before if she had listened—the barking and the shouting and the running overhead—but she hadn't. And now there they were, roaring down into the darkness, making straight for him.

"Missie!" he screamed. "Missie!"

She grabbed a rake, thrashed and thrashed at the dogs, although she knew it would do no good. They were crazed by Coloureds, even someone who just seemed Coloured. And they hated the Sharpener most of all. One had him by the calf, the other snarled and jumped and snapped at his shoulder.

Her mother and the cook came out onto the verandah, shouting for the garden boy to bring the hose, the dogs had got out. The Sharpener dropped to his knees, bloodied and torn, covered his head with his arms.

And then the garden boy arrived with the hose, shouting too, pointing it into the darkness until he could see the dogs. But when he saw the girl standing there, he lowered his head and dropped the hose. He ran out into the garden, screaming for the nanny.

The girl was wet when they found her, her clothes soaking on the floor. And the Sharpener had given up screaming. He lay curled around himself, quite still. And so the dogs had given up too. They stood back, panting.

She tried to save him without answering all their questions. But she couldn't. They decided he was Coloured after all, and they locked him up for good. They'd have locked him up for good even if he weren't Coloured, her mother said. And the girl didn't argue.

But now, lying in bed with her own man or another, she's always down there again, under the house, with the Sharpener. Over the years, he has only got wilder. Sometimes, he brings a friend and they take turns with her. They drink brandy from a bottle and laugh and make one of the dogs go first. And then the Sharpener pulls the dog away. He has to have her for himself. He cannot wait.

# Heartbeats

## Sidney Durham

All the people were old. He did not belong in this place, he thought, although in truth he was not much younger than the others. And like everybody else in the big waiting room, he was there because he had a heart problem. He was certainly too young for that.

Right.

He looked down at his hands, which were slumped in his lap. They were becoming the hands of an older man. There was a web of wrinkles on them, a fine mesh of age-disclosing truth.

A soft electronically counterfeited bell announced the elevator and he turned to watch the doors inch open. Like all hospital elevators, this one seemed sluggish, as if age had overtaken it as well. A young woman emerged. Without hesitation she walked briskly to the center of the large waiting area, sweeping the room with her eyes. A wake of confidence and vitality seemed to trail out behind her like a scent that would linger when she left the room. She was dressed for business, almost colorless in a dark blue blazer and a gray skirt. Her jet black hair hung straight to her shoulders.

He was beginning to wonder if she might be a physician when she turned and walked to the reception desk and signed the patient register. No, it couldn't be. She was too young to have a bad heart. She must have come to the wrong clinic by mistake.

She took a seat near him, smiling briefly as she caught him watching her. The smile was almost an affront. He was harmless, it said. She was the kind of woman who would often have to evade oafish advances from men, but this man was harmless. He was old.

Her lipstick appeared to be fresh. His ill-mannered imagination gave him an image of her lips stretched around his cock. He smiled back at her, a gesture that probably reassured her of his harmlessness. Not too many years before she might have taken his smile as a danger signal.

He glanced at her legs. They were hidden in heavy black hosiery, so it was difficult to imagine their shape. He wondered if they needed shaving. He wondered how they would feel clamped around his head.

She crossed her legs and began to swing her foot slowly, in a rhythm that seemed almost languid. He watched her, not caring if she noticed. After all, he was harmless. He was old. He had a heart problem.

In another time he would have focused intensely on this woman who bounced her foot. His objective would have been simple: her seduction. It would not have mattered much whether he succeeded. He had enjoyed failed seductions nearly as much as successful ones. He had loved catching the quick flash of comprehension that would come to women's eyes when they understood just how serious he was about wanting to fuck them. And he remembered the thrill he had always felt when he saw the first flicker of acquiescence.

But the best memories were the moments of penetration. He had always been attentive with women, heedful of their rhythms, their wants. He skillfully used his tongue and lips and hands to prepare the way, and by the time he held himself above a woman for the first time she was always ready for him, always eager for him. She might have already come, perhaps several times, and at that moment she belonged to him, she was under his dominion. Some women would even bridge up their hips toward him, urging him to hurry.

He would ease his rock-hard cock into the vestibule of her pussy, lodging the thick head between swollen lips and pausing. Some women would sigh at this point; others would hook him with their heels, urging him. Others would even come as his cock began its trip inside.

He had loved to watch the corners of their mouths turn up as he pressed deeper. Nearly all women reacted that way. And if their eyes were open he would hold their gaze as he pressed, and often he would see mischief in those eyes—especially in the eyes of women who were with him illicitly.

Those moments were the hallmarks of perfection in his life.

But his mind, with its brutal realism, reminded him again that the person he had once been no longer existed. He was old. He was harmless, ineffective. Smoking, or perhaps the drugs he took to manage his blood pressure, had made him impotent.

But that was a deception. He knew these were not the things that had ended his sexual profligacy. Something more fundamental had happened. He had fallen in love with a woman named Gracie, a woman who would not tolerate his recklessness, a woman who had left him after only one transgression. He had not recovered from that. She had been vindictive, and losing her had ultimately disabled him. Impotence had sunk long talons into his shoulder and had roosted there, arrogant and haunting.

He wondered if Gracie could be working at this clinic. Probably not, he decided; it was too small to suit her aspirations. Gracie had been different. Strong and self-reliant, she was a professional, a nurse. Unlike the other women he seduced, Gracie had career objectives and ambition.

He caught a hint of perfume from the woman seated by him, and suddenly longed for a cigarette. It had been nearly two months since he'd quit smoking. During that time he had successfully avoided smoking more than two thousand cigarettes, and he'd probably had ten times that many cravings for one.

His heart irregularity began only days after he stopped smoking. The doctors seemed to consider the problem minor, but wanted to do the testing anyway. They dismissed his hopeful idea that he could simply start smoking again.

He heard laughter and looked around. An old man with thinning white hair and a reedy voice was flirting with one of the young women behind the reception counter. Some of the other men in the waiting area had also flirted this way, as if they knew they were considered harmless and were taking advantage of the idea. There seemed to be some sort of unwritten understanding about this. Old men could flirt; younger women didn't need to feel threatened.

He didn't want to be part of that. Flirting had always been a waste of time, unless it produced some tangible result. Fluttering eyelids were no substitute for pulsing labia.

There would be no result, no reason to flirt, no immersion into the folded warmth of a woman's body if his own body continued to fail him. He pressed his lips together in disgust. He had stopped smoking because he had learned it would cause impotence. The result? Still impotent and now a heart irregularity.

The woman in black hosiery recrossed her legs and resumed her slow foot swinging. The top of her ankle was revealed to him, and he wondered how it would feel under his fingertips. Moving up, his eyes fell on the thick swell of her calf, widened by the press against her other leg beneath it, flexing with her movements. He imagined gripping her leg there and lifting it.

Her movement stopped then and he knew she was watching him. Although he did not look up to meet her eyes, it was as if their blackness forced itself into his peripheral view, alerting him that his stare had caught her attention. He did not move his eyes from her calf. She would assume he was simply lost in an old man's stupor.

It worked. Her movements resumed, and he felt her eyes leave him. The thickness of her calf seemed to reach a chiseled perfection as he watched, and he longed to touch it.

In time he heard his name called. He stood and looked around, finally locating a young woman who held a file folder in her hand. As he walked toward her he looked back, hoping to meet the black eyes. She was not looking his direction. It didn't matter; nothing could have happened anyway.

He followed the girl with the file folder. She was certainly pretty. His eyes fixed on her buttocks, which rolled beguilingly as she walked, revealing exactly how she would look naked. Did she know how much she revealed? Did she care?

She stopped at an open doorway. "Have a seat in here," she said. "Somebody will be with you in just a few minutes."

He glanced at her breasts as he passed her, but her attention was elsewhere. She had already forgotten him.

The room was tiny, and the examining table was littered with devices he assumed were heart monitors: black boxes and tangles of wires. An involuntary grimace tightened his face as he realized how awkward the next twenty-four hours would be, burdened with one of those boxes and its wad of wires. He took a seat in a straight chair and waited.

The door burst open with a loud bang, as if it had been kicked. Then he heard, "Well! Look what the cat dragged in!"

It was Gracie. He knew her voice immediately, even before he looked up to her familiar face. "Hello," he said lamely. "I didn't know you worked here."

"Don't worry," she replied cheerfully. "I haven't kept track of you either."

Her voice had the same strong note he'd heard in it the day she left him five years ago. He had never understood what had happened to her. It was as if overnight she had found some new strength, and off she'd gone, never looking back. "How've you been?" he asked, filling a silence.

"Better than you, it seems. Heart misbehaving?"

"A little. Among other things."

"Age will do that to you. Let's get you wired. Stand up. Unbutton your shirt."

He did, not liking it. His pectorals sagged, his stomach bulged. His once trim body was old and dumpy.

She didn't seem to notice, working quickly, impersonally. Reaching inside his shirt, she fastened wires to him, touching with the same hands that had touched him so intimately, so often, in the vanished past. He felt a longing for her and reached to pull her into his arms.

She turned away quickly. "Nothing doing," she said. "That was over long ago."

"You don't have any feelings for me?"

"I feel sorry that you're not well. That's all. You're still the same lying philandering asshole you always were."

He reached, managed to touch the back of her hand with his fingertips before she flinched it away. "Not even a little memory?" he asked.

Her eyes seemed to flicker a deeper shade of green. "Not even a little, Richard. You were a total, complete prick. You used women. You used me, the way you did all women."

"Well, it won't be happening again," he said, unable to contain his bitterness.

"That too? You poor bastard. Get a Viagra prescription. I hear it works wonders. I'm sure your little chickadees won't mind waiting for it to go to work."

"Fuck you."

"Not even in your dreams. I don't know what motivates men like you, Richard, but you should all be hung up by the balls. All you ever cared about was getting laid."

"I—"

"You're done. Just drop off the monitor tomorrow. We'll send a report to your doctor." With that she was out of the room.

He stopped at a convenience store on the way home and bought a pack of cigarettes. The woman behind the counter was attractive and he spoke with her for a moment, expertly assessing her willingness. She was distracted. Her eyes kept drifting to the wires coming from inside his shirt, and to the black box that was strapped to his waist.

He unbuttoned his shirt in the car and ripped the wires off his chest. Then he lit up a cigarette and inhaled, deeply.

# Full House

## David Sedaris

My parents were not the type of people who went to bed at a regular hour. Sleep overtook them, but neither the time nor the idea of a mattress seemed very important. My father favored a chair in the basement, but my mother was apt to lie down anywhere, waking with carpet burns on her face or the pattern of the sofa embossed into the soft flesh of her upper arms. It was sort of embarrassing. She might sleep for eight hours a day, but they were never consecutive hours and they involved no separate outfit. For Christmas we would give her nightgowns, hoping she might take the hint. "They're for bedtime," we'd say, and she'd look at us strangely, as if, like the moment of one's death, the occasion of sleep was too incalculable to involve any real preparation.

The upside to being raised by what were essentially a pair of house cats was that we never had any enforced bedtime. At two A.M. on a school night, my mother would not say, "Go to sleep," but rather, "Shouldn't you be tired?" It wasn't a command but a sincere question, the answer provoking little more than a shrug. "Suit yourself," she'd say, pouring what was likely to be her thirtieth or forty-second cup of coffee. "I'm not sleepy, either. Don't know why, but I'm not."

We were the family that never shut down, the family whose TV was so hot we needed an oven mitt in order to change the channel. Every night was basically a slumber party, so when the real thing came along, my sisters and I failed to show much of an interest.

"But we get to stay up as late as we want," the hosts would say. "And . . . ?"

The first one I attended was held by a neighbor named Walt Winters. Like me, Walt was in the sixth grade. Unlike me, he was gregarious and athletic, which meant, basically, that we had absolutely nothing in common. "But why would he include *me*?" I asked my mother. "I hardly know the guy."

She did not say that Walt's mother had made him invite me, but I knew that this was the only likely explanation. "Oh, go," she said. "It'll be fun."

I tried my best to back out, but then my father got wind of it, and that option was closed. He often passed Walt playing football in the street and saw in the boy a younger version of himself. "He's maybe not the best player in the world, but he and his friends, they're a good group."

"Fine," I said. "Then *you* go sleep with them."

I could not tell my father that boys made me anxious, and so I invented individual reasons to dislike them. The hope was that I might seem discerning rather than frightened, but instead I came off sounding like a prude.

"You're expecting me to spend the night with someone who curses? Someone who actually throws *rocks* at *cats*?"

"You're damned right I am," my father said. "Now get the hell over there."

Aside from myself, there were three other guests at Walt's slumber party. None of them were particularly popular—they weren't good-looking enough for that—but each could hold his own on a playing field or in a discussion about cars. The talk started the moment I walked through the door, and while pretending to listen, I wished that I could have been more honest. "What is the actual point of football?" I wanted to ask. "Is a V-8 engine related in any way to the juice?" I would have sounded like a foreign-exchange student, but the answers might have given me some sort of a foundation. As it was, they may as well have been talking backward.

There were four styles of houses on our street, and while Walt's was different from my own, I was familiar with the layout. The slumber party took place in what the Methodists called a family room, the Catholics used as an extra bedroom, and the neighborhood's only Jews had turned into a combination darkroom and fallout shelter. Walt's family was Methodist, and so the room's focal point was a large black-and-white television. Family photos hung on the wall alongside pictures of the various athletes Mr. Winters had successfully pestered for autographs. I admired them to the best of my ability but was more interested in the wedding portrait displayed above the sofa. Arm in arm with her uniformed husband, Walt's mother looked deliriously, almost frighteningly happy. The bulging eyes and fierce, gummy smile: it was an expression bordering on hysteria, and the intervening years had done nothing to dampen it.

"What is she *on?*" my mother would whisper whenever we passed Mrs. Winters waving gaily from her front yard. I thought she was being too hard on her, but after ten minutes in the woman's home I understood exactly what my mother was talking about.

"Pizza's here!!!" she chimed when the deliveryman came to the door. "Oh, boys, how about some piping hot pizza!!!" I thought it was funny that anyone would use the words *piping hot,* but it wasn't the kind of thing I felt I could actually laugh at. Neither could I laugh at Mr. Winters's pathetic imitation of an Italian waiter. "Mamma mia. Who want anudda slice a dipizza!"

I had the idea that adults were supposed to make themselves scarce at slumber parties, but Walt's parents were all over the place: initiating games, offering snacks and refills. When the midnight horror movie came on, Walt's mother crept into the bathroom, leaving a ketchup-spattered knife beside the sink. An hour passed, and when none of us had yet discovered it, she started dropping little hints. "Doesn't anyone want to wash their hands?" she asked. "Will whoever's closest to the door go check to see if I left fresh towels in the bathroom?"

You just wanted to cry for people like her.

As corny as they were, I was sorry when the movie ended and Mr. and Mrs. Winters stood to leave. It was only two A.M., but clearly they were done in. "I just don't know how you boys can do it," Walt's mother said, yawning into the sleeve of her bathrobe. "I haven't been up this late since Lauren came into the world." Lauren was Walt's sister, who was born prematurely and lived for less than two days. This had happened before the Winterses moved onto our street, but it wasn't any kind of secret, and you weren't supposed to flinch upon hearing the girl's name. The baby had died too soon to pose for photographs, but still she was regarded as a full-fledged member of the family. She had a Christmas stocking the size of a mitten, and they even threw her an annual birthday party, a fact that my mother found especially creepy. "Let's hope they don't invite us," she said. "I mean, Jesus, how do you shop for a dead baby?"

I guessed it was the fear of another premature birth that kept Mrs. Winters from trying again, which was sad, as you got the sense she really wanted a lively household. You got the sense that she had an *idea* of a lively household and that the slumber party and the ketchup-covered knife were all a part of that idea. While in her presence, we had played along, but once she said good night, I understood that all bets were off.

She and her husband lumbered up the stairs, and when Walt

felt certain that they were asleep, he pounced on Dale Gummer-
son, shouting, "Titty twister!!!" Brad Clancy joined in, and when
they had finished, Dale raised his shirt, revealing nipples as
crimped and ruddy as the pepperoni slices littering the forsaken
pizza box.

"Oh my God," I said, realizing too late that this made me
sound like a girl. The appropriate response was to laugh at Dale's
misfortune, not to flutter your hands in front of your face, screech-
ing, "What have they done to your poor nipples! Shouldn't we put
some ice on them?"

Walt picked up on this immediately. "Did you just say you
wanted to put ice on Dale's nipples?"

"Well, not me . . . personally," I said. "I meant, you know, generally. As a group. Or Dale could do it himself if he felt like it."

Walt's eyes wandered from my face to my chest, and then the
entire slumber party was upon me. Dale had not yet regained the
full use of his arms, and so he sat on my legs while Brad and Scott
Marlboro pinned me to the carpet. My shirt was raised, a hand
was clamped over my mouth, and Walt latched onto my nipples,
twisting them back and forth as if they were a set of particularly
stubborn toggle bolts. "*Now* who needs ice!" he said. "*Now* who
thinks he's the goddamn school nurse." I'd once felt sorry for Walt,
but now, my eyes watering in pain, I understood that little Lauren
was smart to have cut out early.

When finally I was freed, I went upstairs and stood at the
kitchen window, my arms folded lightly against my chest. My family's house was located in a ravine. You couldn't see it from the
street, but still I could make out the glow of lights spilling from
the top of our driveway. It was tempting, but were I to leave now,
I'd never hear the end of it. *The baby cried. The baby had to go
home.* Life at school would be unbearable, so I left the window
and returned to the basement, where Walt was shuffling cards
against the coffee table. "Just in time," he said. "Have a seat."

I lowered myself to the floor and reached for a magazine, trying my best to act casual. "I'm not really much for games, so if it's okay with you, I think I'll just watch."

"Watch, hell," Walt said. "This is strip poker. What kind of a homo wants to sit around and watch four guys get naked?"

The logic of this was lost on me. "Well, won't we *all* sort of be watching?"

"Looking maybe, but not *watching*," Walt said. "There's a big difference."

I asked what the difference was, but nobody answered. Then Walt made a twisting motion with his fingers, and I took my place at the table, praying for a gas leak or an electrical fire—anything to save me from the catastrophe of strip poker. To the rest of the group, a naked boy was like a lamp or a bath mat, something so familiar and uninteresting that it faded into the background, but for me it was different. A naked boy was what I desired more than anything on earth, and when you were both watching and desiring, things came up, one thing in particular that was bound to stand out and ruin your life forever. "I hate to tell you," I said, "but it's against my religion to play poker."

"Yeah, right," Walt said. "What are you, Baptist?"

"Greek Orthodox."

"Well, that's a load of crap because the Greeks invented cards," Walt said.

"Actually, I think it was the Egyptians." This from Scott, who was quickly identifying himself as the smart one.

"Greeks, Egyptians, they're all the same thing," Walt said. "Anyway, what your pooh-bah doesn't know won't hurt him, so shut the hell up and play."

He dealt the cards, and I looked from face to face, exaggerating flaws and reminding myself that these boys did not like me. The hope was that I might crush any surviving atom of attraction, but as has been the case for my entire life, the more someone dislikes me the more attractive he becomes. The key was to stall, to argue every hand until the sun came up and Mrs. Winters saved me with whatever cheerful monstrosity she'd planned for breakfast.

On the off chance that stalling would *not* work, I stepped into the bathroom and checked to make sure I was wearing clean underwear. A boner would be horrible beyond belief, but a boner combined with a skid mark meant that I should take the ketchup-smeared knife and just kill myself before it was too late.

"What are you, launching a sub in there?" Walt shouted. "Come on, we're waiting."

Usually when I was forced to compete, it was my tactic to simply give up. To try in any way was to announce your ambition, which only made you more vulnerable. The person who wanted to win but failed was a loser, while the person who didn't really care was just a weirdo—a title I had learned to live with. Here, though, surrender was not an option. I had to win at a game I knew nothing about, and that seemed hopeless until I realized we were all on an equal footing. Not even Scott had the slightest idea what he was doing, and by feigning an air of expertise, I found I could manipulate things in my favor.

"A joker and a queen is much better than the four and five of spades," I said, defending my hand against Brad Clancy's.

"But you have a joker and a three of diamonds."

"Yes, but the joker *makes* it a queen."

"I thought you said that poker was against your religion," Walt said.

"Well, that doesn't mean I don't understand it. Greeks *invented* cards, remember. They're in my blood."

At the start of the game, the starburst clock had read three-thirty. An hour later I was missing one shoe, Scott and Brad had lost their shirts, and both Walt and Dale were down to their underwear. If this was what winning felt like, I wondered why I

hadn't tried it before. Confidently in the lead, I invented little reasons for the undressed to get up and move about the room.

"Hey, Walt, did you hear that? It sounded like footsteps up in
the kitchen."

"I didn't hear anything."

"Why don't you go to the stairway and check. We don't want
any surprises." His underwear was all bunchy in the back, saggy
like a diaper, but his legs were meaty and satisfying to look at.

"Dale, would you make sure those curtains are closed?"

He crossed the room, and I ate him alive with my eyes, confi-
dent that no one would accuse me of staring. Things might have
been different were I in last place, but as a winner, it was my right
to make sure that things were done properly. "There's an open
space down by the baseboard. Bend over and close it, will you?"

It took a while, but after explaining that a pair of kings was no
match for a two of hearts and a three of spades, Walt surrendered
his underpants and tossed them onto a pile beside the TV set.
"Okay," he said. "Now the rest of you can finish the game."

"But it *is* finished," Scott said.

"Oh no," Walt said. "I'm not the only one getting naked. You
guys have to keep playing."

"While you do what—sit back and *watch*?" I said. "What kind
of a homo are you?"

"Yeah," Dale said. "Why don't we do something else? This
game's boring and the rules are impossible."

The others muttered in agreement, and when Walt refused to
back down, I gathered the deck and tamped it commandingly
upon the tabletop. "The only solution is for us *all* to keep playing."

"How the hell do you expect me to do that?" Walt said. "In
case you haven't noticed, there's nothing more for me to lose."

"Oh," I said, "there's always more. Maybe if the weakest hand
is already naked, we should make that person perform some kind
of a task. Nothing big, just, you know, a token kind of a thing."

"A thing like what?" Walt asked.

"I don't know. I guess we'll just have to cross that bridge when we come to it."

In retrospect, I probably went a little too far in ordering Scott to sit on my lap. "But I'm naked!" he said.

"Hey," I told him, "I'm the one who's going to be suffering. I was just looking for something easy. Would you rather run outside and touch the mailbox? The sun will be coming up in about twenty seconds—you want the whole neighborhood to see you?"

"How long will I have to sit on you?" he asked.

"I don't know. A minute or two. Maybe five. Or seven."

I moved onto the easy chair and wearily patted my knee, as if this were a great sacrifice. Scott slid into place, and I considered our reflection in the darkened TV screen. Here I was, one naked guy on my lap and three others ready to do my bidding. It was the stuff of dreams until I remembered that they were not doing these things of their own accord. This was not their pleasure, but their punishment, and once it was over they would make it a point to avoid me. Rumors would spread that I had slipped something into their Cokes, that I had tried to French Brad Clancy, that I had stolen five dollars from Walt's pocket. Not even Mrs. Winters would wave at me, but all that would come later, in a different life. For now I would savor this poor imitation of tenderness, mapping Scott's shoulders, the small of his back, as he shuddered beneath my winning hand.

# Drunkie's Surprise

## Kweli Walker

Mama? Grandma? Maybe when people first look, they might think that, 'cause I'm an average-looking little sixty-year-old woman, boppin' around with a twenty-eight-year-old *Hip Hop Magazine* ad of a brother. The double-take comes when they see him grab my hand in between the fingers, like I like, or kiss my lips and slip me a little tongue, like I like. You see, my lover men will do this . . . no matter where we are or who's lookin', because that's the way I need it and if they don't, they won't see Missy Jankins . . . NO MO'!

Most folk don't even notice, but I catch a couple of 'em sneakin' a second and third peek, especially the women. Some women my age, who know I'm runnin' shit, twist their faces all up, cut their eyes, and stare, but that's just because they jealous, and think I'm takin' advantage. But, most of the forty- and fifty-year-old women just smile and give me a wink. Know what I mean?

I look at it like this, I don't do nothin' . . . to no man . . . who wasn't trying to play a trick on me. Every last one of 'em is legally grown, and I always . . . always . . . always leave 'em off better than I found 'em and that's what makes things *Even Steven*.

Take my new lover, Jared:

If I'da been walking down Western Avenue in my regular clothes, he wouldn't have known if I was alive or dead, let alone smiled and said hello, like he done. He definitely wouldn't have gone up to my place for sex, but . . . a little dark corner, a little short tight pink skirt, a nice snug pink corset to pull me in, a long wavy wig to slang, some nice long eyelashes, a pair support hose, some pink high-heel shoes, some sparkly jewelry, a splash of sweet smellin' perfume, one drink too many at the Chocolate Bar Strip Club, and Jared opened a window for me to climb my old ass right on through.

Jared is your typical single man mess. His money's a mess, and his life's a mess, he dropped out halfway through college, he's back at his mama's place, and ain't got a clue about what he wants to do, other than have fun with his friends and hop from hole to hole. Oh . . . his car and clothes are real nice, though. Sound familiar?

From the time he stepped in the club, I was watchin' and I was waitin' by the bar, with my legs crossed and bouncing. I could feel my little curly gray cat gettin' hotter and wetter every time I looked at the clock. When it got real close to closin' time, it started to meow.

I pay real good attention to who gettin' drunk, what they getting drunk on, and what they hollerin' for the stripper to do, 'cause that's where I learn how to please 'em. I'm kind of a pleasure detective.

Jared looked my way, right when he came around the black felt curtain . . . check! Jared was brown and handsome . . . check! Atlanta Sweets is always the last woman to come out. Beebo does that 'cause Sweet's forty-nine and, well, she's a good-lookin' forty-nine, but forty-nine is fuckin' forty-nine, a'right? When Beebo started doing that, he done me and Sweets a big favor

that cuts my spy work in half. I know that if a man hollers for Atlanta Sweets, I can have that man's dick . . . nooo problem. Me
and Sweets got this thing worked out, where she come out in the
audience and give a "free dick rub" on the man I point out by
stickin' my pinky finger out from my glass of Pepsi. It ain't for
free, mind ya. I pay her a fifty-dollar "finder's fee." Ain't that
what they call it?

I picked Jared 'cause he has a great big dick that stayed hard
the whole time Atlanta Sweets made her booty bounce to the beat.
He hollered out when she stuck that big ass of hers way out and
shook it like a can of whipped cream, so I knew he was comin'
home with me . . . check! I knew it was gonna be doggy-style . . .
check! And Jared was drinkin' waaaaay too much gin to be travel-
ing alone . . . check! check! checkity-check! check! It was all over
but the shoutin'.

Even though he was almost stumblin' drunk, when we come
through my front gate, he said, "Nice yard . . . uh . . . what's your
name?"

I said, "The name's Missy. I do my yard work myself."

Now, I pays attention to that kinda thang. If he ain't too drunk
to notice my yard and ax my name, he could probably use one mo'
drink of gin. You see, I don't need him having no second thoughts
'bout givin' me my dick, 'cause he's soberin' up. No, suh!

My real name's Percola Mae Jankins. My Auntie Tree nicknamed
me Missy, when I was a baby. Missy's short for mischievous. I don't
give out my real name, but I started getting the feelin' me and
Jared are gonna be seeing each other for a while, reason being, he
minds. There ain't nothing better than a lover who minds.

When he walked in my door he goes, "Nice place . . . Missy.
You must really like pink, huh? Where can I put my clothes?"

When I said, "I'll take care of all that, you just sit right over
there, so I can take off your shoes," he handed me his leather

jacket, as best a drunk man can, and sat down where I told him to sit. I kneeled down in front of him, took off his shoes and rubbed his feet a little. Jared kinda laughed and pulled his hard dick out. I liked that, and I didn't tell him to tuck it back in, but like I said, I'm drivin', so I just acted like I didn't see nothing, until I get ready for the dick part. I just dripped a little Love Juice Lotion on it and let him rub it his self.

He goes, "Hey, Missy, don't you wanna ride this dick?"

I said, "I'll be up there in a little bit. You just keep on strokin' it." I love to watch a man choke his chicken. That makes my pussy crackle an' boil. Besides, I get a better idea how to make it feel good to him. Some mens like it hard and rough and some like it slow and nasty. A woman servin' leftovers gotta know how to dish up the plate. Over the years, I learned how to make a man ask what's for dessert in the middle of dinner . . . if you know what I mean.

When I started getting real wet, I stripped down to my corset. I sat on my big brown coffee table, right in front of Jared, and I cocked my legs open so he got a good look up in my pussy, and I started pleasing my pussy like I was by myself. His dick got even harder and he said, "Missy, it's time to get our fuck on."

I said, "In a minute. I ain't quite ready just yet."

I like to tease a man up real good, so I played a game with him. I took it almost to the point where he started gettin' mad, 'cause that way I know I'm gon' get me some good dick. I said, "When you tell me the magic word, I'm gonna suck your dick 'til you can't take no mo'."

Awwww, sookie sookie now! That man started to guessin'! He went, "Abracadabra?" I go, "Naw, that's the word for me to give you a hand job." Right then I start in givin' him a hand job—a good one—that don't leave nothin' out. He leaned on back and took it. I love to give a hand job first. I don't care what he woulda said, that's what I was gon' do anyway. See, when I'm givin' him a hand job, I get to check out his dick real good and make sure he ain't got no bugs and no sores. I slip and slide until he starts guessin' the magic word again, 'cause then I know he's really ready to tear up my pussy. I was jackin' him off like a dick strokin' machine and he was justa guessin'. Every time he guessed a word, I go, "Nope!" Finally he reaches up in my pussy and starts strokin' my clit with his palm. I almost lost my dog-gone mind.

Then he goes, "Alakazam!"

I go, "That's it! That's the magic word!" and I turn to the side, pop out my false teeth, and put 'em in a little wooden box on the coffee table, and go to work on Jared's dick. He th'ows his head back and moans over and over, real loud, callin' on the Lord and all. I can tell he ain't had no gums before. I can tell by how he's actin' that he's definitely gonna want some more. And, I'm gon' give him of that, and plenty more, if he do what I like, and don't give me no back talk . . . ever. I got rules, you see.

1. I want sex at least once a week. Anything less than once a week, without a reason I think is good enough, or a doctor's excuse . . . and it's all over.
2. One public date every month, with sunflowers. In public, you will hold my hand and kiss me in the mouth . . . with tongue, at least once.
3. At least one phone call every day . . . no exceptions. Nobody's too busy to make one phone call, and if they are, they're too busy to get this good old pussy.
4. What I say goes, and when I say it's over, it's done.

You might not believe this, but good gums is hard for a young man to find, and once they got some, it's hard for them to let 'em go. Sometimes guys like Jared leave my place all satisfied, and they think to their self, "That old bitch ain't runnin' nothin'!"

Ha! That's what they think 'til their dick gets hard and starts cravin' them gums and nothing else can hit the spot. Once they figure that out, they call me and do like I say, from then on. I'm just that good. I wasn't always a sexpert, though. I didn't even know I liked sex until my husband Benny died.

Peter Benjamin was fifty-four years old when he asked Auntie Tree for my hand. I was thirty years old and hadn't never really had a man. Auntie Tree knew Pete had a great big house, a brand-new Lincoln Continental, tailor-made suits, jewelry and plenty money. Lookin' back on things, he probably gave her money to marry me, 'cause she was in the middle of building a church. I used to feel bad she done that, but I really was a mess back then. Most religious people would have throwed my ass in the streets way before that. I was tryin' to watch TV and wear Vaseline on my lips, like my wild-ass friend Cee Cee. She was this girl that the preacher's wife adopted.

Auntie Tree hated Cee Cee. She said Cee Cee was possessed by the evil spirit. Cee Cee told me that Aunt Tree was a church devil that turned me into her slave, and that she could go to jail for not lettin' me go to school, even if it was a long time ago. I probably could have stayed with Auntie Tree 'til she died if I wouldn't have told her that, but I was scared she'd make me kneel on rice in the closet again, if she found out from the little birdie. Right after I told her what Cee Cee said, she cried and told me it was time I got married and that she knew just the man . . . Pretty Boy Pete.

Pete had skinny brown legs and a little melon belly and curly white hair that he greased up and slicked down to the side. He had a habit of breaking down crying or laughing real hard without no warning, but other than that, he was a nice old man. He gave me pretty much everything I asked for and all he asked was that I cooked and cleaned, but he never asked for no pussy. Cookin' and cleanin' for him was like being in heaven, compared to all the stuff I used to have to do at Aunt Tree's. I still knew something wasn't right. When Pete got sick and started needin' help, all the puzzle pieces fell right into place.

I was a young woman and my body craved dick. The whole time me and Pete was together, we never fucked one time. It made me kinda mean. I did everything I could to make him want me, but he said he wanted to keep things like they was: I had my room and he had his. I had my friends and he had his cousins that stayed over from time to time. Sometimes I'd rear up and threaten to cheat on him, but he'd always say, "Do whatever you need to do, Missy . . . that's what I'm gonna do."

I couldn't never bring myself to have another man, being married and all. It just didn't seem proper.

The only time Pete ever acted like he was my husband was when his momma flew in from Detroit. His cousins never dropped by when Old Lillie came to town. When she stayed with us, he'd hold my hand, slip me kisses, call me Sweetness, and sleep in my room, but still no dick. Maybe it was for the best.

I guess I coulda left him, but to go where and do what? I figured he kept me even after his momma died, so I stayed 'til he died ten years later. He didn't have nobody in this world but me, and he left me in good shape for a fifty-two-year-old woman with no real schoolin'. He left me his house, his car, and his government pension, and he even taught me how to read and cipher a little. I s'poze I could've done like Pete and moved somebody in, but after livin' with him, I got used to being alone, 'cept for when I need some dick . . . and I need me some dick once a week.

Getting fucked was the first thing I decided to do after Pete died. I made up my mind to learn how to get good sex. I knew I didn't want to get married again, and I didn't really want to take care of nobody else, so that boiled down to finding a willin' man, fuckin' him, and sending him on his way 'til I need some more dick. When I first started out, I made some terrible mistakes.

My first mistake was tryin' to find a man my age . . . with a hard dick. It didn't take but two old dicks to know I needed some young dick. My second mistake was tryin' to find a young man who knew how to fuck and leave. Seems like ever young man I met had some kinda problem or some trick up their sleeve. For some reason, they looked around and saw I had a pretty good life, and they figured I owed 'em something.

Now, I always like big men with great big old arms. I found out the hard way, a lot of them mens been to the jailhouse. Ex-felons ain't exactly lookin' to leave a nice warm place that got a 'frigerator full of home-cooked food. I ain't tryin' to have my house turned into no gym, and I ain't the bank. A coupla of 'em straight out and asked me for money. Call me crazy, but I just can't see payin' a man money to suck his dick.

Here's how I see it: I fucked him and he fucked me . . . that's *Even Steven*, far as I'm concerned. I ain't stingy, but I give when I feel like givin', and that's on Christmas . . . and maybe on ya birthday, if you fuckin' me proper and ain't givin' me no grief. So don't ask me for shit.

Okay! So, I finally figured that I need me a young man, with his own money, who wants to fuck . . . and leave. I had my wheels spinnin' for a while on that one. I gussied myself up and tried lookin' for men at the markets, the car parts stores, the hardware stores, the bowlin' alley, the pool hall, and the golf course. I could always find men, but there was always somethin' that wasn't quite right: a little dick, a limp dick, a dirty dick, a dirty trick, a wife in the wings, or just plain old mean. It was real hit and miss (mostly miss), when I started dick huntin'. I was just about to give up and buy me a bigger vibrator, when some'n told me to talk to Atlanta, one of the older strippers at the club, across the street on the first floor. I figured she knew a whole lot about making men want pussy, and sho' nuff, that's when the good dick start pourin' down from heaven.

Every day when she passed my place, she'd yell over to the porch, "What you cookin'? Sho' smell good!" I'd yell back, "Fried chicken!" or "Pork chops!" Or whatever I was cooking. We done like that for months until I got the idea to take her a plate and ask her 'bout all them fine young men that come to the Chocolate Bar.

When it got close to the time she came to work, I dished her up a platter of fried turkey thighs, potato salad, mustard greens, and two big fluffy scratch biscuits. When I handed it to her, I said, "I need to ax you some'n!" She lifted up the foil and said, "Ax!" I told her what I needed and she told me how to get it. Later that night she brought a handsome little drunk over to my place. While he was passed out on my sofa, she asked me what I thought about him. I told her he was handsome, but I really like big men. She told me that she'd teach me how to come and pick the ones I like. She said she picked a short man, 'cause short men try to make up for being short . . . in bed. When he come to, she went to work on him, while I watched. When I got the hang of things, I jumped on in.

I was right in the middle of tryin' to give my first head job, when my teeth come loose and started wobblin'.

Atlanta said, "You got false teeth?" I nodded.

She said, "You need to pop 'em on out, girl. Don't be shame! This mutha fucka's drunk. He don't give a fuck what you look like. Try it with 'em out!"

I spit 'em out and started sucking him like I saw Atlanta do. She said, "Un-unh! Missy, you goin' too slow. That'd be okay, if he wasn't so drunk. You got to suck fast and hard to get the blood down there, on a drunk." So, I speeded up.

Atlanta goes, "Awww, yeah, now you suckin' dick! See, it's gettin' hard again. He's almost cumin' too. You better stop while you can. When he get where he can talk, that's when you ax for your dick."

I go, "Just come right out and ask?"

"You better, or you can just keep suckin' until he cum in your mouth. What do *you* get outta that?"

"What if he too drunk?"

"Sometimes that's even better. When they drunk like that, you just lay his ass out on the floor, get that dick hard as you can, and slap a cock ring on it, and ride it while you get yours."

"What do I do when I'm through?"

"Shit, wake that fool up and get him out your place. You don't want no strange man up in your house, while you sleep, do you?"

I shook my head.

"Then you don't want him there when you wake up either. Sometimes young men be mad when they wake up and you ain't who they thought you was, when they was drunk. Always keep some'n heavy close by, so you can knock a mutha fucka out if you need to. You can't wait for no man to take the first lick, neither. If they start talking like they wanna hitcha, you just aim right here," Atlanta tapped the front underside of my jaw with her long orange and purple nails, "and then come up wit yo whole body . . . UNGH! Then, all you gotta do is call the po-lice."

Right after she said that, the man on the floor sat up, started rubbing his eyes, and lookin' back and forth between me and Atlanta. She said, "Me and this woman gonna take turns ridin' that big black dick a yours. You mind?"

Atlanta didn't even wait for him to say yes or no, she just hopped on backwards and commenced to ridin'. That man frowned and moaned with his toes curled under. Atlanta said, "You better get that cock ring out of my purse or you gon' be assed out."

That was the first time I got my cum on a dick, not just

dreamin' 'bout a dick. When I got my cum I yelled out and shim-mied. That's when I knew I'd be needin' some more. Atlanta brought a few more drunks by my place, 'til I figured out a few things and learned how to get my own dicks and keep 'em . . . 'til I'm through with 'em. It didn't take long. Like I said, "Good gums is hard to find."

# Fairgrounds

## Peggy Munson

"All's fair in love and whores," said Daddy Billy, spooning me after sex.

"Then all's fair at the fairgrounds tomorrow," I retorted, kissing him on the nose.

I had barely grown out of my colt legs—my wobbly girlish knees that always spread for Daddy Billy—when the carnival grew in spindly metal limbs into a buzzing drove that overtook the Mason County fairgrounds. Things had been rocky between us for a while, but this was the kind of flawless summer day that people nearly trample with enthusiasm. We acted like new lovers. Daddy Billy roused me early with kisses. "Freak Day's here!" he shrilled. He was already clothed. I'd started sleeping naked because Daddy liked to slip beneath the sheets at night. "I need my favorite midnight snack," he'd say, as he was waking me with gropes and sticking fingers into me.

At the carnival, the sun hung with its fake sticky orange of flypaper sap as we wove through kids with droopy snowcones. I was horny and listless, as I always was when Daddy Billy wasn't fucking me. But he was distracted by another yawning circumference—for once, not a lipsticked one. He lobbed Ping-Pong balls at little fish-bowls, trying to win a prize I didn't even want. He seemed uncon-cerned that my thighs might melt together in the heat; but his certain confidence, even against the sun, made me wet. I corkscrewed my hair, shifting on grass ironed flat by weeks of foot-falls. "Be good so Daddy doesn't sell you to the carnival," he said, grinning big. If I wasn't going to ride him, I wanted to ride the rides. I had a pocket full of tickets and a jeweled sky asleep on cu-mulus, just waiting for my eager hands. I tried to pull away but Daddy Billy tugged my wrist. "This is not one of those postmodern Canadian sideshows," he warned, "with adorable, tumbling twins. The inbreeding here makes them ugly and mean. So stay close to Daddy and stay away from the octopus man."

For the past three weeks, the octopus man had been my neme-sis. I was the sole rider who was screaming on the night of an elec-trical storm, when he wouldn't stop the ride and let me down. With a lizard hobble and skin more inked than a letterpress, the octopus man was a surly sadist with an oiled machine. "His octo-pus is his flail," Daddy teased. And that night of the storm, he commanded the throttle and laughed as the lightning unzipped the sooty dark. He flailed me with my fear. He was not as nice as Daddy Billy was, though Daddy had been known to laugh when I screamed. Daddy had been known to do a lot of things.

Daddy Billy—also known as Reverend Billy, Outlaw Billy, and, on rare occasions, Billy Boi—had taught me how it felt to call a lover "Daddy," and then infused the word with sultry power. His naughty drills had turned me from a full-grown woman into an adolescent nymphomaniac. He taught me need that built like summer heat on asphalt. I wanted him explosively. While real girls at the fairgrounds showed their wifely 4-H projects—hand-sewn outfits and fruit pies—I only had a singular ambition: to be the docking station for his giant silicone cock. I sucked my straw to court attention. I rubbed up against him so he'd feel my gumdrop nipple pressing into his sleeve. I watched his last Ping-Pong ball skip around the fishbowl rim and fall. "Harumph," he growled. I loved his Grant Wood–painted brow and every other part of him that hardened at the sight of me.

Daddy gravitated toward the Fun House, where not a single patron queued. The carnie gestured forward like a prison guard. He knew what Daddy was up to, and he didn't approve. Nonetheless, he ogled Daddy's hand cupped around my ass, and the ashy cap of his cigarette dribbled like cum. He saw that we were perverts playing games, and he didn't like that we were civilian freaks instead of rubes. Daddy steered my ass into the spooky dark, then seized my hand in the distorting mirror room. What the mirrors didn't distort, Daddy would pervert. "Today, we're on a date," said Daddy Billy. "But it's secret, because Daddies aren't supposed to date little girls. So let's pretend we're both teenagers. Do you know what teenagers do in the Fun House?"

"Do they tongue kiss?" I asked eagerly.

"They kiss, but in a different way." He grabbed me and pulled me to his body near the wavy mirror. His lips barely grazed my lips and then they pressed against me hard, flash flooding my groin. The kiss was elasticized by the wobbly glass, and then grew wide and tall as Daddy pawed the soft white of my bra. He pinched my nipple, under my shirt, and said gruffly, "Your nipples make Daddy Billy grow long, like our faces in the mirror. Do you want to feel the way Daddy is growing long?" Daddy guided my hand to his jeans and let me feel the dick tunneling down his pant leg. I wanted to put the full length in my mouth. My lips took on its shape automatically, with robotic memory.

"No," chided Daddy. "You'll get that later." He shoved one hand under the waistband of my cutoffs and slid a coarse finger into me. "Mmm. Daddy likes it when you're dripping like a little slut," he said. He kept two fingers on my nipple and twisted it to see if I could hold my scream. "Good little pet," he said. We walked through the rolling barrel and traversed the shaking floor, then spilled into a labyrinthine configuration of mirrors, where Daddy lined me up in front of a replica of me.

"In the carnival," said Daddy-as-benevolent-dictator, "awful things go on. You need to learn to run if anyone tries to do such things to you, so I must demonstrate." He slid his hand down the front of my cutoffs. "See how you have a twin?" asked Daddy, gesturing to my image. "In the carnival, if girls have twins, they're made to fondle each other while dirty carnies watch. Did you know that, sweet girl?"

"No," I said. "But that is wrong."

"Of course. Of *course* it is," said Daddy sternly. "But let's pretend today that I'm your daddy and you have a twin and we are carnies. Aren't you curious about your twin? Don't you wonder what it's like to have the perfect narcissistic fuck? She's just like you."

He forced my hand up to the mirror, to touch my reflection twin's breasts. He watched me stroke her cool, planed face. He kept one hand on his cock as I made a circle on her nipple, then slid my fingers down. My left hand burrowed past the silver button of my cutoffs and down into my drenched white panties. My twin gawked. Her eyes were scared rabbits fleeing a mad scientist's lab. I bent down to kiss and pin her there, a specimen of need.

Behind me, Daddy Billy rubbed against my ass. He wanted his cock inside me so bad. I felt the way that it was homing desperately, yet ramming up against the home sweet home of comfortable clothes. He flattened me against the mirror. I left a trace of lipstick and of steam. Daddy embossed me with cock from behind. His need was hurting me. I wanted so much to let him in. He put

my arms up so my tits pancaked against the glass. He bit my neck
and groaned and fought to push his cock through tiresome
threads. But suddenly, we heard footsteps approaching. Daddy
hitched his belt and pulled away. The twin retreated as we walked
away from her. She backed away like she was running off to join
the carnival.

The sun had morphed into a disapproving eye. My pussy ached for
Daddy's cock, but we could not find any private shaded spots.
Daddy stopped to buy me funnel cakes so I'd get powdered sugar
on my hands and then he licked it off while passersby clucked
meddling tongues. "I need it, Daddy, please," I whispered in his
ear. He got distracted and stopped to try to cop some plush by
throwing rings at a grid of Coke bottles. I saw the octopus man
skulking by but the crowd was cheering wildly as Daddy got a
ringer. "We've got a sharpie!" the carnie yelled, pulling down a
giant blue bear with his shepherd's crook. Daddy told me I could
put the bear between my legs at night when I was waiting up for
him. He said the bear was wicked just like me and liked rubbing
up against the Coke bottles while carnies slept. He asked if I
would like to feel the Coke bottle inside his pants. I grinned and
said, "Yes, Daddy, please." I loved it when he let me know my
waiting time was up. He led me back behind the line of game
booths where the narrow alley filled with aromatic funnel cake exhaust.

He eased the ragged edge of cutoffs to the side and rammed
two fingers into me and made me smell the way my pussy was
burnt sugar. Then he gave a furtive look around and opened up his
belt buckle and asked me if I wanted to feel his Coke bottle, and I
said yes. He took my hand and slid it between denim and his box-
ers. "I don't think that is a bottle," I said skeptically, but when I
tried to pull away he grabbed my wrist.

"I think it is," he said. "If Daddy Billy says it is. Now if you put your fingers in a ring and rub them up and down the bottle, you might win another prize."

"You're trying to trick me like a dirty carnie," I said indignantly. "I know that it's your thing and not a bottle. I'm not some dumb white carnie trash." I hitched my tube top higher and I tightened up the knot that held my gingham shirt above my belly stud.

"Well," Daddy said, "close your eyes and put your fingers in a ring and I will show you that it is. Have you heard of soda jerks? You are the pretty girl your daddy needs to jerk his soda." Daddy Billy took my hand and rubbed it up and down his thing. He had the special Japanese flex-dick on, the one that felt like skin. "Oh honey, you are such a good girl when you do that and you're going to get a *very* special prize," he groaned. I felt his fingers prying up the edge of my cutoffs. He moved my panties over quickly and he rammed the bottle into me. His hips were pushing me against a pole.

"Not here," I said, and tried to push him off, though inside I was squeezing, holding him, and oh, he felt so good. "You're lying. It's a trick."

"I have to fuck you, baby girl. You know you make my cock ache."

He wrapped his arm around the pole and pinned me there and snarled into my ear. "You're such a dirty girl," he said. "To wear these slutty cutoff jeans, so loose that anyone can find a way inside you. What's Daddy supposed to do but pop your cherry with his soda pop?" I closed my eyes and, just to humor him, pretended I believed he had a bottle, not a dick. He fucked me hard against the pole to make me feel the temper of the glass. I wondered what would happen if the bottle shattered in me and I had a bunch of fragments cutting me and liquid spilled inside me until my blood was carbonated. Behind my eyes, I saw a screen of bubbly blood, the little comic bubbles emptied of their words. What if Daddy's shards would never leave, and hurt me every time he pulled away because they wanted wholeness back? And what if I became a mirror maze inside so nobody could tell which me I was, and whether I was inside me or out? He seemed to want to shatter us.

Out of the corner of my eye, I saw a tapestry of moving clothes. Daddy had a way of making raunchy things look innocent, and though I worried, we did not get caught. "You feel so sweet," I whispered in his ear. He moved his cock so gracefully. I thought of standing really still and spreading out my legs so wide that nothing would shatter and there would be no bottlenecking in the thruways of my heart.

"That's right," said Daddy. "Spread your legs so wide for Daddy. Let me in."

I didn't tell him how I felt like glass each time I called him "Daddy." A luminous cocoon that's twirled around a pole into a fire until it takes the shape of something else, until its roundness grows and all of its blue beauty comes to light. I couldn't tell him what it was to be a Daddy's Girl, the way I burned in screaming fires to take the shape of what I had become.

But some distortion from the Fun House cast a spell on me. As good as Daddy felt to me, I was so hollow afterward, like something scraped out with a knife. Maybe the pulsing lights and sounds and sugar shock had made me yearn. I watched the roller coaster ratchet up a hill and thought, some day, the ride must end. It's Newton and the apple. Up goes down.

I realized that I was waiting for a ticket. Some way out. But I did not know why.

"Hey, you," the octopus man called out. I was half tranced with afterglow. I had been watching people rock atop the Ferris wheel, and playing with green rattling beads around my wrist. He cupped a cigarette and slithered out of nowhere, leagues from where he should have been. "I have been trying to corner you all day," he said. I'd heard about the carnies who taught girls to barter blow jobs for a ride. I braced myself and licked my lips. Daddy had strolled off to find a Port-a-Potty and I couldn't see him in the crowd. "I know who you are," he said. "You rode the octopus that night when it was storming. Thursday, right?"

"You wouldn't let me down," I answered curtly.

"Sorry," he said, lighting up his smoke. "But I was high from cotton candy syrup. I was so high the moon was telling puns, and then the storm rolled in."

"I could have been electrocuted! All the other rides stopped long before you let me down." I crossed my arms around my belly, so he couldn't catch a glimpse of skin. I'd noticed that his eyes were drifting over me. One eye was edged with brine; the other one was clear. I licked my lips again, in case I had to lubricate a scream.

"I know, and that's why I have found you now. One time, when I was younger, I was struck by lightning and I died. That's why I thought I should apologize," he said. His whole face frowned into a toady droop.

"You died?" I asked. I wondered if I smelled to him like I'd been fucked. My hands were fragrant as a caramelizing pan. He had an octopus-like quality. His flesh looked pliable, like he could cram himself into a tiny space, or camouflage his freakishness to blend in with a school of sharks that might have otherwise devoured him.

"I died and was resuscitated. When I touch things now, I give a shock," he said. He grabbed my arm and jolted me. He also had a quality of suction. I felt drawn to him and couldn't pull away. "So, miss lone rider, tell me, is that person you are with a guy or a girl?" he asked.

"What do you think?" I said. I felt uneasy. Daddy Billy often passed as male. But secretly, he wore a sports bra cinching both his breasts, and underneath his dick he had an opening we never talked about. He hadn't taken T and had no plans of doing surgery. I loved his body's complex history.

"I think if that's your daddy and he takes advantage of a little girl like you, perhaps you should run off and join the carnival." The octopus man blew smoke in little puffs. I coughed. Had he been eavesdropping? "I told you that I know you, who you are," he said and tapped his chest. "Aversion therapy will not cure a girl like you," he said, and touched my arm again so that I felt a shock. "You're quite the conduit. I saw the way you made your friend light up."

His old tobacco teeth were grinning in a yellow rind.

"You're one of us," he said. "You are a freak. So come tonight at midnight, when the carnival is closed. The carnies meet to ride the rides. Stop by the gate and bring your friend. We'll let you in." He sidled off and ducked behind a tent flap, winking with his wayward eye. "Come one, come all," he said and swept the air. "Before we strike the tents and watch the grand illusion fall." I saw that Daddy had his fists clenched as he ambled up.

"I told you not to talk to carnie folk," he said, and slapped me on the butt. "Don't make me put an apple in your mouth and have you crawl ass first into the Future Farmers of America display. Remember, you are *Daddy's* little pig today." He kissed my cheek and led me off to play.

Daddy was right. I was a little pig who never had her fill of thrills. By that night, I felt as hollow as a whistle made of rotted trees. Maybe the tall, dismembered Ferris wheel began to get to me. When we approached, it was a giant piece of star anise but had no seats from which to kick the stars. The other lights were dimmed to dissuade townsfolk, so rides revolved with minimal illumination. Some carnies worked to strike the game booths down, but others twirled batons of fire, or gave a balding friend a cotton candy hairdo. Everything was shadowy, giving an eerie sense of dissolution. I'd changed into a frilly summer dress, and Daddy wore some pants that bulged out to signify he was a dude. I felt so sexy hanging on his arm. "Come on, you two," the octopus man yelled, and beckoned us with grinning warmth. "I'll stop you at the top and you can hang out there and watch the stars. There's nothing like it."

His girlfriend, Cherry, dangled on his arm. "Frank's right," she said. "Be brave—don't be an octopussy." Cherry stroked a tattoo of a tiny snake behind her ear. Her belly fat filled out the fabric of her dress to make foothills beneath her giant boobs. The octopus man—Frank, she'd said—clamped down the bar of our seat and pulled the throttle back. He watched us spin a bunch of times, then slowly stopped the ride so we were poised on top. The wind was rocking us and then it stopped.

The pod was weighted so we hung half upside down and couldn't look behind us, only up. We hung from spider silk; it felt that weightless. The sky was going to suck the blood right out of me. Then Daddy grabbed me with a clammy hand. I looked and saw the beads of sweat, the way his breath had changed to panic speed. Daddy was terrified. He didn't like to lose control. I pointed to the sky and told him Orion's belt was strapping us in place. "But your belt has to go," I said. "So that you can relax." He nodded gratefully.

I slid the leather from the clasp. I worked my mouth around his cock. "Oh, baby girl," he said, and grabbed my hair. I wanted him to feel that he was in a hammock of my care. Instead, he leaned back and he thought of barber's chairs and sexy women brushing tiny hairs away, or La-Z-Boys and daily blow jobs from a loyal wife. "I saw a shooting star just now," he said, as he continued thrusting in my mouth. "I filled my balls with shooting stars and now you're going to swallow them." I bobbed my head so that he'd know I understood. I took him deep into my throat. "Oh yes," he said. "Eat up the universe from me."

He fed me meteors. "You are the best," I said, and hugged him when his dick was done. I meant it. I was dazzled then.

The moon had turned into a magnifying glass, and it was burning out our insect eyes each time we wandered into light, so we sought shelter in the carnie tent. "It's time for dirty Truth or Dare," said Frank. "Are you two in the game?" At this point, we felt warm, embraced, and Daddy sat beside me with his palm on my knee.

"We're in," he said.

They made me drink enough to numb an elephant, and that's when things got raunchy. On a dare, Frank's girl began to do a sexy dance on me. She hiked her juicy gorgeous leg up on my shoulder. She took my hand and rubbed it up and down her wisp of underwear. Her pussy smelled like dandelion wine and winding wind that grabs at any cloying flower. I rubbed along her pussy lips with the beer bottle. I bent down and I blew a hollow sound into the bottle, then held it like a tuning fork against her clit. She made the oddest little dolphin chirps, then moaned. She looked at me and said, "Now you. Lie back, so I can test how breakable you are."

I looked at Daddy and I shrugged. I rested back against the folding chair and Cherry straddled me. She pried my legs apart and yanked my panties off. I loved how big and rough and soft she was. My folding chair began to tilt. That's when I accidentally backed into the velvet drape that sectioned off the tent, and saw the startled boi behind the velvet shield. The boi was sitting in a wheelchair and his biceps flexed when he rolled back the wheels reflexively. He had an octopus tattoo on his left arm. "J. Monarch Young!" she scolded him. "What are you doing there?" The boi looked sheepish and she shook her head. She said to me, "That's Young. He is the son of Frank. He's paraplegic from a test ride fall. He is a naughty little voyeur too."

Young coughed and shyly said, "Hello."

"You ready for the bottle, dear?" she asked me gently. Young's eyes were tracing me. "To join the carnival, you swallow either fire or glass," she said.

"I swallow glass," I said, and grinned at her. I felt the coolness and the ridges of the bottle's mouth, and tried to open up my hole for her. I wasn't just performing so that Daddy could get off. I was performing for the boi. I knew his eyes were riveted on where he wished he'd put a message in a bottle just for me. As people hooted from the side, I glimpsed the boi's gray eyes. I saw the tension in his skull beneath his perfect crew cut and I wanted to find handholds of his bones. "I think you've had your christening," said Cherry, pulling out the glass. "You're shatterproof and bulletproof. I toast you with my eighty proof." She raised the whiskey bottle and she drank a slug. "As carnies used to say, 'You've got some snap in your garter, sweetheart.' "

Seeing the boi gave me a flutter in my belly, so I thought I'd better wander off to ride some rides alone. I half hoped—fantasized—that Young would find me sectioned off from Daddy Billy but I doubted that he would. I closed my eyes and felt the Tilt-O-Whirl lift up my dress, and then I wandered farther out to the periphery of human noise. The cornfields came right up to where the fairgrounds ended and I strolled up to the edge to stare at them. At night, they stood as still as antelope that know they're being watched. I loved how soft the grass got when it had been broken down. I felt a little dizzy so I lay on the tamped green. It was as soft as puppy fur and then I felt the infamous stealth wind that comes at such a tiny height and underscores the breathy and affected speech that's slung above. I was enjoying how the Great Plains wind felt tickling at my nipples when I heard their stomping feet. The two guys chortled devilishly. I lifted up my head. I saw the two of them, and Daddy said, "I've finally sold you to the carnival." He smirked.

"You've *what*?" I asked. I sat up and I brushed the dirt out of my hair.

"I've sold you to the dirty carnie folk," he said. His face was smug.

Frank gestured with his sucking arms. "I bought you from your daddy for *one* night. To do it with my kid. We made a deal."

I'd promised Daddy, late some nights when he was fucking me, that I would always be his whore. He said these words a lot: *You're Daddy's slut, his whore, his prostitute, his fuck-hole, tricky little trick.* I loved it when he talked to me like that. One time, I dressed up and he dropped me off beside the river where the fags turned tricks. I waited on a bench in ripped-up stockings and a miniskirt and fetish shoes until he came and lured me into the car and gave me twenty bucks to suck his cock. It was so hot the way he forced it down my throat that day, as if he didn't care how much I gagged. We made a lot of promises and deals when we made love. We used a fake fiducial language but I never thought he'd pimp me out for *real*.

"Just one night," goaded Frank. His voice was pitchy, not quite on its tracks.

"How old's your kid?" I asked.

"The kid is nineteen, never had a girl. The kid's shy ever since the accident and not-so-certain gender situation."

He could not say it: *My kid's queer. He wants to make it with a little pervert girl like you.* Frank only had his suction, and he used it to derail me with his voice. "Please?" he begged. "The thing is, Young had picked you out this afternoon. He saw you overturning rubber ducks to win some shoddy trinket and—quite honestly—I never seen his eyes light up like that."

"I can't," I answered. "It's not right." I backed away but was fenced in.

So Daddy Billy turned to Frank and said, "I'll handle her," and herded me against the fence. He rubbed his bulge against my pubic bone. He made me quiver, gasp. He knew my weaknesses. He took his hand—which he had outfitted with one warm leather glove—and held my neck beneath my chin. He traced my jawbone with his thumb. "Won't you be Daddy's perfect whore?" he asked me sweetly. "Daddy was so nice and took you to the carnival." In truth, I thought that Young was beautiful but knew I'd better protest some, or Daddy would be jealous later. I knew that Daddy thought a brother in a wheelchair wouldn't be a threat. This knowledge made me realize the one thing that unnerved me about Daddy Billy: Daddy felt a power over everything he saw as weak, and I could not be sure I wasn't cast in the same caste.

I let my voice get soft, coquettish. "I guess so, Daddy, if it's what you want." I loved to please him anyway.

"Good girl," he said to me, then, "Sold!" he yelled to Frank. They put a blindfold on me and they made me walk in front of them. I had a vague awareness that the plank I walked was pivotal for me. I felt the warmth of light and heard the buzzing insects as we neared Young's tent. "I'll come back when you've sanded down the kid," I heard Frank say. The tent flapped shut behind me and I listened to Young's breathing, and his wheels creaking as he came my way. He traced my knucklebones with fingertips. He pulled me toward his chair.

"Sit on my lap," he said. "Tell me what pity story they gave you so that you'd stay."

When I sat down on him, still blindfolded, I felt what he was packing in his pants. "How did you—?" I asked.

"Idle hands make idle minds, but nimble hands shape ideal packaging," he said. "They told you that I've never done it, right?"

"I find that hard to fathom."

"I've never done it, not the way I want." He wrapped his arms around me and he kissed my neck. "My life consists of dictatorial wheels and all I want to do is reinvent the wheel with this, my dick." I reached down and I put my hand around his bulge. I turned and started kissing him, his salty mouth. I ran my hands over his muscular arms. He slipped the blindfold off my eyes so I could see his grinning face. I touched his bristly crew cut. I stroked the bluish bands of his tattoo. He cupped my hair and pulled me to his lips and gave me an exquisite kiss. "I saw you at the carnival today," he said. "I knew you wanted to be watched." I stood up and walked around his chair.

"I did," I said. "I do." And then I started playing with his buttons and his belt loops, lifting up my leg and pulling back my dress so he could see the vacant place where underwear was ripped away. I touched my close-cropped pubes and stroked one finger on my pussy and then traced it where his barely-mustache grazed his upper lip.

"Smell me," I said. He inhaled deeply, then he grabbed for me. I pulled away and kneeled down so that he could see into the V of cleavage. I pulled his belt out of its latch and started undoing the buttons of his pants. And then I freed it—his enormous cock. "It's huge," I laughed. "Most people who are virgins don't go out and buy Paul Bunyan's dick."

"The carnival believes in grandiosity," he said. I licked the massive head and took his huge cock in my mouth. I swear I felt the ground drop down beneath me, like it did on the centrifugal force ride. I wanted his cock deep, to choke on it, to show the boi his cock was magical. He moaned a little bit. "Now will you ride me?" he asked, timidly. "Will you ride on my chair?"

"I'd love to ride you, Young."

I backed on top of him and slid my pussy down his cock. The head went in, and then I let my weight down so his cock was unilaterally inclined to fuck. "Oh God," I said, "you feel amazing." He wrapped both his arms around me and began to kiss my earlobes and my hair. His fingers started pulling up my dress until he had it at my shoulders. He grabbed my boobs and held me by them so I squeezed against his chest. I rocked back on his cock. Then cleverly, he moved the wheelchair back and forth. "Just ride me, baby," said the boi. With one hand on the wheel, he rocked us in erratic jolts, so that the cock was fucking me—and he was fucking me—despite the fact that he could not move anything below his waist. His other hand was sliding down my soft bare skin and reaching for my clit. He licked his middle finger and he started circling my clit. "You take a lot of cock for such a little girl," he said. And then he fiddled with my clit until he made me come.

"Don't move," he said, as I was gasping from how sweet his fingers felt. He pulled my dress back down. He took his coat and placed it on my lap. "I'm going to wheel you through the carnival while I am still inside you. I've always wanted to do that."

His cock was threading me onto its shaft. His wheelchair did a loop around the grounds. The rides were whirling round. The carnies waved at us, and, when I said hello to them, teased, "Are you a ventriloquist now, Young?" They didn't know that he was fucking me right then, and acted like I was a wooden dummy and he was a star. I ground my pussy down on him and looked back so that I could see his grinning face. He took me to the edge of things, where rides had already been disassembled. The fantasy was breaking down, and Young was suddenly symbolic of my blooming need for change. I wanted something sweet and virginal. I put a blanket down and scooped him from his chair. For hours, we cuddled and we lay inside a circle of the flattened grass, as if the axles of a carousel had broken and we had fallen under the hooves of a wooden horse stampede. I'd been undone by him.

"You look so sacrificial in those savaged clothes," J. Monarch Young exclaimed. "What will you do when all these mechanical illusions drive away?"

"I will go home to Daddy and my real life. Why do you ask?" I touched his face.

"Because my cock wants more of you. I think you want it too."

For just a moment, I felt something rising from the beaten

fairgrounds, a construction not of steel or fantasy but heart. Young braided grass into a ring. I broke off little sticks and made a tiny raft. "Look at the waist-high fields out there," Young said. "I always thought their layout looked like squares on calendars. And yet, you shouldn't have to feel boxed in."

"What if I do?" I asked. "The Fun House has to end."

"Well, sure, but think of the alternatives. Perhaps you need a carnival that doesn't end, with a defector from a land of freaks," he said, and looked at me so earnestly. "I'll stay and be your Tilt-O-Whirl. I'll give you tickets. You can ride on me all day."

The crickets turned their legs into string instruments just then. Something so usual seemed capable of reinvention. I realized why people ran away to join the carnival, and then ran back again: to make the axis turn. "All's fair in love and fairground whores," I said, and took Young's hand and led it to my ragged hem and slid it in.

# From *Villages*

## John Updike

It had been his father who had successfully urged him to get a practical, scientific education. Floyd Mackenzie's experience of the Depression had been that engineers were the last people to be fired; he had seen it happen. "The kid needs to latch on to something practical," he announced. "He's in danger of dreaming his brains away." The boy's brains—demonstrated by stellar high-school marks and his ability, during his years of rural isolation, to entertain himself with books and pencil and paper—could be, he reasoned, best engaged by machinery, if not by the giant knitting machines, as long and heavy as freight cars, whose ill-rewarded servant he himself had been, then by some other kind of construction (bridges, dams, dynamos) whose indispensable utility was more obvious to the world than that of strict, honest accountancy. In a materialist age, matter must be trusted. As events proved, the machines of the future were to be lightweight—rockets leaving earth's gravity and computers quicker than human minds, adjuncts of human subjectivity freeing us into an oxygenless space.

An institution in far-off Massachusetts, a so-called Institute of Technology, offered Owen a scholarship. His being a student from a small rural school system, in a Middle Atlantic state, helped his chances with the bestowers of admissions and student aid. He never saw MIT before he got there. The buildings were set back from an artificially broadened river, the Charles, across from a venerable city, Boston, that held at the summit of a cut-down hill a sallow gold dome from under which the Commonwealth was governed. In the early 'fifties, pre-war shabbiness still ruled Cambridge and Boston, yet they were cities of youth, of students eager to make a future. Sailboats and rowing sculls rippled the river, a glittering sporting site bluer than the Schuylkill, which had been black with coal silt. This Commonwealth seemed toylike and polychrome, compared with the industrial scale of Pennsylvania—its sooty cities built on grids, its row houses climbing the hills like stairs. Boston in its oldest parts was laid out not on a grid but on a pattern, it was said, of ancient cowpaths, widened by Puritan footsteps and then paved in cobblestones.

Back Bay, a filled-in marsh, did form a grid, with a grassy central mall ornamented by elms and bronze statues. A long and windswept bridge misnamed Harvard Bridge connected Back Bay with MIT, its hovering pale dome eerily evoking, from across the river, the flying saucers from which, in those days, extraterrestrial creatures were supposedly spying, with impotent solicitude, upon a benighted planet about to blow itself up with atomic bombs. MIT seemed heroic in the grand and mazy scale of its vast central building: a series of buildings interconnected by passageways, each segment known not by a name but by a number. The main entrance, numbered 77 Massachusetts Avenue, led into Building 7, where six great pillars and a high circumcameral inscription to INDUSTRY, THE ARTS, AGRICULTURE, AND COMMERCE upheld the limestone dome. Fabled Building 20, the "plywood palace" on Vassar Street, had sheltered secret radar researches by which, it was said, the Second World War had been won. Underground infusions of government and corporate wealth continued to enlist scientific intelligence in the Cold War. In the analysis center and the digital computer laboratory—rooms entirely taken up with arrayed cabinets full of wires and vacuum tubes, fed by punched cards—all the radar stations around the United States were linked, undergraduate rumors claimed, and electric circuits calculated missile trajectories that a hundred savants with pencils could not compute in a hundred years.

MIT was a male world, its administrators and instructors all but exclusively male, and a number of them military men. Though the great post-war tide of veterans was receding, uniforms were still common on campus. Of six thousand students, no more than one hundred twenty were women, and half of these were graduate students. Phyllis Goodhue stood out, then, as one of a decided minority, outnumbered fifty to one in the endless corridors—floors of tan terrazzo and doors of frosted glass strictly numbered in black, even the women's lavatory: 3-101-WOMEN. She was yet more noticeable among the spingtime sunbathers in the Great Court, a large sheltered lawn between Buildings 3 and 4 that overlooked the new segment of Memorial Drive, its double row of sycamores, and, in their gaps, the sparkling, playful Charles and the rosy low profile of Back Bay. Most of the female undergraduates were not lovely—driven grinds with neglected figures and complexions, heads down in the hallways as they bucked the tide, trying to blend in with the boys—and Owen had to look twice at Phyllis to verify that she was. Was lovely.

True or false? Was twice necessary? No: from the start, through that river-chilled, sleepless, and miserable first year in which his head was being stuffed with, among other rafts of basic data, introductory circuit theory (Kirchhoff's law and Thévenin's and Norton's theorems, step function and impulse response, resonance phenomena and conjugate impedances), whenever Owen

passed Phyllis in one of the thronged corridors, his own electro-
magnetic field changed, by an amount as subtle but as crucial as
the difference between dø and dt. There was a numbness only she
inflicted. Her presence transformed the odd-shaped cement-
paved spaces scattered among the buildings west of the Kendall
Square subway stop, where bleary students loitered over gossip
and cigarettes; like Ginger Bitting, this apparition had satellites, a
few other girls but, inevitably in this environment, mostly boys.
Owen's eyes placed her at the center of this set, though in truth
she never appeared to dominate. In a boisterous cluster she stood
at the edge and appeared diffidently amused; she never laughed
the loudest. She had a light but clear, carrying voice—he could
overhear her long before seeing her—and careful gestures, re-
strained by a reluctance to impose herself that moved him and
emboldened him. At his watchful distance, her pallor was a bea-
con, a broadcast resonance.

She held her head, with its slightly outthrust chin, erect on a
long neck. Her straight hair, the mixed blond of half-damp sand,
was gathered into a ponytail in back with a rubber band. In the
front, bangs came down to her pale eyebrows, which blended with
her skin, her brows and eyelashes were almost invisible. She wore
no makeup, not even lipstick, and smoked poutingly, her cheeks
deeply hollowed on the inhale and her exhale delivered with a certain dismissive vehemence, upward from the side of her mouth. In
her offhand, underclad (the same dove-gray cloth coat and dirty
tennis sneakers all winter) glamour she came to represent Cambridge for him—aloof, stoic, abstracted, pure. And he discovered
that indeed she was a professor's daughter; her father was Eustace
Goodhue, biographer of the clergyman-poet George Herbert and
editor of variorum editions of the Metaphysicals and lecturer in
English at that other place, the university up the river, where the
humanities, descended from Puritan theological studies, still
ruled, leaving science to the world's worker-bees.

Her distinguished daughterly status was part of the effect she made—made deliberately, he felt. She was like him, he sensed: shy, but with the caution of someone guarding a proud ego. Taller than average, she slouched as if to minimize her bosom, the fullness of which her dowdy winter wraps did not quite conceal. It was even less concealed when, on hot fall days, and again in the sunny breaks of April and May, she took off the long gray coat that made her look like a slender doorman or military attaché and lay stretched on a blanket in the middle of the Great Court with her skirt hiked to the middle of her thighs and her sweater and blouse down to (he could not be sure at his distance) a bathing-suit top or a bra.

She looked like no girl from Pennsylvania, not even the fancy ones from the Main Line. Elsie Seidel, his high-school girlfriend, the daughter of a country feed-and-hardware merchant, was always smartly turned out, with polished penny loafers and ribbed knee socks and sweeping skirts and broad belts in the New Look style, and tortoiseshell barrettes gleaming in the bouncy waves of her light-brown hair. And plenty of lipstick, maroon lipstick that looked black in photographs and rubbed off on his mouth so that, afterwards, it stung to wipe it away with spit on a handkerchief. He didn't want his mother to see; his mother didn't want him to go with Elsie at all, though the girl was respectable, more respectable locally than were the Mackenzies, newcomers to this end of the county and to the school district. The district encompassed several valleys and included families whose first language was still Pennsylvania Dutch. Elsie herself spoke with a "Dutchy" care, slower than girls in Willow talked—her voice seemed older than she was.

There was a country simplicity to her, a well-fed glossiness. The first time they kissed, in the intermission of a dance that Owen had attended because his mother urged him to be less scornful of the region's high school even though it wasn't Willow High, Elsie didn't make the anxious pushing mouth that Alice

Stottlemeyer had during spin-the-bottle but somehow let her lips melt into his, at this warm moist spot where their bodies joined. She was a short girl, in her sweated-up taffeta dance dress, and he, six feet tall at seventeen, the recent beneficiary of the Mackenzie ranginess. She had to tug down at him to keep his face tight to hers; she wanted to kiss more, there behind a broken Coke machine, where the overhead fluorescent light was flickering. Her eager small body molded itself to his; he remembered hearing how Carol Wisniewski had let herself be fucked by Marty Naftzinger standing up in the narrow space between the Rec Hall and the hosiery mill, and saw that it could be done.

Not that he and Elsie ever—in a word they never used between them—fucked. He was too smart for that, too anxious to avoid wasting his one life. He knew that fucking led to marriage and he was not ready for that. In the heat and urgency of that first kiss he recognized that she had had her eye on him, as the phrase went—he had been an exotic, aloof arrival at the school, and somehow the idea of him had wormed its way excitingly into Elsie's head. So between them there was always this tilt, this unbalance: she had desired him before he knew what was up. Nevertheless, he responded; he loved her, as far as he could shake the embarrassment of her not being a Willow girl. She was only, in her swinging skirts and white bobby socks, an imitation, a feed merchant's daughter.

He would afterwards associate Elsie with the inside of a car—its stale velour, its little dim dashboard lights, its rubber floormats and chill metallic surfaces. Chill to begin with: after an evening of driving around, the heater made a cozy nook in the dark. On dates, they took his parents' stuffy pre-war Chevy, the secondhand car the Mackenzies had bought as part of their move to the country house. His father was generally back from Norristown by six, and Owen was granted the car for the gasoline-powered roaming that is, in common American wisdom, a teenager's right.

Before Elsie, he would sometimes drive back to Willow, looking for the action among his old friends and rarely finding it. He
saw Willow now, having left at twelve, with an exile's eyes, as a
small provincial place where life—the social life of his own class-
mates, the bunch at the playground half grown-up—went on without him, out of sight: a deserted village. His grandfather's chicken
house was losing some of its asbestos shingles, he could see as he
cruised by in the alley that bent around their old house. Not that
he was certain to have been happy had his family stayed. Adolescence reshuffles the cards. As a child be had been more spectator
than actor, valued primarily as a loyal follower, an admirer—of
Buddy Rourke, of the girls he scarcely dared imagine naked.

Now, with Elsie in the car, he had real nakedness to deal with.
At first, just kissing, on and on, eyes closed to admit behind sealed
lids a flood of other sensations, an expansion of consciousness into
a salty, perfumed space quite unlike the hushed and headlong
vault of masturbation. In the dark seclusion between cool tight
sheets, his parents' muttering having died away, he would seem for
some seconds to stand on his head, having discovered with his left
hand a faithful mechanism impossibly sweet, an astonishing release, a clench that took him back to infancy, its tight knit of new-
ness before memories overlaid the bliss of being. Into this private
darkness had come another, another seeker, and what was being
found, clumsily yet unstoppably, was a core self explored by another consciousness. Elsie was both witness and witnessed. Her
eyes were the wet, honey-tinged brown of horehound drops. By
the particles of light that entered through the windshield he saw
the dark dents of her dimples when she smiled, and the side of
one eyeball gleam as she studied him across a gap that closed in a
few seconds. Huddled beside him on the front seat, a bench seat
in that era, with her back gouged by the knob of the window crank
and her calves and ankles roasted by the heater, she seemed
cupped to receive him, a nest of growing permissions. With each

date she gave him an inch or two more of herself that he could claim as his henceforth; there was no taking back these small warm territories. Beyond kissing there was so much to touch, so many hooks and tricks among the catches and aromatic coverings, there in the shelter of the car, which sometimes became her car, for, though a year younger than he, she also had a driver's license, and when his poor old family Chevy was under overnight repair or commandeered for some adult evening errand, she would bring a car of her family's, her mother's green Dodge or even her father's new deep-blue Chrysler with its V-8 engine, to pick him up, at the farmhouse where his mother had not without a struggle accepted that Elsie had become his "girl," whatever that meant as the world embarked on a new half-century.

Some of those evenings when Elsie did the driving, pulling up in an impressive machine, she would be invited in, into the little house's front parlor, where the bulky Rausch furniture from the Willow house had suddenly gone shabby and was covered with hairs from the two collies his mother had acquired as part of her vision of rural life. Smartly dressed in this setting of declining gentility, at whose edges Owen's two grandparents made a shuffling, murmuring retreat, Elsie spoke to Owen's mother with a lively courtesy. Her honey-brown eyes flashed; her scarlet lips smiled. Uneasily standing by, in a flannel shirt whose sleeves were too short, in scuffed laced shoes that looked oafish compared with Elsie's polished penny loafers (much on view as she smartly crossed and recrossed her legs), Owen felt like a baton being passed. He felt he was present, as one pleasantly followed another, at a duel. His mother too had once been the smartly turned-out daughter of a successful rural entrepreneur; she knew a certain code, she knew "how to behave." She also knew how people *did* behave, and couldn't do much about it.

When the young people, these social observances discharged, achieved freedom in a car of Elsie's, it seemed perverse, after the movie or the miniature golf was behind them and they had found a parking spot, to have her seated on his left instead of on his right. Come at this way, she felt like a strange girl, with whom he must begin from scratch. Their chins and mouths made angles opposite from the usual, and his hands coped with reversed routes.

"Should we switch?" she asked, when he remarked on this strangeness. Her voice came out breathier, lower in her throat, than the polite, Dutch-flavored voice she used with his mother and the teachers at school. Her lipstick had already begun to smear and flake. Her face was waxily lit by a streetlamp half a block away; they sometimes parked in a hidden place he knew from his childhood walks, at the back of the Dairy Queen lot on Cedar Top. He lived ten miles away, and she four miles more to the south, but Willow was the town whose map he knew and where he felt safest. Other times, they would park up by Shale Hill, near what had been the Victory Gardens, on a dirt road made by recent developers. Always, as the scope of her permissions widened, he searched for even safer spots, where the police would never come up and shine flashlights in their faces, as once had happened, behind the long low sheds of the old farmers' market. As she sat high behind the wheel of her father's expensive car, her mussed hair caught fire in stray loops and strands from the distant streetlamp.

"Let's," he agreed. "If you don't mind my sitting behind your father's wheel."

"I don't mind, Owen. I don't like it poking me in the ribs all the time. I don't see how you can stand it."

"Elsie, when I'm with you, I don't notice such things. Here I go. I'll get out and you slide over."

Thrusting himself into the public space outside the automobile, where adult morality pressed down from the stars, he opened and shut the Chrysler's passenger door (it made that sucky rich rattle-free sound) and scuttled around the broad chrome bumper and white-walled rear tires hunched over, for he already had an erection. Even behind his fly it felt scarily as if it might snag on something, until he settled behind her father's steering wheel, which wore a suede cover. The tang of new-car smell was warmed into freshness by the heat of their bodies. As he slid across the front seat, wide enough for three, into the space where she huddled, the far streetlamp illuminated her blurred face and a small pearl earring and the fuzzy wool of her short-sleeved angora sweater. She let him slide the sweater up and sneak a finger into her bra and stroke the silk skin there, the gentle fatty rise of it. Though Elsie was plump her breasts were small, as if still developing. When he had advanced to taking off her bra and pushing the sweater way up, her chest seemed hardly different from his own; a breast of hers in his hand felt as delicate as a tear bulging in his eye. One night, parked this time up by the Victory Garden wasteland, where the streetlamp was closer than on Cedar Top, he watched raindrops on the windshield make shadows on her chest, thin trails that hesitated and fell as his fingertips traced and tried to stop them, there, and there. She had dear little nipples like rabbit noses. She let him kiss them, suck them until she said in her breathy, un-Dutchy voice, "Ow, Owen. Enough, baby," and touched his head the way the barber did when he wanted it to move. Sitting up, he made circles with his finger and his saliva around her nipples, softly round and round, loving the sight of them so much he felt dizzy, as the parallel shadows of the raindrops faintly streaked her chest and the backs of his hands.

She never touched his prick. It was too sacred, too potent. They pretended it wasn't there, even when their bodies straightened at the angle permitted by the front seat and its heater-crowded foot space and he held her buttocks through her rumpled skirt and pressed himself rhythmically against her, all the time their mouths kissing, until he came, came in his underpants, where the dried jism made a brittle stain he later picked off with his fingernail, hoping his mother wouldn't notice it when she did the wash. In the house they had now she did the wash in a dim cobwebby space under the cellar stairs, on a newer machine than the tub-shaped one that had seized his hand in the Willow basement; this machine had a lid that closed, and a spin-dry phase in its cycle instead of a wringer.

His sense of sexual etiquette was primitive, gleaned from the way men and women acted in the movies up to their huge close-up kiss at the end, and from enigmatic dialogue in a few books, like *For Whom the Bell Tolls* and *Forever Amber* and *A Rage to Live* and *The Amboy Dukes,* that he had looked into, and from a pornographic poem that Marty Naftzinger's younger brother, Jerry, a runty curly-haired kid in Owen's class, could recite, if you paid him a dime. But it was developed enough to ask, after one such climax against her compliant body, "What can we do for you?"

This embarrassed her. Elsie liked to pretend that what had just happened hadn't happened at all. "How do you mean?"

This made him shy in turn. "I mean—just holding still for me isn't enough, is it?"

She said, "We can't do more, Owen. There might be consequences you don't want." She never touched his prick and never said "I love you," knowing it would put him to the discomfort of saying the same thing back, when he wasn't ready. Otherwise she could have explained, *I love you, I like exciting you, it excites me, isn't that enough for now?*

Yet there was more, both knew it, and as his senior year ran out they groped to find it without committing sins so dark and final their lives would be forever deformed. Elsie was less afraid of this than he; he refused to test how far she would let him "go." It had become their way in the car for him to bend over and kiss the silky warm inner sides of her thighs and then press his mouth as far up as he could into the warmth, her warmth, its aroma at times

like the tang his mother gave off on a summer day and at others of
the musky mash bins in the back of her father's store. At first she
resisted, pushing at his shoulders, and then came to expect it. In
those days even teen-age girls wore girdles: the crotch of her underpants was guarded by edges of stiff elastic, and though she
shyly edged her hips forward in the car seat his lips could not
quite reach the damp cotton. Not that he knew enough to make
her come with his mouth, or how girls came at all. The pleasure
was his, in being this close to a secret, in having her yield it up to
him, even her fragrance, which was strong enough at times to
exert a counterforce, a wish to pull his face away. But he loved it
there between her legs, and how hot and sticky his cheeks grew
against her thighs, and the graceless awkwardness this maneuver
asked of her, still wearing her knee socks and loafers.

The summer before he went off to MIT, their experiments
took on a desperate edge. She knew he was slipping away; the
baton had not been passed after all. Owen had got a summer job
on a surveying crew, tending the target marks and chopping brush
out of the sight lines. Elsie had been sent to a Lutheran camp in
Ohio, where she was a counsellor, for six weeks. He would get
rides with the crew to far corners of the county and have to be
fetched from Alton when he could not hitch a ride south; he
would come home exhausted and dirty, and tried not to think that
college in a foreign region was swooping down upon him and
would carry him away—for good, he both hoped and feared. His
grandparents were ailing and his parents were no longer the young
couple on Mifflin Avenue into whose bed he would climb when a
dream scared him.

After Elsie returned from Ohio, it seemed almost too much
work to take a bath in the farmhouse's one tub and go out again,
into the dark. He and she needed the dark now. With the free-
doms they had granted each other they needed such privacy that
even a distant streetlight or the remotest chance of a Willow cop

with a flashlight and barking voice could not be borne. Where could they go, with their maturing needs and fears of eventual desertion? His summer had not been so distracted that he had missed the implication, in her letters from camp, that she had found companionship with the boy counsellors, or the gossip, when in August she had returned, that while he was cutting brush in future housing developments she was to be seen at the township public pool, lounging in a two-piece bathing suit on a towel on the grass, with another boy, a boy her age, in her class, who would be there with her after September.

"My father owns a hundred acres of woods not that far from Brechstown," she told Owen, after an hour of directionless cruising one evening. "There's an old road in. Nobody ever comes there."

"Sounds perfect," he said, but did it? He let her direct him, turn by turn, on narrow roads he had never driven before. He was frightened at the road entrance, with its No Trespassing sign and rusting remains of barbed-wire fence; there was a sandstone boulder that with his summer muscles he rolled five feet to the side so they could get by. They were in the fragile old black Chevrolet that his father, mocking his own poverty, called "the flivver." As branches raked the creeping car's sides, Owen felt guilt, yet less than if it had been her father's Chrysler, which was kept so shipshape and Simonized. A litter of cans and wrappers in the headlights revealed that others had been here before, also pushing aside the boulder in their strength of desire. The road was rough; the old car rocked. Suppose they broke an axle or got a flat tire? The scandal, the disgrace would stain his charmed life forever.

"Isn't this far enough?" he asked. He felt a trap closing behind him.

"It goes in for a long way but gets worse," Elsie admitted. He turned off the ignition and the headlights. Such darkness! It pounced upon them with an audible crackle; it locked around the

windows as if the car had plunged into a black river. As Owen's
eyes adjusted, he saw a star or two high in the windshield, in the
spaces between the great still trees overhead. Occasional headlights on the dirt road a half-mile away twinkled. Their own headlights must have been equally visible. Elsie's face was a mere
glimmer in the cave of velour, rubber, shaped steel, and shatterproof glass. His lips found hers, and they were full and moist, but
the old melting, one mouth into another, met impediments, things
he couldn't put out of his mind. Suppose the Chevy didn't start
when they wanted to go? Suppose he couldn't back it out on this
overgrown road, the bushes a solid mass behind them and he
without the machete he used on the surveying crew? He felt life, a
silent vegetable life, enclosing them, on this her father's land, this
man present in every leaf and reaching branch. Owen was still
young enough to invest the darkness with spying presences; they
distracted him when he should have been purely bent on the
treasure at hand, in the deepest privacy he and Elsie would ever
know.

It was August; she wore shorts and no girdle. As their embrace
gained ardor and flexibility her crotch came into his hand as if rising to it. She lifted her hips on the car seat so he could slide her
shorts down: through his clumsiness her white underpants came
off with them and Elsie did not try to grab them back. She seemed
to stretch, elongating her belly. Even in this darkness he saw wet
gleams upon her eyeballs like faraway fireflies and the pallor of
her long belly descending to a small soft shadow. Frightened of
that shadow, he turned his attention to her breasts; with a touch
more practiced than with her underpants, he unhooked her bra
and tugged up her short-sleeved jersey. She crossed her arms and
pulled the jersey the rest of the way, up over her head, with the
bra. Her hair, cut shorter this summer so she could be in and out
of the lake at the Lutheran camp, bounced, releasing a scent of
shampoo. The bony smooth roundness of her shoulders gave him

the shock of her nakedness; he hid his face in the side of her neck, saying, "Oh God. I can't stand this."

Her cheek tensed, smiling. "Now you, Owen," she breathed into his ear. "Your shirt."

Quickly, not wanting to let go of her for a second, he pulled it off, wishing he had bathed more carefully at home, for the smell of his armpits joined that of her shampoo and her skin in the close air of the car. He could see more and more, as if light were leaking from the patches of sky in the gaps between the trees, shedding glimmers into the woods, where faint noises were reviving and becoming less faint. He kissed her breasts, trying to be delicate, trying not to bite as the nipples grew hard, while she pressed into his ear a voice that seemed made up, enlarged and rehearsed, like something in the movies: "Owen, I used to take off my clothes in my room and walk around looking at myself in the mirror, wishing you could see me."

"You're beautiful—amazing," he told her, meaning it, but, as if her voice had swabbed out his ears, he now heard other things, whispers and stirrings around them, on the other side of the glass and metal. From somewhere not too distant there was a hoot, an owl or possibly a signal from a murderous, demented gang that lived here in caves and came out at night. *Suppose the car doesn't start?* he thought again. It often didn't, in rainstorms, or on cold mornings, his father frantic, flooding the engine in his panic, so the wearying starter turned it over uncatching, *cooga cooga*. "Did you hear something?" Owen asked Elsie.

She had left her loafers on the gritty floor of the car and had risen up, bare now even to her feet, to kneel on the seat beside him, stroking his face as he tongued her breasts; even in his state of growing terror he marvelled, holding her tight, at the *give* of a girl's waist, at the semi-liquid space below the ribs and then, behind, the downy hard plate at the base of the spine and the glassy globes of her buttocks, smooth into the cleavage, all of it unified like the silvery body of a fish, all so simple and true, the simple truth of her, alive in his arms. He heard the distant hoot again. Something rustled near the car tires. She felt his mouth losing interest in her nipple, and began to listen with him. Behind the skin between her breasts her heart was beating. "I don't think so," Elsie answered him, her voice losing its movie-screen largeness and becoming small, with a childish quaver.

For reassurance she added, "He says nobody ever comes here except in hunting season." But she too must have seen the cans and wrappers in the headlights, evidence of others. *He:* her father, the owner, all around them, hating Owen, what he was doing to his daughter, striving in every twig and trunk to eject the two of them. They listened and heard a noise so faint it could have just been saliva rattling in their held breath. Owen's hands began to move again, gathering her tender taut nakedness closer to him, his fingertips finding a touch of fuzz in the cleavage behind. He wondered how to get his head down to kiss that soft shadow he had glimpsed; it had seemed shyer, gauzier than what he had seen in dirty photographs and drawings, the few he *had* seen. His prick was aching behind his fly, and her hand dropped and, the first time ever, began rumbling at his belt buckle to release it, its imperious pressure, its closeted sour smell.

But he had spooked her, he had spooked them both, and the desire that dominated him, bare-chested though he was, was the desire to escape, to see if the car could start and he could back it up that narrow road without hitting a tree or deep hole. Her father's land, and her nakedness in it like a shout: Owen was vulnerable, criminal even—trespassing, and she a minor. He must restore her intact to society. The rustling he had imagined near the tires became a sudden thrashing, a distinct lunge of the unknown.

"Elsie," he whispered.

"What?" Perhaps expecting some avowal, some earthy plea.

"Let's get out of here."

She hesitated. He heard her heart beat, her breath whistle. "It's up to you," she decided in the mannerly voice that she had used with his mother. Then, catching his mood, she whispered, "Yes, let's."

Often afterwards he would remember details of this hour (her shorts and underpants in one sweep; her gleaming eye-whites; his sense of her slithering into the space above his head like a silken kite, like an angel crammed into an upper corner of a Sienese Nativity) and regret his lack of the boldness that would have let him linger with her gift of herself, and taste it, and let her continue undoing his pants. But his nerves had poisoned their privacy. Naked or not, she was a person, and now a frightened one. His retreat was cowardly but he felt brave and cool, successfully managing the maneuver. He started the engine—thank God, it started, drowning out all those other sounds—and backed down the overgrown road by the wan glow of the back-up lights while branches scraped metal and Elsie scrambled into her clothes. He would have backed up right onto the paved road, not bothering to roll back the boulder, but she said in a voice whose calmness sounded stern, "Owen. We should put it back the way we found it."

Her father's precious land. This had been her show, he realized. He got out angrily and in the glare of his own headlights heaved the rock back into place, for the next trespassers. "Sorry, sorry, sorry," he said when the Chevy was safely running down the highway, to the village, Brechstown, where she lived. "I chickened out."

Elsie said, after lighting a cigarette (rare for her, but girls in Willow smoked, and he had taught her), "You're more citified than I am. Woods don't frighten me. My father and uncle hunt in the fall. There are no bears or anything, not even bobcats anymore. I felt safe."

"You should have told me that while we were in there."

"I *tried* to distract you, to keep you interested."

"You did, you were stunning. I loved it. You."

She was silent, putting his jerky speech together.

He told her, "It's just as well. We might have fucked."

Not a word they used, with others or between themselves: it was a kind of offering. But she held her silence. It occurred to him, his face heating in a blush, that he hadn't been prepared even physically, with one of these rubber things he had seen years ago up by the abandoned Dairy Queen. *Don't touch it!*

She at last spoke: "I wouldn't have let you, Owen. I intend to be a virgin for my husband. It was just, like I said, I wanted you to know me, to see me as I see myself."

"You were beautiful. Are beautiful, Elsie."

Was she crying? "Thank you, Owen," she brought out. "You're a nice person."

Too nice, was the implication. Still, he couldn't blame himself. Her body like that of a slithering cool flexible fish in his arms had been a revelation, but it had been revelation enough for one night.

Were there other nights, to follow? There might have been, but when he looked back, trying to recall each underlit detail, it didn't seem so. Their futures came upon them fast. Elsie had another boyfriend for her senior year, and married yet another boy she met at the local Penn State extension. Surprisingly, they left the region, settling in the San Francisco area. If Owen wouldn't take her away, another would.

They must have driven around that night, burning up gas, letting their heartbeats slow down, trying to talk into place what they had learned about each other and their own lives, before he drove her home, to Brechstown. It was a village almost in Chester County, an erratically spaced cluster such as Willow must have been before the advent of trolley cars made it a suburb of Alton. Right behind the houses were fields and farm buildings, barns whitewashed white by their Amish owners and silos built of a brown-glazed oversized brick. Mr. Seidel's feed-and-hardware

store, with its loading platform and checkered Purina ads, sat between a gas station and a one-man country barbershop, closed, its
striped pole not turning. Elsie waited on store customers on Satur-
days, and Owen had more than once shaken her father's hand in
there; Mr. Seidel was a muscular man bordering on fat, and even
though he lifted eighty-pound feed sacks into the Mennonite
trucks and Amish buggies he wore a shirt and a necktie and a gold
tieclip. He would take Owen's hand with an expert lunge, flashing
a mischievous smile beneath a small, squared-off mustache. His
house was a quarter-mile away, up a long crunching driveway, an
old farmhouse like Owen's own family's but fussily improved. A
new addition held a two-car garage below and a family room
above, with a TV and built-in loudspeakers and furniture that all
matched; the addition was covered in aluminum siding. The original house was built not of sandstone but of limestone, because
that was what the earth yielded here, near the Chester County
line.

When he and Elsie kissed good-night, again there was not that
melting together, though he took the liberty of stroking a breast as
she leaned toward him getting out of the car. Owen felt he had
failed but no one could take from him his stolen treasure, how far
Elsie had "gone," leaving him with a kind of home movie his mind
could run and rerun in a rickety projector, not just in bed but in
inward moments of daylight, flickering bits and pieces of her—her
shampoo, her heartbeat like a stranger knocking on the other side
of a door, the surprising elastic give and stretch of her waist.

# Beatings R Me

## Mr. Sleep

My specialty is choking and savage beatings. So, as a man of the sensitivity required to deliver the best misery money can buy, I have certain pre-stated strictures that will make my time, making your time miserable, just a little bit nicer. For me, of course, you ass.

1)   Lose the Jennifer Lopez CDs before I come the fuck over. Nobody wants to hear them, much less see them, and it just serves as a constant reminder to me that I should have gotten an MBA, instead of squandering my time on MBAs with ass-lashing fetishes, such as yourself.

2)   No sandals. I hate them and you should too.

3)   Don't act like you forgot this is a cash transaction. We're not friends. You don't do it on the bus, so don't do it here.

4)   No sudden moves. It might get someone hurt. And I'm not talking about feelings.

5)   Same goes with "surprises." We don't like them in real life and certainly not while doing outcalls.

6)    Your asking me if you can suck my cock fifteen times in a row is one way to meet Mr. BallGag, because:

7)    *No sex* in our ads means *no sex.* Not a Clintonesque variant of *no sex,* but no cocky, no sucky.

8)    *No,* I do not want anything to drink. I don't trust you that much.

9)    Telling me how beautiful I am won't get me to let you suck my cock.

And last but not least, we'll end this on a positive note:

10)   Fight back all you want. It won't help.

# Ukiyo

## Donna George Storey

It begins respectably enough.

My longtime colleague and friend, Yutaka Yamaguchi, invites me to dinner at one of Kyoto's oldest restaurants. We're celebrating. He's published his second Tanizaki volume, I just got tenure. Along the way I lost a husband, too. Work kept me so frantic this past year it took a month to notice he'd moved out.

My goal this summer, I tell Yutaka, is to rediscover pleasure. Not in books or dreams—I've had plenty of that—but in something I can savor, something I can hold in my hand. The real thing.

For the moment I've found it. We have a table on the terrace to catch the river breeze. The evening sky stretches over us, a bolt of violet silk fading to silver. Young waiters murmur excuses as they bring course after course: slices of sea bream and fluffy, snow-white conger sailing on a miniature boat of ice, eggplant and broiled river eel, wisps of ivory-colored noodles in chilled soy broth.

Yutaka pours more cold sake into my cup, a small work of art in itself with frothy air bubbles suspended like jewels in the depths of the thick glass. "What other pleasures shall we rediscover tonight? We're in the right part of town for it."

"I don't know. How about one of those image clubs where I can play company president and screw my 'secretary' on the desk? Or maybe a soapland. How much would it cost to have two or three naked women soap me up with their bodies?" The sake is clearly taking effect.

He laughs.

"Gion is for men," I remind him. "Rich men."

"Perhaps, but foreign women are the 'third sex.' Legend has it you possess magic powers."

It's true enough my status as honorary male has come in handy in my profession, but I never considered matters of the flesh. I feel a surge of warmth between my thighs as if a cock is dangling there, thick and florid. The sensation is oddly exciting.

"No magic I know can turn me into a gentleman profligate. Not even for one night."

Yutaka smiles.

We drift through the canyons of the pleasure district. Signs for bars and clubs twine up dark glass buildings like neon ivy. Two college boys hold up a friend, his body sagging like martyred Saint Sebastian, his chin glistening with vomit. A gray-haired man and a young woman in an office lady's uniform hurry down a side street toward a blinking lavender sign for a rent-by-the-hour hotel.

Suddenly the sky shrinks and blushes. I'm inside a tiny room. Everything is red, the ceiling, the floor, the banquettes, the leather-upholstered bar. Only the mirrors on the walls lend a silvery glint to the infinite reflections of red. A man in shirtsleeves with a loosened tie sits at a table near the entrance, his face ruddy with drink. Two young women, one thin and feline, the other with a round, luminous face, lounge on either side of him.

It's a hostess bar, the classic choice for the evening's "second party"—if I were a man.

A handsome middle-aged woman in a kimono walks out from behind the bar to greet us. Yutaka introduces me as his colleague from a prominent American university. Her eyes flicker with new respect. In an instant I've changed from foreign girlfriend into a member of that inscrutable subspecies—the third sex.

Bowing, she gestures to an empty table. A tuxedoed waiter brings out a tray with ice, mineral water, and a bottle of Chivas wearing a silver necklace on its glass shoulders printed with the name *Yamaguchi*.

The moon-faced woman slinks over from the other table and introduces herself as Kazumi. Her modest silk dress only accentuates her curves. I've glimpsed my share of female flesh in the public baths here, but never anything so lush. In spite of myself, I imagine her kneeling before one of those low faucets, her heavy breasts dangling like cones of white wisteria tinted dark rose at the tips.

I blink and swallow hard.

As Kazumi busies herself mixing us whisky-and-waters, she chides Yutaka for not visiting her in so many months. Who else can recommend good books to her? Then she turns her sloe eyes to me, the honorable American professor. How young I look for a lady of such marvelous accomplishment; how perfectly my summer dress becomes my fair complexion. Her low, husky voice makes my skin tingle as if I'm being stroked with a piece of velvet. It's a long time since I've been courted. I admire her skill, but I don't believe a word she says. Even though I'm not the one paying.

My eyes wander to the next table where the slender, catlike hostess is doing something strange. She is touching herself—first her ears, then her eyes, nostrils, mouth—and counting. "Eight," she says, tracing a small, coy circle where her dress creases in her lap. She pauses, eyes narrowed, as if struggling against the urge to pleasure herself then and there, but she shifts her weight to one haunch and trails her finger around to the cleft of her ass. "Nine." I hear the word *ana:* hole, orifice.

If I were that man, I think, I'd touch her now.

But he only stares, his face flushing scarlet.

Back out on the street, we float through the summer night. The sky is black satin, embroidered with points of silver thread. Eleven-thirty and it's still warm, so warm it's hard to tell where the night air ends and my body begins.

"That hostess was lying through her teeth," I tease Yutaka. "Only a man would be fool enough to believe it."

"Carolyn, you're resisting."

"Maybe a pink salon would do the trick? Some throbbing music, a quick hand job from a stranger in the dark?" To my surprise, I'm half-serious. I've always wondered about those places, with the flashing photo galleries of women in tawdry lingerie and the permed gangster barkers calling out to men's crudest, most desperate desires.

"It's a bit early for such extreme measures." Yutaka claps me on the shoulder. "I think we need another drink. A little liquid courage?"

He leads me down a narrow side street. Glass and neon turn to weathered lattice doors illuminated by plump red lanterns. The oily, bittersweet fragrance of *yakitori* hangs in the air. As we move deeper into the maze of alleyways, even the walls vanish. In a haze of cigarette smoke, we pass gaming parlors, noodle stands, and tiny pharmacies hawking condoms and vitality drinks for every blood type. The stylish young women of Gion proper have suddenly grown older, their bodies thickened by childbirth, their smiles flashing gold. The men, grizzled and bent over mahjong tables, might have been frozen in place for fifty years. A final turn and Yutaka ducks under a blue curtain into a tiny bar, no different from its neighbors.

"*Irasshaimase!*" The aproned proprietress glances up from the low wooden bar. Her harried expression melts into genuine pleasure. "*Yamaguchi sensei. Ohisashiburi desu ne!*"

Her smile enfolds me, pulls me in. Any friend of Yutaka's is a friend of hers.

All six seats at the bar are occupied by middle-aged salarymen, some grinning, others soulful depending on the number of drinks they've consumed, but there's space in a *tatami* alcove tucked beside the bar. The mama-san sets a plate of cold soybean pods between us and returns with two tall glasses of *chuhai,* a cocktail of sweet potato liquor that goes down as easy as lemonade.

I catch myself studying my friend across the table: lean, high cheekbones; fine, leather-grained lines around his eyes; elegant fingers, the color of old parchment. Catholic girl that I am, it's no stretch to make him into a confessor after a *chuhai* or two.

"Everyone thinks it's easy being an academic. You teach a few classes a week, have the summers off. What a joke. I haven't had a break from work since I started grad school. Jason never got it."

Yutaka murmurs that his wife, too, can be less than understanding at times. We're talking in English, the natural language of complaint.

Of course it only got worse when Jason's dot-com company went belly-up. I was at the computer all day and most of the night, racing to finish the revisions on my book so I could have my contract in hand for the tenure committee. At first I scheduled regular breaks in the evening to be with him, but if I tried to get romantic, he'd snarl something about being tired. Then, when I was back at work, he'd creep into the study and start massaging my shoulders. I'd shrug his hands away—I had no time for games—and he'd go off to mope. But one day last fall he didn't go away. He only pressed down harder, kneading my muscles with brisk, defiant strokes. I was surprised how good it felt. After a minute or two, I closed my eyes and relaxed into it. Soon I felt a hand moving down my chest, undoing the top buttons of my shirt.

I asked him what he was doing. As if I didn't know.

Hush, he murmured into my neck. He pulled my shirt down over my shoulders and yanked up my camisole. The cool air licked my nipples.

Open your eyes, he said. Watch me play with your tits.

I winced, but did as I was told, gazing down at his big tanned hands squeezing my flesh. They looked foreign—a stranger's hands—but, oddly enough, I liked that. My chest was already speckled with flowery pink blotches of arousal.

Does the Japanese scholar like to have her nipples pinched?

I bit back a moan.

I think you do. Look at the way you're rocking your hips. Is it possible Madame Professor might have other things on her mind right now than work?

I glanced at the computer. The lines of text trembled and blurred.

Let me help you out of these pants, Professor.

I tilted my ass up to make it easier for him. Leaving my jeans and panties dangling around one ankle, he slid his hands between my knees and spread my legs wide, then wider still until they hung over the sides of the chair. He started to strum my clit—that much he could still do just right—and I bucked against his hand, whimpering as my tender asshole rubbed against the scratchy fabric of the chair seat.

Jason clicked his tongue. My, my, what would the tenure committee think if they saw you now, squirming around in your own juices?

*Fuck me.*

I'm sorry, I didn't hear you, Professor. Let's have a nice loud voice so the students napping in the back row can hear.

*Fuck me, you bastard.* Forget the kids in the back row, my shouting probably woke the neighbors two blocks away.

Jason reached down and fumbled with his zipper. His cock sprang out, an angry red baton. He lifted me to my feet and positioned me against the horizontal filing cabinet. We often used to do it standing up in the early days, me on tiptoe, Jason crouching a bit to get it in. I loved the sensation of his cock moving in and out, pressing up against my clit. I felt like I was flying. This time was different, though. Rougher. The denim of his jeans chafed against my tender pubes, and each thrust knocked my ass cheeks against the cabinet drawer. We weren't making love. He was punishing me, spanking me with a chilly, rattling metal hand, but I wasn't a helpless little girl, I was fighting back, grinding into him, soaring up higher, a witch on her broomstick. I came before he did, shrieking sweet victory.

It was the last time he touched me.

Will I ever have sex again?

"You're a very attractive woman, Carolyn."

I jump guiltily, but Yutaka's face holds nothing but mild concern. I must have been drifting off, mumbling to myself in drunken reverie. *Ukiyo,* the floating world, that's what they call it in Japan. Dreams and sex and sorrow all mixed up together. If I did say it all out loud, Yutaka is friend enough to forget in the morning.

I lean toward him. "You see, Yu-kun, it's not working. I'm still a woman. Even if I just want a little comfort, the warmth of another body beside me, I have to find the right guy who loves and respects me and fits in at the department's wine and cheese parties. I have to follow the goddamn rules."

"There are no rules here," Yutaka whispers back. His eyes twinkle.

I know a dare when I hear one. There it is again, that strange, tugging warmth between my legs. I go to smooth my skirt, but stop, suddenly afraid of what I will find.

A cell phone call and a taxi ride later, we're sitting on cushions in a well-appointed *zashiki*. Yutaka sips cold sake. I nurse a glass of barley tea. The place doesn't look like a brothel. We could be guests in any traditional inn with tasteful pretensions, except for the fact that my heart is pounding in my throat.

The *shoji* door opens with a whisper. A young woman kneels on the glossy straw matting and bows low, first to me, then Yutaka.

She is lovely.

"This young lady will perform a traditional dance for us," Yutaka explains. "Her name is Ohisa." I bite back a smile. Ohisa is the name of a character in a Tanizaki novel, an old man's doll-like mistress, who, even in 1928, was a relic of the past. We've both published articles on her, mine a feminist reading of her submissive behavior as theater, masking a deeper rebellion. In private, on lazy afternoons, I'm less politically correct. I sometimes pretend I'm spying on her and the old man as he forces her to act out arcane sexual practices from erotic prints; beneath her dainty protests, I know she enjoys it.

And now she sits before us in the flesh.

The wizened grandma in the corner strikes up a geisha love song on her *samisen*. Ohisa rises to her feet. By some trick of the hand, her red sash slithers to the *tatami*, a gaudy, sleepy snake. Her summer kimono follows, pooling at her feet in ripples of midnight blue cotton and morning glories. What's left: Ohisa in a robe of nearly transparent silk that hugs her slender hips, her small round breasts. The nipples, a pale tender pink, poke through the thin cloth.

This is no ordinary dance.

My face grows hot, my hands throb and twitch in my lap. Has it finally happened? Am I seeing with a man's eyes?

I reach into my bag and pull out my sketchpad, full of amateur renderings of a fox shrine tucked beside a tofu shop, a corner of the iris garden at the Heian Shrine. I draw quickly, the curves of her buttock and shoulder, a faint shading of aureole. The kind of sexy picture a voyeur who thinks he has talent might dash off as a souvenir. But I also see what few men would in the proud tilt of her chin, the precision of her gestures. Ohisa—or whatever her real name is—is an artist.

When the dance is over, Yutaka stands, flashes me a smile and disappears. The *samisen* player leaves, too, but not before she removes the screen in the corner to reveal a futon, the top quilt folded back in invitation. A small brigade of sex toys stands ready by the pillow, all for a lady's pleasure. Images flash into my head, cartoon obscenities. Ohisa trussed up in the dildo harness, her vein-brocaded rubber tool bobbing with each wanton thrust. Or myself, the mad professor, leering over her supine form, a vibrator wand buzzing in each hand.

I catch Ohisa's eye. We both look away. Right now this room is a foreign land to us both.

Flustered, I push the drawing toward her. My offering for her putting up with Yutaka's absurd joke.

Ohisa studies the picture. She looks up at me again. Then she smiles.

It is Ohisa's idea to pose for me. She vamps, makes silly faces. We giggle like girls at a slumber party. I find, to my surprise, I'm having a very good time. Of course for her it might be nothing more than an act, a canny reading of a novice customer's mood. She's a professional woman. Like me.

At last she kneels on the bed with her back to me, her head turned in profile. Connoisseurs claim no vision is more erotic: the contrast of pale, slender neck and rich black hair.

It's my best sketch yet.

"Very nice," she murmurs.

It is now that I allow myself one indulgence. I touch her. Lightly on the shoulder, then again on her cool, smooth hair. I mean to stop here—and give her what I hope is an easy night's work—but for what she does. She sighs. A sound of such melancholy yearning, I feel it in my own body, an ache like hunger, but lower. Suddenly I want to comfort her, give her something, even if it's selfish. I wrap my arms around her and pull her back against me. She doesn't resist.

"May I touch your breasts?" My voice is strange, deeper.

"Please," she whispers. Her chest rises in quick, shallow breaths.

In the cups of my palms, her skin is padded satin. I circle the nipples with my fingertips, feel tiny goose bumps rise. Once, as if by accident, I brush the stiffened tips.

She sighs again. The sound makes my fingers sing like electric wire. I understand it now, how a man can get so hot and bothered just by touching a woman.

My hand skates down the curve of her belly.

"May I . . ." I want to say ". . . play with your cunt," but the proper words escape me.

She seems to understand. She parts the robe, drops her legs open.

The hair down there is slightly damp as if she's fresh from a bath.

"How do you make yourself feel good when you're alone?" I'm fumbling for words, absurdly polite. "Teach me. Please."

Obediently she guides my finger to a soft hollow just to the right of her springy little clit. As I strum, I flick her nipple with the pad of my thumb, the way I do when I masturbate. She moans. I drink it all in, the slurpy kiss of finger on pussy, the spice-and-seawater smell of her. Or is it me? Rubbing her in her secret place is enough to make my own cunt drool like an old drunk. My skirt is hiked up to my waist and I'm pushing myself against her ass and she squirms back and we're riding together on a wet spot as wide as the ocean, floating in that place where only sex can take you. No rules. No boundaries. Only pleasure.

Suddenly Ohisa's body goes rigid. *"Iku, iku wa."* The Japanese don't come, they "go," but I need no translation as she sways in my embrace, mewing and shuddering.

I hold her until her breath is even and soft.

The curbside door of the taxi opens as if by magic. I slide in, lean back, glide through the summer night. The whine of an *enka* ballad drifts from the radio.

Heedless of the white-gloved driver, I bring my fingers to my nose. In novels and floating world prints the journey from pleasure back to ordinary life is the time of contemplation. The lies I'll tell Yutaka. The way I'll remember her cunt, soft as wet rose petals, when I bring myself off later in my bed. A touch of teenage-boy glee—*I made a girl come!*—though I know I didn't touch Ohisa in the way that counts.

I take a long, slow breath. A woman's pleasure. The perfume those libertines of old ruined their fortunes to possess. I have it right here in my hand. The real thing.

# Grifter

## Carol Queen

I wouldn't have gotten involved, except that Joe was such an old friend. I've known him since college, long enough for either of us to have raised kids if we were the marrying kind. He certainly never was—I've watched him go through a succession of blondes, the hairstyles changing with the decades, from long and straight to big and fluffy and back again. If any of them loved him, I'd be surprised. He was a success right away—in fact, he came to school with enough money to impress any girl he wanted, and they just lined right up. It was never that easy for me back in those days, and it didn't help my opinion of women, watching them cuddle up to his bank balance and not to him.

Then I started meeting women who didn't care about that. The entire sex was redeemed by one barefoot girl who liked to smoke pot and recite poetry to me before I tied her to the bed.

Joe and I could never double date because our girls couldn't get along. Blonde bubbleheads or connivers setting themselves up to be Mrs. Money struggled to make small talk with kinky grad students. It was partly my influence that none of them ever grabbed the ring, though a few of them earned themselves a few years at his side, shacked up, playing house, and then leaving him—if the leave-taking was civilized—with a car or a condo or a no-strings loan to start a business. They were all gold diggers, as near as I could figure, but mostly honest about it. As one of my ethereal bondage-queen girlfriends explained, it was just what their mothers had taught them to do. It was how the whole straight world worked. He had fun with them, they looked good on his arm—and it wasn't really my business.

Until Alice came along, and we're not talking Wonderland. My old pal Joe, now something like the seventeenth-richest man in the country, came face-to-face with the kind of succubus that wants nothing more than to eat a man like him, spit out the husk, and pick her teeth with his bones. He'd finally stumbled into the sights of a grifter.

None of Joe's friends noticed anything different at first: She was blonde and gorgeous, and could keep up her end of any conversation. She said she was an attorney, but had a surprising amount of free time, always ready to take Joe's arm for an outing, and the more caviar or ski chalets involved, the quicker she could go. Like I said, there was nothing so different about that. But where Blondes One through One Hundred were eager to put out, understanding the connection between their visits to the money tree and their ability to keep Joe well fucked—and God knows there was someone nearby to take the place of any doll with too-frequent headaches—Alice seduced and then dangled the prize just out of Joe's reach. He strove for that sweet carrot like the dumbest mule who ever plodded through Tennessee dirt. It might just have been a new technique—the latest Blonde Strategy, passed along in tony ladies' rooms as guys smoked their fat cigars—and it's true he fell for it hook, line, and sinker. He was used to dropping his pants when and where he wanted, but Alice wasn't having any of that. My babe du jour—an aspiring-if-decades-late Beat poet when she wasn't singing the older laments and praises to the tune of my cat—speculated that maybe she had read *The Rules*. Joe wasn't the marrying kind, true, but he wasn't getting any younger. Maybe his mother'd been pressuring him about an heir.

You could see it unbalanced Joe. Alice was there at his beck and call, always dressed to eat caviar. But she never put out, teasing him with very un-Joe-like notions: "You have no idea how much better it can be," she purred, "when you wait."

My little beatnik and I got a good laugh out of that. We had waited a good fifteen minutes our first time, though it's true I hadn't gotten out the bondage gear till our third date. Joe was entering his own kind of bondage, beginning to get a little sloppy. He was already offering her things. We worried he'd buy the cow without tasting the milk. Sure, I know that's crass. But love or no love (and I've been around the block enough to know this wasn't any kind of love I'd ever seen), before you go buying diamonds don't you want to know whether tab A and slot B are a righteous fit? Joe used to think that way, but his brain was not working the way it ever had before.

Anyway, what's a nice fur coat between friends? It wasn't like it hurt him to spend the money. She hinted at more esoteric pleasures if he'd only equip her for them. In his circle, I'm the acknowledged expert on esoteric pleasures, so he came to me.

"I've never felt so . . . enthralled! So ready for something new, something I've never experienced!" Joe wasn't the pay-his-way-up-Everest kind of rich guy, exactly, but it came out that he was planning to set her up in a condo, complete with everything money could buy. He simply had to experience it all for himself, and she was his key, his Beatrice.

I didn't think so. Hey, if Joe had ever wanted to play slap and tickle, he'd have been welcome at my place: a pretty nicely tricked-out dungeon if I do say so myself, even if I did have to build most of it from scratch. Joe knew he was always welcome—he could bring any blonde he liked. In a pinch, I knew a blonde or two who were at the top of their game. If ecstatic torture was this year's new flavor, it could be had, with girls dressed in any color of black. Most of them even had their own outfits, unlike Alice, whose trendy dominatrix look was courtesy of Joe's credit cards.

But by now Joe had swallowed the bait. He wouldn't place his lily-white ass in anyone's hands but Alice's, much as I tried to convince him he ought to have at least one good experience to compare to her chat-room-tutored ministrations. I was pretty sure this girl was a gold-plated phony, but he wouldn't even let her out of his sight to play with me. I tried to explain how important it was that she be road tested, but no such luck. By now he'd convinced himself that her piss tasted like high-class chardonnay.

Not that she'd let him near her piss, even.

So I invited him to bring her over to my playroom. Then I called Micki, an ex who worked for a private eye.

She ran Alice every which way, and guess what? She wasn't a lawyer, though let's just say she'd been close to lawyers in the past . . . and I mean that in both the biblical and the jurisprudential senses. She was nearby a couple of rich old men when they bit the dust, and close enough to see some of the profit. My hunch about her S and M credentials seemed to play out—no one had ever heard of or played with her. Although, of course, she could have an Internet alias that regularly committed unspeakable acts upon the absent, insensate bodies of her submissives. Speaking of aliases, Micki found a couple, one that claimed Alice to be just once-removed from deposed European royalty. Well, whatever—she *did* have the cheekbones. But way past that, she had the cheek—it turned out she wasn't even an American citizen, although she would be, of course, if any rich schmucks like my old friend Joe saw fit to waltz her down the aisle.

"Right," said Micki, "if he lives that long."

"Oh, he'll live that long, all right, though odds are pretty good they won't grow old together." I pondered this setup. Did I give a shit? Was this, on some level, what Joe deserved? He'd had decent luck with blondes so far; maybe the inevitable bad apple had just turned up, and it was meant to be.

Naaah, I finally decided. Joe wasn't a bad guy. No, in this picture, the bad guy had 38DDs.

Our double date was set up, and we still had a week to go. This gave Micki time to do a little more digging. She had a real prejudice against blondes, Micki did, and I saw a predatory side of her emerge that had never come out while she was tied to my rack. On Wednesday she hit pay dirt—she turned up a real boyfriend in Alice's closet. Not in her past—Alice was giving away plenty of milk, just not to Joe. He subconsciously honed in on her well-fucked radiance, wanting whatever it signified. But Joe had no idea it signified a small-time thief with big brown eyes and a really big cock named Johnny. Johnny had one strike to go—no wonder Alice was head-of-household.

It turned out that I was the lightest-weight guy Micki ever played with. She'd been on both sides of the fence and had a friend or two who still owed her favors. On Friday afternoon, a couple of them popped up on either side of Johnny's bar stool. He got an early start at the Dew Drop Inn, or whatever his joint-of-choice was called—obviously no one had taught him the finer things, like no cheap whisky before noon. Only one trip to the alley, a view of a different kind of 38, and a couple of well-placed suggestions later, and Johnny decided to go home to Chicago. Micki paid for the bus trip. Damn, she really got involved with her work.

So Alice came back to the abode to find it cleared out—no Johnny, no note. Also absent was a fair amount of the jewelry she'd already gotten from Joe—good-quality trinkets, really, but Johnny'd need some walking-around money when he got back home.

You'd have had to be looking closely to see that Alice wasn't quite herself when our big date rolled around on Saturday night. Joe obviously didn't notice—she had him so snowed, nothing would have sunk in. Maybe a shaved head, but she was done up as flawlessly as ever. If mascara had raccooned around her eyes last night as she sobbed over the loss of her bunny-boy, she'd had time to put the toner on. And in fact, Joe was even more obsequious than ever, trying to get into what he thought was the proper mood for his kinky date. His slavish attention stabilized her somewhat. That, after all, was the name of the game.

This was a double date only because we were using my space and my gear, and I insisted that Micki and I chaperone. Alice had no time for us, intent only on trussing up Joe. Micki muttered under her breath that this was Alice's way of keeping Joe's hands off her, and indeed, she had him in cuffs in record time. In a perfect X on my St. Andrew's cross a naked Joe was soon immobile, Alice purring around him as she tied half-assed knots and tweaked his tits. Micki and I occupied the other side of the room, managing to look busy while we kept an eye on things. Joe was hard as a rock—this was probably true nearly all the time when Alice was around, she got him so worked up—and she even deigned to put a cock ring on him and run her nails along the engorged flesh. This was almost certainly the closest he'd gotten to scoring with her after all this time, so he paid complete attention.

Micki and I were of two minds about strategy. One option was to wait until Alice fucked something up, as we were pretty certain she would. But our plan as it unfolded would seem like a pretty extreme overreaction to a bondage faux pas. It didn't really have any logic connecting Alice's eventual mistake to what we planned to do, and besides, when you got right down to it, Alice's very presence in Joe's life was mistake enough. So Plan B, we decided, was simpler: Just do it.

Micki was integral to this. I'm a pretty nice guy. Sure, I like hurting women, but only the ones who want to be hurt. I'd just as happily lick a girl's clit until tomorrow morning as whip her—as long as she's tied up, anyway. The bondage is really my lech. Pain is an extra, and like most nice guys, I take the concept of consent very seriously. I don't even know if I could inflict nonconsensual pain or distress—even on Alice, despite my dreams of tying her wrists and dangling her over the balcony.

Micki was another story. Micki liked pain, and she liked both sides—she was an equal opportunity woman in that respect, as switchable as it gets. Some of the things she'd gotten me to do to her would qualify as horrific, if it hadn't been for the look on her face—pure nirvana, a sensation slut in her true element. And Micki usually played fair when she topped, but the plain fact was, she didn't care whether or not her willing victim liked the games she played. The fact that her bottom had agreed to play was what mattered. And there was one final, secret side to Micki—when she got irritated, it didn't really matter whether you were a willing victim at all.

"I could be on the other side of the law pretty easily myself," she told me once. "It's all a rush. A little vicious part of me doesn't give a shit about consent. I just have too much superego to go all the way—most of the time. I keep that side of me in a pen, but that doesn't mean it's not there."

I pictured that part of Micki, which I had heard about but never met, as a snarling weasel—a cute but feral powerhouse with sharp, sharp teeth. Micki had a special way of thinking about wrongdoing, and for her, taking Alice down was logical in two ways: Alice was asking for it by fucking around and grifting, and Micki deserved to do it, because there were so many times she'd

wanted to do something like it and never had. It was like cleaning
your room on a sunny day when you'd rather be outside: You
cleaned it, and then you got to eat cake. Except this time, she was
going to eat Alice.

Joe was trussed and hard, and Alice buzzed around him like a bee
on a flower. They were paying no attention to Micki and me at all.
We could have gotten into a nice loud scene and the lovebirds
wouldn't have noticed. So it was ridiculously easy for me to slip up
behind Alice and grab her wrists. Micki, right there with the cuffs,
slapped them on and shoved. Between us we quickly had a
spitting-mad Alice bent over a horse, blonde as Gwendoline and
just as immobile. I held her there while Micki grabbed a portable
set of stocks that chained to the legs of the horse. Over her neck
and locked into place, Alice could rage and wiggle, but she
couldn't go anywhere. Red-faced and furious, she spewed some
pretty impressive invective—hadn't learned talk like *that* in any of
the courts of Europe—but Micki shut her up momentarily with
several hard thwacks to the ass.

Joe hadn't said a word. Still tied up the way Alice had left him,
he stared at the new tableau, dumbfounded.

Micki bent down so she could look Alice in the eye. "Wondering why we've convened this little meeting?"

"You shit-sucking bitch, what the fuck are you doing?" Damn,
Alice seemed so much less elegant when she was pissed. It became easier to see what Johnny saw in her.

"Show a little respect, babe," said Micki, punctuating it with a
resounding slap. Alice's eyes went involuntarily wide. "We're holding a little tribunal, that's what, babe. A truth-telling commission,
how does that sound?"

I stepped over to Joe and uncuffed his hands, though he was
still wound to the posts of the cross like a kid who got on the
wrong side of a rough game of cowboys and Indians. He wasn't

going anywhere. I patted him on the shoulder and interrupted the resumed flow of Alice's swearing. "See, Alice, we've been really concerned that you don't fit in very well with our crowd. Joe deserves the best, and he doesn't seem to be getting it from you. He doesn't seem to be getting anything but a snow job, to tell you the truth."

Micki cut in. "As a matter of fact, you really remind me of somebody who'll only put out after the wedding day, and only if well-stocked with Viagra and poppers." Joe was oblivious to this, but Alice's expression changed just enough to make me think that this possibly lethal combo might in fact be in the medicine chest, just waiting for Joe to sign the right papers. Micki ran a spiky nail across Alice's throat while she stalked back and forth in front of her, leaving the fine pale length marked with a glowing red slash. "Foxglove takes too long, huh, baby? We wouldn't want to whore ourselves out *too* long, just to get our hands on some money. That's just so bad for a girl's self-esteem, isn't it?"

Alice hissed.

"Hey, speaking of whoring, where's that little fuck-boy you lived with up until day before yesterday? Where'd he go?"

Alice started up with the verbal vitriol. Joe's eyes went a little wider in their already-evident confusion, kind of like a dog who twists its head sideways and you could swear it just said "Huh?" Instead, what came out of his mouth was, "What the . . . ?" I figured we should let him stay trussed to the St. Andrew's cross for at least a little while. It was a ringside seat, after all; but also, I wasn't sure this was going to feel any more consensual to Joe than it did to Alice. At least, not at first.

Micki saw Joe's doglike confusion and lifted Alice's chin with the point of one nail so Joe could look her in the face. Alice's eyes darted around, like she was looking for the magic key that would let her out of this predicament. She sure didn't seem to want to meet his look, into which a certain mix of hurt and almost-but-not-quite-anger had begun to seep. But Micki's sharp direction wouldn't let her look away. Alice's expression began to resemble a teenager whose overindulgent mom has finally found her little darling's stash of coke, hash oil, and stolen pharmaceuticals.

Micki wasn't overindulgent at all, except occasionally to her own dark side. "Why don't you tell Joe about Johnny, Alice? Don't you think he deserves to know that he's helping support a no-good, big-cocked fucklush who isn't even his own goddamned illegitimate kid? That he's paying some guy's rent so you can take it in the ass all night after sending him home with blue balls? It seems to me, any guy who's taking you on ski vacations and buying expensive champagne would want to know that kind of detail, you little cunt."

This last statement finished with a stinging slap, as punctuation. Joe was starting to look maybe a little less confused and maybe a little more irritated—after all, Alice hadn't opened her mouth to deny any of it. Her considerable conversational skills seemed reduced to calling Micki a fucking bitch.

Micki had a lot more verbal acuity than this. "So is this little scam all your plan, missy? If Johnny was pimping you out, I can't imagine he'd have cut out on you quite so fast. Hasn't called yet, huh?" Nothing but a glare from the trussed-up blonde—plus an attempt to struggle her way out of the bondage.

"Hey, Alice," I cut in, "when you try to get away, it makes your ass look really hot. I'm beginning to see what Joe likes about you." Alice roared, with just the hint of unintelligible invective at the center of the noise.

Micki took over again. "You know, what you're doing with old Joe here *reeeallly* irritates me, Alice. Would you like to know why?"

Alice was beginning to get back up to speed, expletive-wise. Micki rummaged around in a toy bag and came up with a ball gag.

The verbiage continued to spew as Micki dangled it a few inches from Alice's eyes.

"Sweetie, when you took your little Internet correspondence course on pro domination, did they mention this? It's a really handy toy to have when someone just won't shut up." Micki's considerable professional skills included takedowns, and the gag went into Alice's mouth with almost no fuss. Micki just waited till the yowling blonde reached a particularly open-mouthed yell, and in the gag went. It had a buckle, so she didn't need to call upon her knot-tying abilities as Alice tried to Linda Blair her head out of Micki's reach. In a few short seconds, the gag was in and the tirade had turned to muffled bellows of impotent rage.

"Alice, shut the fuck up. I want to explain something to you." The next slap *did* shut Alice up, at least briefly. "You know, cunt, in a perfect world, it would be no big deal if you wanted to suck rich guys' souls. We wouldn't even have cared this time, except Joe's not an asshole. When you do your little game on assholes, the world stays balanced. When you do it to decent guys, you fuck things up. It makes bad feng shui everywhere. It makes your karma suck and it makes it harder for decent women to get what they want."

Did I mention Micki was a very spiritual person?

"I don't know if you learned this shit from your mother or made it up as you went along, and I bet *you* think it's the law of the jungle. But I want something really different from the men in my life, and if you've been through the room before I get there, it makes the men turn into jerks. A rich jerk can cause a lot of trouble. A rich jerk who wants revenge on women can *really* cause a lot of trouble. So while you move on to the next mark, other women get the backwash. You're fucking it up for everybody. And what makes it worse is you're smart. You could be doing something useful." The word "smart" was punctuated by a sharp movement—Micki plunging her fist into Alice's hair and jerking up, as

close to her brain as Alice could get—for now, anyway. I wasn't
sure how much Hannibal Lecter she had in her when she got this
way.

"You have completely fucked up your abilities. You have let me
and all other women down. You're not even doing anything useful
with the fucking money you do get. You're a blonde fucking
bleached fucking leech."

Joe finally sputtered into action—sort of. "Alice, er, is this
true?" Alice only glared at him, which was its own sort of simple
communication. I would almost—almost!—have given up the
pleasure of doing this to Alice, if it meant I'd never had to see my
friend look so dispirited. But I'd gotten him into this, and I figured
he deserved an answer.

"It's true, Joe. Micki ran her, and she's a class-A grifter. While
you fed her filet, she was getting porked by a punk she kept in
style, courtesy of you. After you married her she was probably
gonna set up the kid as your driver. If you lived long enough to
drive anywhere."

Micki looked up from her ministrations. She'd been doing quietly
fucked up things to Alice, who was finally looking a little scared—still
pissed, but scared. "Joe, I'm sorry we couldn't just tell you. But I've
been around a lot of guys, and I don't think you would've bought it if
we'd just told you over lunch." Joe shook his head a little. "We're not
going to do anything drastic to Miss Gold Digger here, don't worry—
but when I'm done with her she might be less willing to fuck up the
life of the next five rich guys she meets."

"Joe," I said carefully, "do you want to help us out here?"

"Yeah, we thought you might like to throw one good fuck into
her before you never see her again." Micki was remarkably
cheerful-sounding; she just wasn't willing to grasp that Joe was in
love with Alice, or had been until three minutes ago. Besides,
Micki would have loved to provide the soundtrack while Joe finally
tasted the milk. You couldn't have wanted a better trash-talker in

your bed than Micki, and just opening her mouth she could have doubled the indignity for Alice—Joe's cock hammering somewhere down south, Micki reading her beads like only a truly vicious girl can do.

But Joe was, as I told you, a decent guy. What were the odds, I wondered silently, of two such decent guys as me and him getting caught up with two evil women like Alice and Micki? Though Micki *did* keep a lid on it most of the time, I had a feeling the lid would come off pretty soon.

"No, let me leave," said Joe. Though it took the next five minutes for me to get him out—Alice had clearly never heard of panic snaps, and he was tied to the cross in an absolute gnarl of ropes—I was finally able to support him as he lowered his arms, get him some water, and help him find his coat. "I don't want to know what happens after I go," he said, and closed the door quietly on his way out. He never once looked back at Alice.

Although it would have been sweet porn indeed to see Joe throw a savage fuck, Micki was actually, I suspected, a tougher fuck than Joe would ever be—and she was still in the room. Part A of the mission had been simple—get Joe out of this bitch's thrall. Part B was really Micki's primary agenda: Teach her a bitter and thorough lesson. Micki cared very passionately about right and wrong, probably because her own self-control was fairly hard-won. This is the kind of superego that, when blended in a perfect yin-yang with one's id, makes for a diamond-hard and implacable top. In fact, I was pretty sure that while she punished Alice, she'd be sending an internal message to herself: Crime doesn't pay, babe. Is that the secret motivation of sadistic cops and prison guards everywhere? I'd have to remember to ask her this later, when we were doing one of three logical post-scene activities: enjoying a drink and going back over every little element of the evening, fucking like crazed, power-drunk weasels, or running for the border after we dumped the body.

But I'd made Micki promise she wouldn't kill her.

"Don't worry, sweetie," Micki was in fact saying, "we're not going to kill you. I don't even think we plan to disfigure you, but you might want to try to hold still, just in case."

Alice gave her a look that was reminiscent of an alley cat wrapped in duct tape.

"We might talk a little about whether you *deserve* to be killed," Micki continued, "but we won't actually do it. However, I fervently hope that when I get done with you, you will never—*never*—ever pull another scam. I want you to walk out of here tonight, if you can walk at all, thinking you can't wait to take a Greyhound to Chicago, move back in with Johnny, and get a nice job at a Krispy Kreme."

The cat started to hiss.

"Because you are never going to use your skills to fuck with people," Micki said, *"ever"*—she punctuated this with a ringing slap—*"again!"*

Alice's eyes filled with tears, though none of the rage left them.

"You're also not going to turn us in, and do you know why?" Micki pulled a computer printout from her pocket, folded multiple times and scored down the sides with the regular pattern of holes that said "old funky printer in a PI's office." She unscrolled it and began to read all the dirt she had on Alice, including birth name and the year she first got sent to juvenile court. "Alice, if there's anything that's not on here, it would just make me want to fuck you up worse. So take your medicine and crawl home, and no later than tomorrow, get out of this fucking town."

"Unless you like this so much that you want to ask Micki if she'd pretty please keep you," I added with a smirk. "Stranger things have happened. Micki has a lot of charisma."

Duct-tape kitty's eyes had narrowed. "Oh, aren't you bisexual? That could change."

Now that Alice knew the parameters of the scene—she'd most likely live, and there were no safewords—Micki got to work. "Go fix yourself a drink," she said to me. "I won't need you for a while." And indeed, when I returned from the bar that stood at the far end of my little rumpus room, Micki had upped the ante on Alice's bondage—everything tighter, elbows jutting up at a painful looking angle because her wrists were tied more tightly behind her back, and rope in a neat harness fixing her chest securely to the horse. Her ass and cunt completely accessible, spreader bars keeping her high-heeled feet thrust as far apart as they would go—Micki had made a tableau straight out of John Willie. Anybody in the S and M community who said fucking wasn't important had never seen this little setup. This was *all* about fucking.

"You know, we could do a lot of things to you here, Alice," said Micki, "and maybe we will. But it seems to me the most poetic justice would be a nice hard fuck. We'll tape it, of course, and if you ever come up on my radar again, your spread-wide ass is going into the video stores. Don't think I can't get it there. And remember, I know your real name. It'll be on the cover in a real big font." Micki wasn't kidding—Alice was on the horse because my rumpus room digital recorder was pointed right at it. I liked to document my best rumpus experiences, and this was surely going to be right up there with the first time Micki came to visit me here.

I told you I'm a nice guy. I am. But Micki—well, she always had a sort of mesmerizing, awful effect on me. It's why I asked her to do this job. And I would never, ever rape anyone—unless Micki pointed her scarlet nail and said, "That's your end." My cock was suddenly ready to do anything to anyone, and Micki's cock came out of her tote bag at just about the time my pants hit the floor.

Micki assigned me to fuck Alice's face. She took up the rear, and I noticed the dick she'd strapped on was not one of her smaller ones. Maybe Micki didn't actually have any smaller ones. Whenever she'd lay trussed up under me, spread painfully wide

to my own somewhat-better-than-average meat, she would eventually, mewlingly, beg me to get out one of her toys and finish
her off. And her toys—well, they gave *me* penis envy. So wherever she was shoving that thing, into Alice's fore or aft, she'd definitely notice. And though more than willing to do Micki's
bidding, I let her start first before I slipped Alice's gag—I
needed her in a haze before she had a chance to use her perfect
white teeth on me.

Micki knew how to put a person in a haze. And though I'm
not sure Alice liked what Micki did to her, exactly, she looked to
be going under. A cock as big as Micki's will focus a woman's attention, I guess. But as soon as I saw a bubble of drool appear at
the edge of the ball gag, I knew it would be safe to take it out
and slip myself in. I'd fucked face more than once—sometimes
it's just what a tied-up woman wants, and I pride myself on being
able to judge the sometimes tiny space between "not quite hard
enough" and "just a little too hard." Of course, I gave Alice the
latter right away, slipping into her saliva-slick throat and using it
almost as savagely as Micki, on the other side of the horse,
slammed Alice's ass. I fisted my hands in her hair and thrust so
hard the horse rocked a little—or was that Micki's doing? Alice's
gulps and sobs around my meat made me so fucking horny, the
nice guy I've been protesting I am had taken a complete hike.
Her drool slicked me up so that I could have fucked her throat
all night. And there was one more thing: Micki and I could look
right into each other's eyes while we slammed our bodies at the
completely helpless blonde tied between us. We fucked each
other, in that crazed-weasel way, right through Alice's immobilized
form. It was so hot that every so often I had to close my eyes and
scrape my cock over Alice's teeth, just enough reality check and
discomfort to keep me going. Because this was better than any
fuck Micki had ever thrown me, even at her most cat-in-heat moments tied to my bed. This made me real glad that there was a

woman between us who needed and deserved to be punished, because I don't know if I could have taken all that heat directed just
at me.

At length Generalissima Micki called me from my post. She pulled
out of Alice's ass with an audible pop—her dicks were usually the
big-headed kind, and this battering ram was no exception. She got
me to support Alice's weight while she levered the three-quarters
fucked-out bondage victim to the floor—still in range of our camera, in fact Alice's cunt pointed right that way—where my job was
to hold her down while Micki worked her efficient hand into
Alice's cunt while she continued the evening's comportment lesson. This time Micki could look right into Alice's eyes, and from
the look in them as Micki slid in past the knuckles, not bothering
to do more than spit on the pink cuntflesh first, Alice had never
realized anything much bigger than Johnny's dick could fit in
there.

"I love surprising sophisticated people," said Micki with real
satisfaction, giving her wrist enough of a twist that Alice gasped
and yelped. I knelt down firmly on the wrists that had suddenly
started to flail.

"Now Alice, here's where I make my point in a way that you
just might hear," said Micki, focusing all her feral-beast-in-a-cop-
suit presence on Alice. "What we're doing here is sex. It's not especially consensual, which would ordinarily be a problem. In fact,
I'm really using sex as a weapon here, which I don't condone, not
at all, but sometimes you just have to fight fire with fire. You don't
respect sex or desire, Alice, you use it. That's not right. I don't care
how you got this way, because you are smart and calculating
enough to do anything you want, and you seem to want to do this.
And when I get done with you . . ."—and here Micki began to
thrust, achieving a surprising amount of movement in and out of
Alice's presumably very tight and very full cunt—". . . you'll never

again get filled up enough by a rich guy or a skinny big-dicked punk. You're going to need something else. You're going to need to think about what your life is about . . ."

Micki was fucking hard now; her words were coming out in gasps.

". . . and what you're doing with it . . ."

Under my knees, I felt pressure; Alice's body was tightening up like a bowstring bends a bow.

". . . and you're not going to use your cunt to get you furs and caviar anymore, because your *cunt* . . ."

Micki punctuated "cunt" with an especially powerful thrust. I could see her biceps working.

". . . your *cunt* is going to have some needs of its own. From now on, you fucking grifter bitch, your *cunt* is going to talk to you . . ."

Alice came with a howl and I could barely hear Micki's final words: ". . . *twenty-four hours a day!*"

Just like Micki's cunt, I bet, talks to her.

Micki didn't kill Alice, though I can't swear to the behavior of her goons—the same two guys who ushered Johnny off his bar stool gave his erstwhile girlfriend, fucked-out and sloppy and reeking of come, a ride home, or a ride *somewhere.* I spent the rest of the night with Micki, fucking in full-out crazed-weasel mode, which was just as scary without Alice between us as I'd thought it'd be— just not scary enough to stop. When Micki got like this, it was too confusing to figure out who should get tied up, so for once neither of us did.

I don't know what became of Alice. She hasn't shown her face in this town, and every online pervert in the country knows her story, thanks to Micki. That woman loves telling tales out of school, but only when it's appropriate. She has a superego like a fucking steel trap. She also put the word out on the PI wires, so if

Alice turns back up in Bangor, Maine, or Tupelo, Mississippi, someone will have a shot at figuring her out before she goes too far with the next rich schmuck.

Micki and I had a good reason for breaking up the first time, and we didn't get back together over Alice—except that one night. I'm a nice guy, but let me tell you—I'm keeping a close eye on Joe's girlfriends now. I'll know if any new grifters try to get their meathooks into him. And if anyone does . . .

I'm sure Micki and I will be able to handle it.

# From *Little Children: A Novel*

## Tom Perrotta

Though it had lasted for almost twenty years, Richard's first marriage had been wrong from the start, based as it was on a serious misunderstanding. Peggy had become pregnant during their final semester of college—this was in 1975, two years after *Roe v. Wade*—but they'd decided, in a fit of self-defeating undergraduate bravado, to do "the difficult and honorable thing rather than the shameful, easy one." Actually, this was Peggy's formulation; Richard just wanted her to get an abortion, though he never quite got around to stating this preference in so many words.

His silence and passivity in the face of an event that so profoundly transformed his life was something that still baffled him. He didn't love Peggy, didn't want to become a father. And yet he married her and accepted the burden of parenthood without a squeak of protest. To make matters worse, "the baby" turned out to be twins, a much more difficult and honorable project than even Peggy had bargained for. Their domestic circumstances were so chaotic and relentless for so long that Richard was in his mid-thirties before he realized how badly he resented his wife and children for imprisoning him in a suburban cage and forcing him onto the hamster wheel of corporate drudgery while his college buddies were off backpacking through Asia and snorting coke in trendy discos with high school girls who looked much older than they actually were.

By this point in his life, Richard had a night school MBA and a series of professional triumphs under his belt, mostly in the fast-food sector—The Cheese-Bomb Mini-Pizza™ and The Double-Wide Burger™ were two of his notable achievements. He traveled a fair amount on business and consoled himself with a string of hotel flings, as well as a long-term affair with a client's receptionist in Chicago that went sour after he forgot her birthday for the second year in a row. She retaliated with a long, informative letter to Peggy, complete with surprisingly well-written excerpts from her diary.

His daughters were sophomores in high school when this bombshell struck; Richard and Peggy agreed to stay together until they graduated. Oddly, those last two years were their happiest as a couple, though they rarely slept in the same bed and kept their social calendars as separate as possible. Something about the expiration date on the marriage made each of them more generous than they'd been in the past—your spouse's annoying habit becomes a lot less oppressive if you don't have to imagine putting up with it until the day one of you dies. By the time they split, he'd developed a real affection for her, and still called once or twice a week to see how she was doing.

The envelope in the bag contained not one but three Polaroids of Slutty Kay wearing the polka-dot thong, each of them bearing a scrawled inscription. In the first one *(Hi, Richard!)*, she was standing otherwise naked in front of what must have been her bedroom closet, looking unusually contemplative as she brushed her hair. In the second, she was wearing a sleeveless turquoise minidress and sitting in a car in such a way—open door, one leg in, one leg out—that you got a very clear glimpse of her crotch *(Hope this gets you hot!)*. The trio concluded with a rearview shot of Kay bending over and smiling up at the camera from between her knees *(Love and Kisses, S.K.)*. The enclosed sex log was written in the same girlish cursive on a sheet of plain yellow legal paper:

> 7 A.M.—*Up and at 'em . . . first orgasm of the day (silver bullet vibrator) . . . mmmm . . . quick shower*

> 7:30 A.M.—*Put on Richard's thong*

> 8 A.M.—*Coffee at Java House . . . Window seat so I can flash the businessmen . . . Hope they like polka dots!*

> 8:30 A.M.—*Stuck in traffic again . . . Why not masturbate? (Wow, these panties are getting moist!)*

> 9 A.M.–12 Noon—*Work (illustration of frowny face)*

> 12:14—*Lunchtime sex with girlfriend Trudy from Personnel Dept—all she can eat! (Ha-Ha)*

> 12:46—*Tuna sandwich, light mayo, Diet Coke*

> 1–5 P.M.—*Work (frowny face)*

6 P.M.—*Masturbate while cooking dinner (roast slightly burned)*

8–11 P.M.—*Hotel room orgy with members of Slutty Kay Fan Club—and I do mean members! (panties off for most of this time, but back on for drive home)*

12 Midnight—*too tired to remove panties before falling asleep . . . but NOT too tired for one last orgasm (trusty blue dildo)*

7 A.M.—*Up and at 'em . . . remove yesterday's thong, still wet and very fragrant, and seal them in bag for my good friend, RICHARD.*

*p.s.—They're autographed too!*

Richard had been divorced for almost two years when he started seeing Sarah. They hit it off right away, though he suspected later that this instant intimacy had less to do with any real connection between them than it did with the fact that they were both desperately lonely and waiting for someone to rescue them. At the time he'd been drawn to her bitter sense of humor, her youthful body, and her enigmatic sexuality (she claimed to be "basically straight," but spoke frequently about the Korean woman she'd been in love with in college). She seemed to appreciate his social ease, his liberal politics, and, though she never actually said so, the promise he held out of liberation from Starbucks and long-term financial security, at least once his daughters graduated from college.

They'd been married for less than a year when she got pregnant. This time around Richard had no mixed feelings—he was thrilled with the idea of bringing a child into the world, consciously and without regret, correcting the mistakes he'd made with the twins (they blamed him for the divorce and were no longer speaking to him, though they were happy to accept buckets of his money). He vowed to himself and to Sarah that he would be involved and available in this new child's life. He would work less, spend more time at home. He would coach soccer, sing songs in the car, organize memorable birthday parties. He attended Lamaze classes, read a slew of child care books, and coached Sarah successfully through labor and delivery, a miraculous (but also disturbing and horrible and nearly endless) event that he had completely missed out on with the twins, whose birth he'd spent pacing the hospital waiting room like Ricky Ricardo, and then passing out cigars to the other expectant fathers when the doctor gave him the thumbs-up.

He tried, he really did, at least for the first year. He said all those things new fathers are supposed to say and changed his share of diapers. But sometimes he found himself wishing that Lucy was a boy. He'd had two girls already, why did he need a third? And sometimes, when he was stuck at home with the baby on a rainy weekend, he found himself overcome by a familiar sense of claustrophobia and resentment, as if he were once again a young man throwing away the best years of his youth.

His sex life suffered, too, of course. How had he forgotten about that? Sarah was too tired, her nipples were sore, she couldn't even think about it. When he suggested leaving the baby with her mother for a few days so they could take a quick getaway to the Caribbean, she looked at him like he was crazy.

"My mother can barely take of herself," she said. "How's she going to care for an infant?"

It was around that time that he started logging on to swingers' web sites and thinking, *Why not? It looks like fun.* He printed out a list of "house parties" in their area and decided to approach Sarah about the possibility of attending one, just to see what it was like. *They love bisexual women,* he would tell her. *You don't have to do anything you don't want.* But when he went downstairs to talk to her, she was sitting at the kitchen table, expressing milk from her engorged left breast with a loud electric pump, looking pale and haggard as she flipped through the newspaper, and for a second or two, he felt an emotion toward her that was a little like contempt.

He still hadn't gotten over how completely he'd misread his own needs. He'd assumed he was evolving and improving as a person, but all he'd really done was repeat his own failure, this time with his eyes wide-open and no one to blame but himself.

The panties weren't working as well as he'd hoped. It wasn't that the thong wasn't as fragrant as Kay had promised—that was definitely *not* the problem—it was just that the fragrance wasn't as distinctive or evocative of Kay's unique sexuality as he'd expected. For all he knew, it could have been worn by any woman in the world, including Sarah.

Which got him thinking, at a very inconvenient time, about a troubling possibility: What if Kay *hadn't* worn it? On her web site, she claimed to provide the panties to her devoted customers as a labor of love, but Richard wasn't sure he believed her. After all, didn't Kay have an advanced degree in business? For the panties to be really profitable, she would have to deal in bulk. She couldn't just wear one pair per day, as the sex log suggested.

*If I were Kay*, he thought, *I'd subcontract the panty-wearing.* It was all too easy to imagine a sweatshop full of bored women— Chinese and Latina seamstresses—all of them wearing polka-dotted thongs as they worked their sewing machines, then wearily slipping them into plastic bags at the end of the day, along with a completely fictional "sex log." What kind of fool would that make Richard?

He pressed the thong over his mouth and nose and inhaled deeply, trying to banish these inappropriately commercial considerations. This was no time to be thinking about business, his pants around his ankles, his palm slick with Vaseline Intensive Care.

*These are Kay's panties*, he chanted to himself. *These panties belong to Kay.* But then, just when he got himself going, he'd think, *Maybe they're not. Maybe they're outsourced.*

It was hard to know how long he'd hosted this dialogue in his mind before the whole issue of authenticity suddenly became moot. His eyes were darting in a regular pattern from the sex log to the Polaroids to an image on his computer screen of Kay leaning on a guardrail overlooking Niagara Falls, discreetly lifting her dress to give the camera a glimpse of her bare ass. He was breathing deeply, taking her essence deep into his lungs, into his bloodstream—

"Ahem."

He whipped his head around, the panties still pressed over the lower half of his face. Sarah was standing in the doorway, her expression wavering between revulsion and amazement.

"Is this going to take much longer?" she asked. "I'd really like to go for my walk."

Richard understood that something terribly embarrassing had occurred, but all he felt just then was a profound annoyance at the interruption.

"You could have knocked," he said, his words disappearing into the undergarment.

"I did."

It took an effort of will for him to remove the thong.

"I'm sorry," he said. "This will just take a minute."

"I think we need to talk," she said, but to his immense relief she backed out of the room without another word, pressing the door shut with the gentlest of clicks, not unlike the sound your tongue makes against the roof of your mouth when you think something's a shame.

# Fifteen Minutes

## Gwen Masters

She was in her early twenties, John guessed. Her body looked young, but the hard living made her face look ten years older. He watched her from the sidelines, took note of her bleached blond hair, her long painted nails, her tank top that was just a little too tight and a little too short. Her jeans were cut off just below the hip. When she turned just the right way, she flashed anybody who cared to look. She wasn't wearing any panties.

Girls like that were a dime a dozen. They were a joke in the music world, referred to as "germs," because that is what they were. They would follow the band around like a sickness that sticks to the skin. They were good for the occasional nightly release, the blow job that left a bad taste in both their mouths. When they spread their legs it was with a practiced desperation. Anybody who fucked a groupie knew they were fucking somebody who had been indiscriminate with hundreds of guys before them. It had nothing to do with the man behind the microphone or the keyboard player's talent or even the bus driver's gift of getting everybody there safely. It had to do with comparisons between friends and one-upmanship.

"Is he a good lay?" one would ask.

"He's after his own pleasure," another would snarl, as if they really cared.

Tom had asked for a blond this time. It was rare that the front man wanted a woman after the show. He was more careful than most, usually refusing to feed the game that was played out on tour buses and backstage stairs and the occasional pricey hotel room. "A little something for me and then for the boys," he said this time before he climbed onstage with guitar in hand.

The blond would do. Her legs were long and lean. Her tits were bouncy under the tank top, her nipples hard as rocks while she watched the band do their thing. She wasn't jumping up and down or cheering them on. She was bopping lightly along with the music and studying the players as if they were her favorite kind of treat. She had been down the groupie road before. She would do.

Beside Blondie was a young kid, perhaps no more than thirteen, dressed even more provocatively. Where was her mother? Her father? In a few years she would be lifting her skirts for anything with a guitar. John took in the overdone makeup, the thigh-high boots. Maybe she had already had her cherry popped by some undiscerning roadie.

John scanned the crowd one more time. There were a few other possibilities, but Blondie kept pulling his attention. He flipped the all-access pass out of his jeans pocket and over his head. It was easier to mingle when he wasn't wearing it, but he needed to make a quick impression. John circled around behind the stage. The sound of the band was muffled back there. He picked his way carefully along the outer walkway, stepping over amp cords and nodding a hello to the roadies who sat idly near the waiting trucks.

"Big man wants some road nookie," John told them. "Anybody up for blond?"

Charley took a drink of something in a paper sack. He lifted his hand and wiggled his ring finger at him. The wedding band flashed in the dim light. "Already got me a blond," he drawled.

John smiled. Charley was one of the few who took the wedding band seriously. "Not you, then."

Rick boosted himself up onto the walkway. "She prime?"

"Let's find out."

The blond glanced over at John when the men came out beside the stage. She gave him the once-over and started to look away, uninterested, until she saw the all-access pass around his neck. Her smile didn't quite reach her eyes. They were green, big and pretty. Her chest was a little on the small side but even perkier up close. She smelled like marijuana and perfume.

"Hello there," she drawled with the slightest hint of a southern accent. John smiled and casually looped his arm around her shoulders. No need for pretense. He pointed up at Tom.

"You a natural blond?" John hollered into her ear.

"You'll just have to take my word for it, since there's no hair down there," she hollered back, her voice barely audible over the screaming sax solo.

John nudged her toward Rick and she went obediently. John fell into step behind her and watched her ass move under the denim. Her legs were even longer than he thought. Coltish. She had a tattoo on the small of her back, a little butterfly spreading its wings.

Behind the stage the music was quiet enough that John didn't have to yell. "Want to come back to the hotel?" he asked, straightforward.

"Depends. Do I get to see Tom?"

"Among others," Rick promised. Blondie looked him up and down and smiled. Licked her lips.

"I just want an autograph," she purred.

She didn't balk about wanting to stick around to watch the encore. She simply nodded when he opened the door of the limousine, slid in with those long legs trailing. The door closed with a luxurious thump and immediately they were in motion, headed for the hotel. John reached for the bar and she caught his hand in midair.

"You weren't on this tour last year. What do you do?" she asked, her eyes pinning him to the seat.

"I'm a manager."

"Not the road manager. Publicity? Merchandising?"

"Equipment."

She reached for the front of his jeans. She wasn't too eager, but not too methodical either. Her mouth was soft and warm. John jerked when he felt the surprise of her tongue ring against his cock. It made him instantly hard.

"Nice," he whispered. Her hair was silky smooth. She moved up and down on him, flicking that warm metal stud against his head when she pulled all the way up. John leaned his head back against the seat and closed his eyes. He thought about Blondie kneeling on the hotel bed, sucking his cock while she took one of the other guys up her cunt.

He didn't bother to tell her he was going to come. He just grabbed her hair and held her steady while he shot off. When he felt her swallow, he knew he had picked the right one.

"You're good," he said as she sat up. She looked him in the eye and wiped her lips with the back of her hand. Sat beside him in the seat and crossed those long legs, watched him zip back up. Leaned over to kiss his neck.

"That's my thanks," she told him, flipping his all-access pass on the lanyard.

"I want to fuck you last. After they have all had a go at you."

Her eyes widened but she didn't look surprised. "You like that, do you?"

"How many times have you done this?"

She thought for a moment, biting her full bottom lip. There was a lipstick smear on her teeth. "A whole band? Only once."

"How old are you?"

"Old enough." She leaned over and flicked his ear with her tongue. Brought his hand up under her shirt, let him feel her up. "Can't you tell?"

The hotel room was huge. Blondie wandered around, taking it all in. John answered his cell phone. He found dozens of bottles in the complimentary bar, tossed tequila to Blondie. She downed it in one swallow while John stared. One of the record label guys walked in and within minutes she was trailing one long painted nail down the front of his shirt.

One by one they trailed in, stopping by before they headed to their own rooms to call wives or girlfriends back home, maybe both. It was a rare night in a hotel, with a warm comfortable bed and room service and a late schedule to get to the next town. Most of their time was spent on the buses, trying to sleep and doing anything to keep the hum of the wheels from driving them insane. Movies were watched so many times they could be quoted, line for line. Sometimes the guys would take different parts and talk out the whole movie, just because it was something to do. There was the occasional woman, usually up against the side of a trailer or in a discrete corner of the venue. No women were allowed on the buses, ever. Band rule.

However, women were definitely allowed in hotel rooms.

Tom got to the hotel an hour later. By then Blondie had said hello to almost everyone who worked the tour and some who didn't. John watched her sidle up to Tom. She played the shy card, which was transparent as glass. Tom listened to her talk all through the room service delivery, the signing of a stack of photos for radio station giveaways, the phone call he took from somebody important enough to be calling the great Tom Myers at one in the morning. When he clicked the phone closed and reached for Blondie's thigh, John ushered out anyone who wasn't on the pay-roll.

Tom always used condoms, and tonight was no exception. John turned to see Blondie rolling one onto Tom's cock with her mouth. From the doorway of the bathroom, Rich watched. Rich was the bass player, married with three kids at home. John watched as Rich unbuttoned his jeans. Alex stood a few paces behind him. Alex was a newlywed with only two weeks of blessed matrimony under his belt. John wondered what he would do.

Scottie, the drummer, ambled out of the small kitchen with a sandwich on a paper plate. He stopped dead in his tracks at the sight of Blondie, who was now standing in front of Tom and gy-rating to music only she could hear. The tank top landed on the floor. Her breasts might have been fake, but they were sensa-tional.

"Well, we get a free show," Scottie commented. He leaned against the wall to watch, his sandwich completely forgotten.

She was wearing panties after all, but she might as well have been bare. The G-string covered absolutely nothing. Tom slipped his fingertips under the straps and pulled her to him. His tongue played with her belly button ring while he worked the panties down her long legs. Blondie tossed her hair over her shoulder and looked straight at John as she lifted her hands, played with her nipples. Her eyes told the whole story. She was high as a kite.

So was Tom, John noted with dismay. So much for keeping the front man clean. John didn't know where he got the powder, but he would make sure to find out before the next gig.

Blondie pushed Tom back on the bed and straddled him. Rich moved closer to get a better view. The slut wasn't wet, but she started to grind on Tom's cock anyway. One slow inch at a time, she impaled herself on him. Tom squeezed her nipples and watched her face as she watched all the other men in the room.

"I can't believe I'm fucking Tom Myers," she giggled like a schoolgirl.

"You're not fucking me yet," Tom pointed out. "Come on. Make me come."

Rich stepped up and touched Blondie's ass. The effect on her was electric. That's what she needed, John realized. She didn't get turned on over just one guy. She really was into it for the thrill of fucking the whole room. She suddenly slid down easily on Tom's cock, and he moaned out loud.

"Yeah. Just like that," he encouraged.

Blondie started to fuck him in earnest. She gazed down at Tom while Rich shoved his jeans down to his knees. His shirt came off. "Care to have another?" Rich asked, the question directed more toward Tom than Blondie.

"The bitch wants it," Tom said. He grabbed her hair, pulled her head back. "Only question is *where* does she want it, isn't that right?"

"Anywhere," Blondie gasped.

Rich stepped up behind Blondie. Her ass was at just the right height while she rode Tom. John watched as Rich coated his cock with something complimentary from the bathroom—shampoo, hand lotion, he wasn't sure.

"Condoms are in the duffel bag," Tom said, then groaned as Blondie began to slam down harder.

"I'm not in the mood for condoms," Rich growled, then grabbed Blondie's hair. She arched her back, putting her nipples in perfect alignment with Tom's mouth. She squealed as his mouth closed over one of them. "You gonna make me use a condom, sweetheart?"

"No . . . no condoms," Blondie agreed.

Rich began to push his cock between her ass cheeks. It took a moment for him to get the angle right. John's cock surged, fully hard, when he heard Blondie's cry and Rich's moan of satisfaction.

"There you go, just like that . . . all the way up," Rich taunted as he pushed relentlessly. Tom groaned under the two of them.

"Hurry up and come," Scottie murmured under his breath. "I want my turn."

John reached down and brushed his hand across the front of his jeans. He had never quite gotten into letting the other men see him naked, but he reminded himself that it didn't matter. Nobody was really paying attention to the equipment. They were all paying attention to the three holes and which one they were going to fuck next.

Rich sawed in and out of Blondie's ass. John watched it from the corner of the room. Alex, the newlywed, had taken a seat near the bathroom door. He was slowly stroking his erection through his pants.

Suddenly Tom tensed under Blondie's grinding body. She looked down at him and unleashed a line of moans and taunts. "That's it, fucking come for me, shoot that jism for me, make me your little band whore," she begged, and Tom's handsome face contorted as he came. "I just made Tom Myers come," Blondie practically chortled, and Rich slammed her hard enough to make her shut up.

John watched the changing of the guard. Tom eased out from under Blondie. Scottie's cock disappeared into her mouth while Rich's movements started to get jerky. But John's eyes were on Tom, who was walking none too steadily to the kitchenette.

"Where did it come from?" John asked, stopping him in the doorway.

"What?"

"The blow. Where?"

Tom shook his head, looking down into the mini-fridge. "You brought her here, man."

John's mind raced. How the fuck did she do it? She wasn't even carrying a purse. In the other room, Blondie laughed when

Rich groaned that he was going to come. Scottie said he wanted that pussy next. Tom's eyes were glassy.

John pointed at him, his finger inches from Tom's nose. "We aren't doing this again, Tom. I've put you through more than enough goddamn rehab."

Tom waved him away.

Rich was in the bathroom. Scottie was going at Blondie, fucking her mouth like there was no tomorrow. Alex stood at the edge of the bed, watching, waiting his turn. John kicked the hell out of a mandolin case and slammed the balcony door behind him as he walked out. It was really fucking *hot* out there for two in the morning.

He stood there for a long while, watching the lights far below. Four years on the road was a long time, and more and more often John thought that maybe he was done with that life. But every time he tried to walk away, there was something else that kept him there. More money. That one shining gig in the one venue that he always wanted to work. But mostly it was the thought of going back to his empty house every night and going to work at the record label every day, getting his ass kissed in a world where they just pushed paper and hung platinum records on walls. This was where he belonged.

Scottie was laughing. John wondered again where Blondie had that blow hidden all that time. He should frisk these fucking groupie whores, *that's* what he should do.

He walked back into the room just in time to see Alex sink his cock into Blondie's cunt. The sound told him exactly where Scottie had come. Young Alex shot off in minutes. Blondie acted disappointed until Rich stepped back up to the bed. Another round.

By the time the three guys left for their own rooms, the sun was streaking the sky outside. John stood at the wall of glass and watched the colors change. He listened to Tom and Blondie going at it one more time. He was disillusioned as hell, but he knew that in a week or two this would happen again, and he would be all for it. The anger was just a passing phase. It always was.

"You ready for her, John?" Tom's voice was harsh. Almost hoarse. John raised an eyebrow, lost in thought. He could get him into the throat specialist, get him checked out on Tuesday, the one day they had free . . .

"John?"

Tom's voice was definitely a little off. It was that goddamn coke. Blondie was a bitch.

John turned and unzipped his jeans. Stepped out of them. Walked to the bed. Blondie had just finished with Tom; her face was covered with him. John was disgusted at the fact that he got hard as a rock immediately. A handful of hair in one hand, one firm tit in the other, John went at her like an animal. He ignored her squeals of protest. He stared at her face, her eyes wild with excitement, her face sticky and wet. She reeked of sex.

The thrill of how wet she was brought him to the edge far too soon, so he slowed down. Rammed her. "Ugh," she uttered, and John realized just how ugly she was now that all the makeup was gone. Did these groupies really think that they would be remembered fondly? Did Blondie really think she was anything more than just a piece of meat, a distraction for men who had been on the road a little too long without any woman to relieve the burden?

John closed his eyes and snapshots of the last few hours flew through his head while he came. He pushed as deep as he could and let himself go where so many others had been. He thought of her spreading her legs for the whole band and he came so hard he saw little bursts of light behind his eyelids. He was left shaky and weak. Then Blondie was moaning for him to get off her, he was too heavy. So he did, and pushed her out of the bed at the same time. She didn't seem to mind.

An hour later Tom was sitting on the edge of the bed. John blinked up at him. "She gone?"

"Yeah. She took all the coke with her."

John sighed and rubbed the bridge of his nose, his eyes. "Good."

"You know, it's funny," Tom said. "I don't even remember what she looks like. It's been thirty minutes and I already couldn't pick her out of a crowd. How many women have we had out here, anyway?" Tom mused. "Thousand?"

"In four years? Nah. Five hundred."

"Do *you* remember any of them?" Tom asked. John thought about that for a long moment. He shifted under the sheet. Ached just a little from the pounding he gave Blondie.

"Yeah," John said. "For a little while. Then they fade."

"Kinda like us," Tom sighed, and John looked at him. In the morning light his friend looked ten years older than he really was. John supposed that he did, too.

"Everybody has got to have their fifteen minutes," he said.

# The End

## Rachel Kramer Bussel

*Do you see her face*
*when she's gone*
*sometimes so bright*
*your heart just stops*

*did she answer you*
*your other half*
*you know they say*
*she comes just once*

—Sleater-Kinney, "Jenny"

It doesn't help that she looks more beautiful now than ever. Her face glows with a natural tan and the sweetest smile I think I will ever see, her blue eyes shining at me with need and want and love and pain. I want to feel as if we are our own entity, existing in a private universe that nothing and no one else can pierce. That life is all about looking at her, in her, nothing more, nothing less. Without makeup, she is the perfect combination of girl and woman, and she fills me with a need to hold and protect her that leaves me raw and open and more vulnerable than any person should ever be.

I know all the right moves to make, the ways to touch her, the strokes that will make her melt and move and clutch me as if she will need me forever. I know how she wants it. I need to feel as if I'm the only one who can give it to her. I live for those times when she grabs me and looks as deeply inside me as I am inside her.

As she lies there, so small, so seemingly fragile, her doll's body looks like some alluring creature, one that I might break if I handle it improperly. I can easily forget the core of strength and stubbornness she possesses. Spread out in front of me, she is truly the girl of the dreams I never knew I had. I slide my fingers inside her, pushing deep into her core, knowing just where to curve and bend to get to where I want to be. I've never known another woman's body quite like this, navigating her pussy as easily as I trace my fingers over her face, reading her like a well-worn page of a beloved book, instantly, easily.

At this moment, with her hair messy and tangled like an overworked Barbie's, I want to grab it as I've done so many times before, to pull fiercely and then bring her head down into the pillow, to live up to the violent promise of this situation. I almost pull away, because I am not that kind of girl. I'm still getting used to being the girl who wants to hurt someone else, who feels a distinct kind of awe when I hear the sound of my hand slamming down against her ass. I'm still getting used to being the girl who likes giving it rough, who likes to claw and scrape, who sometimes wants to slap her across the face. The girl who got the slightest thrill when she cried the other day while I spanked her.

I see the collar next to the bed glittering brightly. It meant everything when I fastened it around her neck those countless weeks ago, transforming the airport bathroom into our own private sexual sanctuary. Now, it is too bright, too accusatory, a mistake in so many ways. Like the sweetest of forbidden fruit, her neck beckons, so white and exposed, pulsing with veins and life and want. Now when I see her neck, tender and ever-needy, I can barely go near it. The pleasure would be too great. It would be too easy to press a bit too hard, to enjoy it for all the wrong reasons, even though I can feel her angling toward it, begging me to obliterate her for a few blessed seconds. I know what it does to her, and for the first time I don't want to know. That's never been the kind of power I've wanted, even though she'd gladly give it to me, give me almost anything except what I need the most.

I want to slide back to that simple starting point, our bodies blank canvases on which to draw magnificent works of the most special kind of art. Maybe there is still some power left in this bed, something that flows from one of us to the other rather than simply inward, something that binds us together. The ways I thought I knew her have all vanished, lost in a mystery too complex for me to solve. Too many silences and unspoken thoughts war for space between us. She is just as much a stranger to me as she was on our first date, perhaps even more so now, her mind locked away in a box with someone else's keys. Knowing only her body leaves me emptier than if we'd never even met, giving me a hollow victory, a prize I'm forced to return, undeserving and unwanted.

My fingers grant me nothing except access to a disembodied cunt, separated from all reality, the way the old-school feminists described pornography, parceling out body parts at random without context or meaning. I wish I could erase my sense memory of how it feels to fuck her, love her, and know her all at the same time, in the same motions. I am somehow back to square one, vainly hoping, praying, that I can make her happy.

Only this time, we have so much more to do than just fuck, than slide and scream and bite and whisper, than twist and bend and push and probe. The stakes are so much higher that no or-gasm will ever be enough, but I try anyway.

No matter how far I reach inside, I cannot crack her. Those eyes are a one-way mirror, reflecting a surface of something I can-not see and probably don't want to. I want to tell her I love her, show her everything inside me, but I open my mouth and just as quickly close it. I can feel her body shaking, the tears and pain ris-ing up like an earthquake's tremors, and I shove harder, grab her neck and push her down, anything to quell the rising tide that will be here soon enough. This may look the same as all those other times, my fingers arching and stroking, her eyes shut or staring at me, needy, grabbing me when I touch her in just the right way that is almost—but not quite—too much. But it is nothing like those other times, nothing like anything I've ever done before. It is like touching something totally alien, someone I never even knew, someone not even human. I feel lost as I touch her, my heart so far away I hardly know what to do or how to act. I can see that this is not bridging the gap, but I can't stop myself. I try to pretend that her moans, her wetness, these external signals of de-sire actually mean she is truly mine. There is no way to make her come and erase the other girl's touch entirely. I am not yet think-ing about her and the other girl, wondering how she touches her, not wanting to know but needing to, drawn to that deadly fire with a car-crash allure, though that will all come in time, in those free-standing hours of numbed shock, those lost weekends when she invades my head and will not leave.

She has written me a letter, as requested, given me exact blueprints for how to fuck her. How to take her up against the wall, how to tie her up, tease her, taunt her, and hold out even when she protests. I want nothing more than to be able to follow these instructions, which by now I don't even need because I know how to trigger her, how to get her to go from laughing to spreading her legs in the briefest of moments. I know exactly how to touch her now, where to stroke and bite and slap to give both of us what we need, but that is no longer enough. I don't have it in me to be that kind of top, to blank out all the rest and fulfill only that viciously visceral urge to pummel, pound, and punish. That urge is too clearly real, too close to the unspoken pain, the words that will come later, the ones right underneath the tears. I know when I hit her what it means. There can be no erotic power exchange when she holds all the real power, I have enough soul left in me to know that sex should not be a mechanical obligation. It should not be the only thing you can do to stay alive, compelled with the force of something so strong you're powerless to resist.

I reach, reach, reach inside her, desperately searching, hoping to wrench us back to wherever we are supposed to be, back to where we were—a week, a month, a lifetime ago. I draw out this process, watch myself as if from afar as my hand slides inside her, as I lube myself up and try to cram all of me into her, make a lasting impression. I have my entire hand inside her, yet I feel more removed from her than I have ever felt. She might as well still be in Florida. She might as well still be a stranger, this might as well still be our first date when I laughed so much because I was so nervous. I'd rather this be any of those nights, even the ones when I was so drunk and afraid, so powerless and unsure; anything would be better than this slow death, this slow withering until we are nothing more than two girls in a room with tears in our eyes and an ocean of questions and scars and hurt between us. I can't predict what will come after this most pregnant of silences, can't know the depths of pain that will puncture me beyond the horrors of my imagination, can't know that I will regret everything I might have, could have, done wrong, or did do wrong.

She turns over on her stomach, face hidden from my searching eyes, and I fumble to reconnect, to slide into her as if nothing is wrong, as if it's just a matter of finding a comfortable angle. I finally have had enough, cannot keep going with the charade that pressing myself against her will fill all the gaps that still exist between us. But for whatever twisted reasons we need this, this final time. And this is the last time, because nothing is worth feeling so utterly and completely alone while you're fucking your girlfriend before you break up. No power trip or blazing orgasm, no heart-pounding breathless finish, no sadistic impulse or mistaken nostalgia is worth this much pain.

I don't know how to say what I have to, what I'm terrified to, how to ask questions whose answers I know I won't want to hear. There's no book I can read that will teach me how to make her G-spot tell me her secrets, tell me those fantasies and dreams that don't come from her pussy but from her heart. The end, it turns out, is nothing like the beginning. There is no promise of something more, some grand future of possibility, the infinite ways of knowing each other just waiting to be discovered. There is no hope that we can merge, in all the ways love can make you merge, into something so much greater than the sum of our parts. The end is like what they say about death, when your whole life flashes before your eyes. I see moments, fragments—my hand up her skirt on the street, taking her in the doorway of a friend's apartment, so fiercely she can barely sink down to the ground, her on her knees in the bathroom, surprising me as she buries her face into me, no room to protest, grinding the edge of a knife along her back, slapping her tits until they are raw and red—but they seem so far away right now, like a movie, like someone else's pornographic memories. They don't make me smile, and I don't want them anymore. I want to bury myself in her and never let go, hold on to something that has just fluttered away in the wind, fine as the glittering sparkles she wears on her eyes, minuscule and almost opaque, too minute to ever recapture. But all I can do is back away, as slowly as I can, so slowly that it seems as if I am hardly moving, and before I know it, I, and she—we—are gone, almost as if we never existed.

# Granny Pearls

## Salome Wilde

My most memorable experience? Oh, that's easy. Gather round, little jewels, and let me tell you a story.

Life in the Box can be dull if you don't get taken out much, but it can be just as bad when you only see light on "special occasions," like weddings or funerals. (Diamond Brooch can brag all she wants about meeting the governor, but that story is so old she can't even remember what color dress she was pinned to.) Some days I'd give a lot to be an amethyst ring or even a tie tack. Despite the respect, I tell you: it's tough to be Granny Pearls.

But you wanted to hear about my adventures, not an old gal's complaints. I could tell you about the time I slipped off and ended up under the front seat of the Town Car for two weeks, conversing with gum wrappers and lint, but I can see by your frowns that's not what you're asking for. Impatient trinkets: you can't wait to get out and swing from earlobes or dance on fingers shoved deep into sticky crevices you've only imagined in your sparkling dreams. Ah, I remember that time of life so well, and how little hope I had—

being such a costly necklace—of ever being in the right place at the right time. But, my time did come, as will yours—and soon enough, you wicked little baubles.

It was a lovely spring afternoon, and I was aglow with expectation, though I'd not been out of the Box in ages. Easter services that bored me to sleep, chaperoning at proms: life was not what my friends the Bangle Bracelet Quintuplets had said it would be. However, my expectations and my life changed forever that one crisp May morning. I was lovingly clasped over a tight pale blue sweater that showed off the Mistress's eyes, and out we went. In the car—a cramped, unfamiliar vehicle that smelled of lemons— her fingers lingered over me, twirling my beads in a most stimulating way. I called to a big gold ring on an unfamiliar hairy finger curved around the steering wheel, and he told me in his loud, guttural voice that he wasn't sure but could probably guess where we were going and that he'd definitely seen the Mistress before. He said he had talked to Wedding Ring, but found her a "stuffy bitch." I ignored the crass insult to our most venerated *Grande Dame* (who else never sleeps in the Box but she), but I looked about and realized that she was not where she ought to be. Imagine! Wedding Ring was missing from her proper place on the finger: the world was topsy-turvy!

I tried to figure out what was happening, but my mind was muzzy from the way the Mistress's soft, pale fingers kept playing over me. Without warning, the car stopped and out we went. The sun was bright and filled me with lustrous pride; my head swam with pleasure and anxiousness. Gold Ring's "Buck up, toots, this could be fun" was hardly reassuring. Nor could I relax when we walked into a dark, musty-smelling room before I'd even found my bearings.

Gold Ring hinted he knew this room well and had seen "plenty of action" here. I tried to pretend I did not grasp his meaning, but, of course, I did. Before I could offer a cutting retort or even a gasp of outrage, I felt myself smashed against the dress shirt of the man who was crushing the Mistress to his chest. I whispered "What is happening?" to a nearby button, but I could not understand its dialect. The two bodies ground me between them, and though the tight darkness was frightening, I began to enjoy the soft noises they made, the way their bodies swayed, and the way I was twisted and twirled so casually. I'd never been used so before: always, I'd been handled reverently. From the moment I'd been taken from the jewel case and placed around the Mistress's neck, I'd known I was born to a high station and must keep up appearances. Even when she'd put me in the Box with the wonderful little ornaments and costume pieces that came before your time, I'd still felt special. But now, here I was, entirely ignored. No one to show off my delicate, translucent radiance for. Just two bodies in a small, dark, stuffy room, pressing me between them. I felt less treasured than I'd ever been in my young life, but I also felt more aroused than I'd ever been. The heat of their alien passions left me dizzy.

I thought I'd faint when Gold Ring's owner reached his bulky fingers around to remove me from the Mistress's neck. He was certainly not gentle. But it did stimulate me; I cannot deny it. Gold Ring snickered from his place on his owner's finger, and I felt myself blush and giggle in return. Foolish strand!

My moment of exposure became a sudden rush of embarrassment when those hands dropped me casually to the floor. My mood snapped like a broken clasp as I fell with a thud to the moldy carpet. The Mistress and her strange bedfellow disappeared from my sight. Countless moments passed as I lay there, forgotten, their discarded clothing piling on top of me as I listened to their occasional broken moans and throaty fragments of speech.

I waited, utterly alone, for the end of their fervor, when I would—I hoped—be returned to my place around the Mistress's slender throat, and we would go back to the familiar sights and smells of our home and the Box. Endless minutes passed as I lay, smothered in perfumed sweater, rumpled dress shirt, slacks, skirt, hose. I could not decide whether I was more angered at being left out of the mysteries they enjoyed or at their disregard of my beauty and preciousness.

I must have fallen asleep for a bit, for I woke with a start to find myself suspended over the floor, held in the man's coarse grip. "I think you're in for it now, girlie," Gold Ring said with a twinkle, but I couldn't imagine what he meant. Even if he were a more cultured gentleman's band and not an electroplated thing with a faux sapphire for a heart, I do not think he or anyone could have prepared me for what came next.

The Mistress, naked and on all fours on the bed, was uttering some sort of half-hearted protest as the man dangled me before her eyes and then ran me down the curve of her back, all the way down to her derriere. I was shocked beyond speech to find her in this position. How could she! And how could she let me be used as part of this impropriety! Despite my silent protest, I found myself again in that space between shame and surrender, knowing I shouldn't like to be handled this way, but enjoying it nonetheless. If the Mistress was not mortified, why should I be?

But being dragged along her naked body was not to be my ultimate role in their strange scenario. After a few passes over her back, the man concentrated on drawing me back and forth between her buttocks. This made her writhe and moan, as I grew ever more radiant and warm. And then his movements became rougher: he began to use me to strike her backside. Over and over I was flung through the air, only to slap down against her flesh again. I grew disoriented, vaguely nauseated, and certain I would break. Surely, I would be torn apart and my pearls scattered all over this dirty room. Never again would I see my jewelry family and friends again.

Somehow, I held together. Through minutes or hours—I could not tell which—the Mistress never demanded that he stop misus-

ing me, and he never concerned himself with my delicacy. Instead,
he ceased his whipping and began to press my clasp to her anus.
Do not gasp at what I tell you, sweet trifles. It is best you learn
now that there are no places in the human body that those of us in
the Box may not eventually come to know. And I came to know
this space intimately, as he pushed first one then another and then
another and yet still another of my pearls into the space beyond
that dark pucker while the Mistress cried out until I could hear
her no longer. I was crushed into that tight netherworld, dank and
rich with wild and earthy smells. In the end, only my clasp and a
bit of silk thread still remained outside. I felt her body clench
against me and his hand tugging gently at the thread, reminding
me I was still attached. I was grateful for this small gesture, as I
began to lose the sharpness of my senses as I gave myself over to
this moist, silent place. Huddled in on myself, I saw life anew: I
was no better than the flimsiest dime-store plastic, no worse than
the most perfect diamond. We are all just here to bring pleasure,
my luminous lovelies, whether as gaudily paraded excess or subtle
shows of wealth, whether visible to all or hidden in our Box,
whether around necks or shoved into body cavities: nothing is beyond us, nothing is beneath us. The Mistress and I both learned
that lesson that day.

How did I get out, you ask? Well, what is pushed in must be
pulled out, my fellow trifles. And so I was, bead by glistening
bead.

# High Risk

## Bob Vickery

It's a little after eleven o'clock, late enough to draw a decent bar crowd, but early enough, if I'm lucky, to score and still catch a few hours' sleep. I have to be in the hiring hall by eight o'clock sharp tomorrow morning if I'm to get a crack at a job. It's crazy to be cruising on a weekday night, but I haven't been laid since I moved out here, and my cock is giving me a hard time about it. Springsteen is playing on the jukebox, and the boys are lined up against the walls, checking out any new action that walks through the door. I feel their eyes draw a bead on me, and it's gratifying to see how they track me as I push my way through the crowd. I need a little tender loving tonight; I'm feeling lonely and more than a little depressed about not finding work.

I make my way to the bar and order the cheapest beer they got, which is still four goddamn dollars. As I pull the bills from my wallet, I realize that I'm going to have to nurse this sucker for the rest of the night. That is, unless I can get someone to buy me another. This is very possible. I'm muscular and hairy, with the face of a back alley thug, perfect fodder for all those guys out there with fantasies of getting it on with a knuckle-dragger. And they *are* out there. I found out long ago that by just leaning against a wall and looking stupid, I can usually draw in someone looking for a little walk on the wild side.

Within half an hour I've hooked up with a couple of boyfriends who have a place in the Village. One's a humpy little dago with a tight, compact body and dark soulful eyes. He tells me his name is Lou, short for Luigi. His buddy is lighter, with blond hair, a kid's face, and the tall, lean body of a competitive swimmer. They both fall into the "sex candy" category, and I'm quite happy to be their stray mutt for the night. We talk the usual barroom bullshit, and I answer their questions as politely as I'm capable of, waiting for them to make up their minds. When the blond guy, whose name is Charley, asks me what I do for a living, I tell him I'm an iron man. Well, that tips the scales in my balance fast enough; I can see they're about creaming in their jeans at the thought of making it with *a construction worker.* They exchange glances, raise their eyebrows, and give each other a silent nod, with all the subtlety of a two-by-four between the eyes. It's funny, but they seem to think I'm too clueless to notice any of this. Or else they just don't care. They finally ask if I want to go home with them and I say, "Sure."

Riding in their car, I pick up signals that these guys want someone mean and stupid. I think about calling this off, but decide to just go ahead and play the game. When we get back to their place, I throw them around the bedroom, rough them up a bit, rip their clothes off, and then make them strip me naked. Lou pulls my pants down; when my dick springs out to full attention he looks like a kid who just got a new bike for Christmas. I grab his head and start fucking his face hard while Charley eats out my ass. Lou is no slouch at giving head. I close my eyes and let the sensations sweep over me of having my dick *finally* in some place warm and wet. We play out all the expected riffs on the theme of the big, bad construction worker. I call them "faggots" and "cocksuckers" and knock them around some more. But later on, I let them turn the tables on me. Charley "pins" me down as Lou slowly works a greased dildo up my ass. I snarl and spit, cursing threats at them, with all of us just having a grand old time. I end up fucking them both in retaliation; first Lou, then Charley, then Lou again, because I find him the hotter of the two. I shoot my load while plowing him, and as I squirt it deep into the condom up his ass, I throw back my head and bellow like a bull. A neighbor pounds on the wall and shouts at us to shut the fuck up. I lie back while Lou and Charley kneel over me and shoot on my face. They beg me to spend the night, but I tell them no, I got plans tomorrow morning. When they don't give it up, I kick over an end table and tell them to go fuck themselves. They love it.

On the subway back, I think about how easy it was to give them what they wanted. Hell, if things get desperate enough, I could always try hustling. Christ, I hope it doesn't come to that.

I luck out. The next morning I finally land a job up on Lexington Avenue. One of the iron men there took a flop yesterday and fell two stories, breaking his leg. Tough luck for him. Lucky break for me. Oh, does that sound callous? Excuse me, I'll be more sensitive when I have more than fifty-seven bucks in my checking account.

I show up the next day right at eight o'clock, like I was told to; I'm not about to do anything to blow this gig. The building's a big motherfucker all right—already fifty-four stories worth of iron up, with another twenty-two to go. I take the lift up to where the crew is punching in. By force of habit, I zero in on the bumpiest guy there, some Irish piece of tail with a red crew cut, alert blue eyes, and a tight, sexy body that's just screaming for a serious plowing. I ask him what the foreman's name is and where I can find him.

He gives me a quick look-over. "His name's Jackson," he says. "Last I saw him, he was over by the derrick bull wheel."

"What does he look like?"

He gives a hint of a smile. "Think pit bull on steroids." He buckles on his tool belt and hoists a coil of cable on his shoulder. "Just go over there. You can't miss him."

It doesn't take long to find Jackson. The guy was right. He does have the small bloodshot eyes and sloped head of an attack dog. I report in, and he looks me over, his eyes pausing for a second on the four gold rings pierced in my left ear. He doesn't look too happy with what the cat dragged in. We're standing just a few feet away from the bull wheel and have to shout to hear each other. "The hall tells me you're a connector," he growls. "Is that for real?"

I nod. "For five years. Out in L.A."

Jackson squints his eyes, a third-rate Clint Eastwood. "Oh, yeah? Why'd you come out here?"

*What,* I think, *I need a passport?* But I know how crews guard their turfs like junkyard dogs. I give my best shit-eating smile. "Construction's gone to hell out west. All the trades are scrambling for work. I thought I'd try east for a change."

Jackson's squint doesn't lighten up any. Then again, maybe that's how he always looks. He points up to a figure balanced on an eight-inch beam overhead, guiding down a twenty-foot I beam hung from a derrick cable. Even from this distance, I can see that it's the red-headed guy I talked to earlier. "That's Mike O'Reilly. You're going to be working with him bolting those headers." I start climbing up the column next to Mike's, but Jackson grabs me by the arm and pulls me back. By instinct my hand clenches into a fist, and I unclench it just as quick. I don't think slugging the boss would be such a good idea.

"I'll be keeping my eye on you," he says, giving me the fisheye. "If you can't cut it, your ass will be off the crew by tomorrow."

*Thanks for the pep talk,* I think. I shimmy up the column with my eyes trained on Mike. He's perched on the beam, wrestling a header into place. I take a few seconds to take in the sight: his shirt off, his body packed with muscles, his powerful arms lifted up and struggling with all that steel against the backdrop of clear blue sky. Pure poetry. Enough to set my dick thumping. God, I love construction!

Mike is still humping the header when I finally get level with him, though with twenty feet of empty air still between us. "Howdy!" I call out to him.

He glances my way and then back at the header. He gives it a mighty whack with his spud wrench and then looks back at me again, his gaze bold as brass. His mouth curls up into an easy smile. "I wondered if you were Pete's replacement. How ya doing? Did Jackson chew a chunk out of your ass?"

"I still got most of it left." I grabbed my end of the header. "You need some help with that?"

"Yeah, if you feel so inclined."

I get the header lined up just so, slip a few bolts in, and tighten the nuts. I glance over to Mike. "You secure?" I call out. He nods. I hoist myself up onto the beam, trot out to the center and cut the choker loose. A gust of wind blasts me and I sway to compensate, nothing to fall back on but empty air. Girder surfing, we call it back in L.A. The building foundation pit is a tiny patch of blackness fifty-four stories below. Far enough down that if I took a dive, parts of me would splatter into Brooklyn. This doesn't bother me any. If it did, I'd be selling shoes for a living.

Mike and I pace ourselves like dancers, matching our rhythms and moves as we line up the headers and start bolting them down. I can see Mike knows what he's doing. He works the iron good, moving the beams easily where he wants them, and bolting them down quick and skillful. It doesn't take long before we get a good heat up and are snapping those beams into the columns like they're from a kid's erector set.

I find myself sneaking glances at Mike from time to time. He isn't exactly cocky, but he handles himself like a man who knows he's good and just lets his body take over to do what has to be done. It's late in the morning now, and the sun is getting hot. Streams of sweat trickle down his torso, making it fuckin' *gleam;* drops of it bead around his nipples, which are as big as quarters and the color of old pennies. I think about what it'd be like chewing on them, flicking them with my tongue, nipping them with my teeth as Mike's muscular body squirms under me. His torso is nut brown, but when he leans down to spin in a low bolt, I see his tan line and a strip of creamy skin beneath it. His ass must be a very pretty thing, pale and smooth like polished ivory. The fun and games a couple of nights ago haven't taken the edge off my hunger; if anything, I'm stoked for more of the same.

We're on our fifth header by the time the lunch whistle blows. Mike pulls off his hard hat and wipes his forehead with the back of his hand; I watch as his biceps bulge up and dance. He stands there for a few seconds, his left knee bent, his weight on his right hip, that muscle-packed torso so nicely slicked. I feel my throat squeeze tight just looking at him. He's a slab of prime beef, all right, and my brain goes overtime thinking of all the dirty things I'd like to do to him. He suddenly turns and looks at me, and there's this second when my face is still naked, my thoughts written on it for anyone to see. I couldn't have been more obvious if I'd reached out and grabbed his basket. Mike's eyes burn into me, and it's clear he *knows* what's on my mind. But he turns his head and gazes out toward the Jersey shore, like he's searching for something. Slowly, carelessly, he reaches up and scratches his balls, giving them a little extra tug. The signal is so fuckin' blatant that my brain buzzes with confusion. I'm surprised smoke isn't coming out of my ears.

Mike and I eat lunch together sitting on a girder with our legs dangling over eight hundred feet of nothing. Mike is relaxed and friendly, so open and at ease that I begin to wonder if I misread what was going on between us just a few minutes ago. I ask Mike how Pete, the guy whose place I'm taking, happened to fall.

Mike shrugs. "We were working a little late. I guess he was tired and just got sloppy. It happens."

After a while, we run out of conversation. I lay on my back and close my eyes, feeling the sun beat down on me. I think about what Mike looks like naked, and I give him a dick that's meaty and thick, just to keep the fantasy interesting. My dick gives a hard thrust against my jeans, but I don't do anything to hide it.

"Thinking about pussy?" Mike asks. I half open my eyes and see him looking down at me, grinning. "I was just wondering. It looks like your dick's about to split your pants open."

"It's been a problem lately," I say, keeping my voice casual. "I seem to be horny all the time."

Mike's grin widens. "Well, maybe you'll get lucky soon." He winks his eye at me, and again I get that weird feeling he's sending me some kind of message. He stands up and dusts himself off. "Time to get back to work."

For the rest of the afternoon it's like that, Mike joking around, giving me these looks that may mean something, but then again maybe not. He's got me wound tighter than a clock, and I don't like it. For one thing, it's affecting my work now. A couple of times I fumble the bolts, stupidly watching them slip between my fingers and drop down all that space beneath us. I almost lose my spud wrench the same way, just grabbing it in the last half second before it's gone for good. I glance toward Mike, and he's watching me, grinning. "Uh-oh," he says. "You almost killed a businessman that time." His smile is good-natured enough, but his eyes gleam with a bold light that misses nothing. He's just having a good ol' time at my expense. I feel like pushing him off his beam.

At four forty-five, Jackson signals for us to start wrapping it up. Mike cups his mouth with his hands. "Send another beam up!" he shouts. Jackson shakes his head and points to his watch. "We can do it!" Mike shouts back. "Al and I don't mind working a little

late." Jackson shrugs and signals for the crane operator to hoist another beam up.

I glare at Mike. "What the hell's got into you?" I call over to
him. "I want to go home."

Mike just grins. "The way you been fucking up this afternoon,
I figure you owe the company a few minutes' extra work." The
beam swings down overhead, and he guides it into place. Pissed, I
help line up the holes and slide a few bolts in. By the time he cuts
the choker loose, the rest of the crew has taken off, leaving us
alone. I spend a few more minutes bent over my end of the beam,
slipping in the remaining bolts and tightening the nuts. I'm working as fast as I can so that I can just get the hell out of here and
put an end to this day. I turn to see how Mike's doing with his end.
He's still out there on the middle of the beam, only now his pants
are down around his ankles. He's slowly stroking his stiff cock, his
face as calm as if this is the most natural thing he could be doing. I
almost drop my wrench for the second time that day.

"You ought to tie that thing around your wrist," Mike says, "before you kill someone."

I just stare at him. "What the fuck are you doing?"

Mike laughs. "What does it look like?"

I watch him standing there on the beam, beating off. My own
dick starts beating against my zipper, yelling to be let out. "Come
on down to where there's some floor beneath us," I say. My
throat's so tight I can barely get the words out.

Mike shakes his head. "No, I got a better idea. Come up here
and join me."

The beam he's standing on juts out over the side of the building. I look down at the fifty-four stories' worth of empty air beneath us. If we fell, I just might be able to shoot a load before
hitting bottom, but there'd be hell to pay afterward. I shake my
head. "No way, Mike. I only practice safe sex."

But Mike just stands there grinning, stroking his dick. He stops for a minute and peels off his T-shirt. His sweaty torso gleams in the late afternoon sun, cut and chiseled in such a way that every muscle stands out. He tosses the shirt into the wind, and I watch as it floats down into oblivion. The street below is deep in the shadow of early evening, but up here it's still bright day. I spend a couple of seconds watching Mike standing there buck naked except for his hard hat, and I know I'm going to get it on with him or die trying. I jump up on the beam.

"Hold on," Mike calls out. "I want you to get naked first."

*What the hell.* I shrug. I'm ready for anything now. I do a careful strip, draping my clothes over the column head. Seconds later, I'm bare-ass naked. A slight breeze plays over my body and I can feel the last rays of the sun on my skin. The steel's cool and smooth under my bare feet; everything else around me feels like miles of empty air.

Mike's lips curl up into a slow smile. "You look fuckin' great, Al," he says. He kicks off his shoes, and I watch as they disappear into the darkness below. He steps out of his pants, leaving them piled on the girder behind him.

I walk across the girder toward him like a man crossing pond ice on a sunny day. I've been walking for years on narrow beams above open space, and I feel my body automatically make the tiny adjustments that keep me from losing my balance. When I reach Mike, I run my hands over his chest and torso, as much to steady myself as to feel his naked body. He leans forward and kisses me lightly, then not so lightly. We play dueling tongues for a while, and then Mike reaches down and wraps his palm around my dick. He glances at it and then back at me. "Jeez, you got a beautiful dick, Al."

"Yeah, I get a lot of compliments on it."

Mike grins. "I bet. Look how thick it is. And long, too. And how big and red the cockhead is." He laughs. "Not many men have a dick this pretty, Al. I hope you appreciate what you got."

He glances down again. "Your balls have a nice size to them, too, even though they're pulled up a little tight."

I smile stiffly. "Being scared shitless has a way of doing that to me, Mike. Maybe we should just skip the commentary and move on to what's next."

Mike looks amused. He carefully bends down and picks up his jeans. He pulls a condom out of the back pocket. "All right, let's get to it. How 'bout plugging my butt hard?"

I have to laugh. "Well, I'm glad you take every precaution," I say, as I slip the condom on. Mike turns around and bends over, hands on knees.

I have never fucked with such concentration before. My mind is alert to every movement we make, and my body is as tuned as if each nerve ending has a mind of its own. I begin pumping my hips, first with a slow, grinding tempo, then faster and deeper. Everything is reduced down to one word: *balance.* Mike knows this, too, and he meets me stroke for stroke, his body reacting to the thrusts and pulls of mine like we're both well-oiled parts of one moving machine. I hold on to his torso, not roughly, but with a touch light and cautious enough to just barely feel the squirm of his muscles beneath my fingertips. We fuck like we're defusing a bomb, in carefully controlled terror. I have never had sex that felt so goddamn exciting.

I spit in my hand and begin stroking Mike off. Mike groans loudly and squirms against me, a move I wasn't expecting. For a second, we sway to one side and I feel the beam slip from under my feet. Mike and I both quickly shift our weight and regain our balance. "Sweet Jesus," I mutter. But I never miss a stroke.

The lights are beginning to go on in the buildings below us. The city spreads out beneath us to the horizon and I feel like I'm fuckin' flying. Even this far up, I can still faintly hear the sounds of traffic from below. I plunge deep into Mike again. Mike's groan trails off into a long whimper. His balls are pulled up tight, and his dick in my

hand is as stiff as dicks get. I know he's not far from squirting his load.
Each time I pump my hips, Mike's groans get louder and more heart-
felt. I pull my dick out just to the head and then slide in with a long,
deep thrust. Mike cries out, and his body spasms against me. His dick
pulses in my hand, his load gushing between my fingers and dripping
down into the darkness below. I hold on tight as his body shudders in
my arms, keeping the control and balance for both of us. When he
quiets down, I give my hips a few quick thrusts. That's all I need to
get me off. I ride the orgasm out like a surfer on a killer wave, getting
off on the thrill but concentrating on my balance all at the same time.

When the last shudder is over, I carefully pull out. Mike turns
around and we kiss each other lightly, our bodies pressed tightly
together. Mike makes a sudden jerking movement to the side, and
I feel a half second of pure terror before I regain my balance.
Mike laughs.

I glare at him. "You dickhead."

But Mike just keeps on grinning. He picks up his pants. "Come
on, let's get off this damn beam."

Back by the foreman's shack, I give Mike my undershirt to re-
place the one he tossed over the side. But he's going to have to
take the subway home barefooted. He just shrugs this off. As I get
dressed I start thinking about what a fuckin' insane thing it was we
just did. To my annoyance, my hands begin to tremble as I tie my
shoes. I make sure Mike doesn't see this.

I look up at him. "Did you ever do anything this crazy before?"

The muscles in Mike's face twitch, like he's trying to decide
whether or not to say something. Finally he breaks into a slow,
easy smile. "Sure. How do you think the guy you replaced, Pete,
fell?" He sees the expression in my face and laughs. "Hey, I was
*joking*, okay? I've never done this before."

We ride down in the lift in silence. Mike is idly looking out toward the city skyline. I stare at his face, trying to figure out just exactly how Pete did fall off that girder.

Down on the street, Mike kisses me lightly. "See you tomorrow, Al. You're great to work with." I watch as he walks barefoot down the sidewalk to the subway station on the corner, his arms swinging jauntily by his side. I shake my head. Jamming my hands in my jeans pockets, I thread through the crowds of people. When I get to the first street corner, I wait for the light to turn green, looking both ways carefully before crossing.

# Stalin's Mustache

## Will Heinrich

One morning Aloisius Weinberg woke up and discovered a mustache on the end of his penis. It was thick and black but neatly groomed, and it lay just below the very tip, as if the orifice of his urethra were a single nostril. A mustache on a penis being something that Weinberg, despite a full and exciting life, had never so much as imagined, let alone seen, he did not know what to do. For thirty minutes or more he stood mesmerized by it, naked before a full-length mirror. It was undeniably fascinating, he felt drawn to it. But there was also, to his eye, something threatening about the little black rectangle, and he did not want to touch it. Omitting, therefore, his usual Sunday morning bath, he slipped on a pair of pants and went out to buy some bialys.

Standing in line at Kossar's he made the acquaintance of a beautiful young Vassar girl who had just finished her creative writing thesis on Henry Miller and pre-post-feminist pornography. She had curly dark hair and breasts like wineskins. Though they had never met before, and though Weinberg had not spoken a

word nor made any gesture more than a small epileptic bobble
that might have been mistaken for a nod, the girl greeted him ef-
fusively, asked him how he was, and immediately put two hands on
his ass. "Fine, thank you," Weinberg said. Before he knew it they
were on the floor of the Vassar girl's dead grandmother's rent-
controlled apartment, Weinberg with three black socks in his
mouth, making love like animals. They spent all afternoon in an
orgy of groping, fondling, fucking, and whitefish, and she never
once mentioned her schoolwork. It was too good to be true. Finally at seven o'clock, when Weinberg's oily face had begun to
itch, and after the girl's dead grandmother's fourteen cats had
been mewling for their dinner for six hours, the girl took the black
socks out of Weinberg's mouth, wiped the chopped onions off his
underpants, and showed him the door. "That was fantastic," she
said. "Don't call me."

Only when he had returned home and after he had poured
himself a cup of coffee and lit three cigarettes did Weinberg remember the mustache. Had it been a hallucination? Was it still
there? If so, why had the Vassar girl said nothing about it? Had
she seen a penis mustache before? "Well," Weinberg said to himself, "if anyone *has* ever seen a penis mustache, it's bound to be a
Vassar girl." Chuckling over this pithy truth, Weinberg dismissed
his early-morning vision and went into the kitchen to begin washing a large pile of dirty dishes. For several hours he splashed happily while listening to a loop tape of Bob Dylan singing
"Hurricane," but at last, while attacking burnt-on tsimmes with a
spackle knife, he was assailed by doubt. He did not take hallucino-
gens or yoga and had never had visions before. Besides, it had
seemed so real. Meditatively, Weinberg pulled out the waistband
of his aquamarine sweatpants and lifted his unit in his left hand—
he gasped, letting fall from his lips two lit cigarettes and thereby
setting his tsimmes pan on fire. The mustache was still there.

For the first week he simply ignored it. His habits of bathing

and personal hygiene were such as to allow him a considerable degree of ignorance concerning his private areas, and he took full advantage of this. He went about his usual business with as
unconcerned an air as he was able to counterfeit, and he was aided
in this by a series of unlikely sexual conquests. On Monday night a
Cuban waitress with a backside that could knock over a telephone
booth took him to an apartment somewhere in the Bronx, tied him
to a water heater, and made love to him until he passed out; he
woke up in an idling taxicab on Riverside Drive. On Tuesday afternoon he had hardly worked up the nerve to bid the green-eyed
girl in the bakery "good day" before they were in the storeroom,
naked and covered with flour. She was long, slender, and working
her way through Sarah Lawrence. On Wednesday evening he went
to a bar in Midtown and was picked up by a high-powered business supplies saleswoman who took him to a suite at the Royalton
and physically threw him into the bathtub. On Thursday morning,
as he stumbled out of the Royalton, he bumped into a muscular
lady bike messenger who pedaled him to a high school playing
field on Staten Island, where they made love in the dirt like Adam
and Eve. On the Staten Island ferry on Thursday afternoon, a
short Hunter College anthropology student with a broad face and
a long black braid down her back led him by the hand into a bathroom stall, where they violated each other and a soft pretzel with
mustard. While walking home he picked up a ringing pay phone,
which, it turned out, had been called by accident by a hip young
photographer from Oneonta who lived in a studio in Long Island
City. Before he knew it, it was Friday afternoon and he was loping
bowlegged down Jackson Avenue, squinting into the sun and trying to find the subway. Because he was very tired and had not
been home in two days, he resolved not to leave his apartment at
least until Saturday morning; that evening, he was made love to by
a sexy Shanghainese delivery girl. Uncertain what to tip in this situation, he handed her ten dollars, and she gave him in return a

free order of crunchy fried wontons that she evidently kept about her person for just such an occasion.

So far, so good. Weinberg was not a reflective sort; and while most men—even those, like Weinberg, whose college degrees read "Film and Video"—would have hazarded a guess by now at some connection between the mysterious black penis mustache and the subsequent wave of sexual serendipity, Weinberg simply chalked it all up to a long-overdue karmic payback for the sincerity of his devilish good looks. In fact, by the time he fell asleep Friday night, he had convinced himself that it was not the past few days that were anomalous, but the entirety of his previous experience. The world was finally working the way it was supposed to. By the time he woke up Saturday morning, after dreaming about a soccer stadium full of naked women weeping and pleading for their lives, Aloisius Weinberg was thoroughly convinced that not a single one of the previous week's sexual adventures had *befallen* him—he had, rather, in some subtle and unknown but indubitable way engineered them all himself; they were all, therefore, not luck, but just deserts, and he could make them continue. He resolved that not another day would pass in his life without a minimum of three random sexual conquests. And so, after taking a shower—in the course of which he shampooed and conditioned his new nether mustache, and only masturbated a little—and dressing himself in pink flip-flops and a terry-cloth bathrobe, Weinberg exited his tiny Grand Street apartment and rang for the elevator. The doors opened to reveal the Lifshitz girls, twin sister dental hygienists who had never before seemed likely to give him the time of day. This morning they were all smiles. "Isn't your name Aloisius?" said one girl. "Aloisius rhymes with delicious!" said the other. Then both girls giggled, and Aloisius remarked to himself that three a day might be setting the bar too low. Five minutes later the twin Lifshitz girls stumbled out into the lobby, dazedly straightening their short-shorts and tube tops, and Aloisius Weinberg strode regally behind them, ostentatiously retying his bathrobe and smoothing down his eyebrows.

The following weeks continued apace, and each day found Weinberg's johnson better traveled, but as time passed Weinberg began to notice three disturbing trends. The first was either the deterioration of his sexual morality, or the gradual abandonment of the pretense that he had any in the first place. For example, on Saturday morning, after bopping the two Lifshitz girls and then detouring to the basement for a brief but satisfying round of old-fashioned Cape Cod-style three-hole pennywhistle with a zaftig Hasidic hausfrau, Weinberg found himself and his white bathrobe moseying across town toward Stuyvesant High School. He spent a pleasant stroll considering whether he wanted a kasha knish for lunch or a sweet potato, and then, before he knew it, he was sticking it in the knish of a seventeen-year-old Chinese-American club girl in the bushes of Robert F. Wagner Park. He talked spontaneously about electronic music he had never heard of and drugs he had never taken, and the whole thing took less than twenty-five minutes. And it only got worse: on Saturday he asked this Stuyvesant girl if she was eighteen, and let her lie; on Tuesday he *told* the three Dalton girls that they were eighteen and dared them to disagree; and by Friday at the roller rink he just let it pass. Nor was age-of-consent the only shattered taboo: he began sleeping with mothers while their babies cried, wives with their husbands on speakerphone, and schoolteachers on lunch breaks in playgrounds. One afternoon he walked into a Jungian clinic and seduced six female psychotherapists, then left without paying the bill. By the second weekend it took all his little willpower and a great deal of alcohol to keep himself in check at his niece's bat mitzvah. A corollary to this disturbing trend was that he did not even find it disturbing except after the fact and in principle; he was more concerned by his own lack of concern than anything else. It seemed out of character. The second disturbing trend

Weinberg noticed was also amply evidenced at the bat mitzvah: his gluttony was extending itself to realms beyond the sexual. That he drank a great deal was nothing new—nor, for Weinberg, was it un- usual to wake up in the middle of the night to have a cigarette— but culinarily, at least, he had always favored quality over quantity. But now he found himself consuming sixty-five broccoli quiches, half a dozen whole whitefish and three buffet dinners, then curs- ing out the manager of the Massapequa Marriott for stocking only six kinds of ice cream. When the manager offered him tofutti, Weinberg threatened him with a bottle of Galliano and had to be wrestled down by his Uncle Itchy, who subsequently broke his dental plate and began to cry.

Even so, none of this would have really bothered him if not for the third disturbing trend. Unbeknownst to Weinberg, who re- fused to read authors unless they had demonstrably hairier chests than he did—which meant, in effect, that he could not be counted on to discuss any authors at all except Norman Mailer and one or two Sicilian pornographers—this trend had been predicted in the work of the eminent economist Thomas R. Malthus. (Malthus claimed that population grew geometrically while the means of subsistence improved only arithmetically, and that therefore the odds of finding something decent to eat decline towards zero the further you drive into Connecticut.) Every day brought Weinberg more conquests than the last, but the growth of his tally sheet was dwarfed by the increase of his ambition. His eyes became keener and more predatory, his lust more brutal and wide-ranging, until finally the mere sight of any woman, regardless of her attractive- ness, availability or physical proximity, became intolerable to him if he could not penetrate her immediately. He could not watch movies or television, he could not stroll down Fifth Avenue, he could not attend high school field-hockey games. Finally, he could hardly leave his apartment at all, because it was simply physically impossible to have sex with every woman he saw, even taking into account his rubbery skin and phenomenal *ejaculatio praecox.* For a few days he made do by hampering his vision with dark glasses and a floppy hat, but quickly the problem reasserted itself mentally: it got so that Weinberg could make love to thirty-five women a day and barely notice it—let alone feel grateful, or remark on the sheer physical prodigy of his feat—because he was so tormented by the thought of the hundreds of millions of other women that he was not having sex with at the same time. At first he was downcast at the impossibility of bedding the whole world, but despair quickly tamed to bitter, jealous, fanatical anger: the Queen of Norway had betrayed him! Edith Wharton was cheating on him! Isabella Rossellini was denying him his conjugal rights! Duplicitous cunts, all of them! Counterrevolutionary sows! Petit-bourgeois sluts! At the same time, his imperial sexual ambition overflowed all the boundaries of his culture and upbringing. For the first time, he felt sexual desire for men—and not only for men, but also for giraffes, dolphins, musk melons and male and female ginko trees; and not only for living creatures, but for all conceivable conquests, real and imaginary, living and dead. One night, trembling and unable to sleep, he tried to soothe himself with a cup of weak tea and a favorite old children's book, only to find himself shortly paralyzed with rage, brandishing a fish knife and screaming at Cinderella and Prince Charming for two-timing him with each other.

Clearly the time had come to do something. In a rare moment of clarity, while exhausted and lying on the cold bathroom floor, Weinberg finally realized that it was the mustache. The whole thing—starting from the very beginning with the Vassar girl in her dead grandmother's rent-controlled apartment, and all the way up to and including the handicapped bi-curious Con Ed man's helper monkey who had just left—it was all the mustache. In a cold sweat Weinberg dragged himself to his feet and opened the medicine cabinet. He undid the drawstring of his Ecuadorian basket pants and took down a straight razor. His penis, once exposed to the air, leapt immediately to erection; he steadied it with his left hand. Slowly he lowered the razor. He thought he saw a dark shadow pass across his penile crown. No, he told himself, he was hallucinating, get it over with. A drop of sweat fell from his nose and deafeningly hit the floor. . . . In the end, Weinberg's hand trembled so badly that instead of slicing off the mustache, he slashed his left wrist and fainted, hitting his head on the bathtub. He woke up briefly in the ambulance, his penis and its mustache in the mouth of a buxom nurse-practitioner, and then passed out again.

At this point Weinberg gave up. He relinquished all personal agency and let his schmeckel do what it liked. To begin with, it bedded everyone in the psychiatric ward and single-handedly started a small tuberculosis epidemic. Next was Sutton Place: in one wild and crazy week, Aloisius Weinberg's penis leapt and slashed its way across one hundred and fifty-two permanent missions to the United Nations while Aloisius Weinberg's mind miserably fantasized about holding hands and watching *Jeopardy!* with some nice uptight Jewish girl from Tenafly, New Jersey. The following week was Fashion Week: somehow gaining entry to all the best shows and parties, even though Weinberg himself was by now dirty, malnourished and dressed in rags, Aloisius Weinberg's penis gave herpes, genital warts, chlamydia, and fleas to seventy-eight assorted supermodels and socialites, including three of Mick Jagger's girlfriends and two of his daughters. He also fucked nine cheese blintzes and a panda bear. On Sunday night his penis allowed Weinberg an hour's rest, in a corner of the Plaza Hotel drinking verbena tea and sobbing quietly. His penis was biding its time. Sure enough, the following week, after a visit to the offices of the *New York Observer* that Weinberg found particularly shameful, his penis was the toast of the town: it was scheduled for three magazine covers and a buddy movie with Warren Beatty, and had hired six secretaries to handle all the phone calls from

Hollywood, Milan, and the White House. Weinberg was wretched.
Broken of rebellion and without appetite, he smoked more than
ever and tried to stay out of the way.

It has recently been claimed that as many as a third of the men
of central Asia can trace their paternal ancestry directly to
Genghis Khan. That may be so, but Khan had nothing on Weinberg. Over the course of the next two years he, or rather his "San
Francisco frankfurter," traveled to every corner of the globe and
impregnated not less than six hundred thousand of the likeliest
and most fertile girls that could be boasted by the human race. At
the same time pictures of his penis, which a Russian expatriate society reporter had ironically nicknamed "Stalin," were plastered
over every available surface. Discussion of this new Stalin dominated the public media and even worked its way into the bedrock
of the most basic human discourse, so that every Friday night in
bars across the world men could be heard to say to women, "It
may not be Stalin, but it does all right." It all seemed like it would
go on forever—Weinberg's cock striding across nations, Weinberg
slouching and smoking Merit Ultra Lights—until one day, all of a
sudden, while reviewing a parade of Bulgarian hookers, Stalin
caught his mustache in a zipper and ripped it clean off.

For a moment, no one moved. Then the hookers began to
dance and sing folk songs. Soon the news had traveled the world;
parties broke out, statues were toppled, and lapel buttons cast
away. Weinberg, ignored and unwanted, meekly crawled home to
take a bath. He congratulated himself on having had the foresight
to stock up on Mr. Bubble. As he sat in the bath drinking chocolate milk and listening to *A Prairie Home Companion,* Weinberg
jiggled and jiggled and jiggled his piece—not from neurosis or for
masturbatory pleasure, but simply because he was so tickled at its
newfound flaccidity. "Hot dog!" Weinberg said. "I'll never jerk off
again!" The next morning he woke up early, discerning birdsong
behind the car alarms and smelling fresh cantaloupe underneath

the car exhaust. He slipped on a pair of fuchsia yoga pants and went out to buy himself a celebratory bialy, or maybe an onion roll. Standing in line at Kossar's, Weinberg noticed in front of him none other than the very same dark-haired Vassar girl he had met there two years before, the first of Stalin's conquests. He could not help but notice that this girl still had an awfully nice tush. She stepped forward to the counter and he watched it ripple. "But no," Weinberg said to himself, "enough is enough," and he took his onion roll home and jerked off.

# Bad Education

## Stephen Elliott

I was new in San Francisco and screwed up inside. I was living in a white Ford Fiesta with a blue stripe along the doors, parked on top of a hill above the Castro District, wheels lodged against the curb. I had a blanket (a present from my ex-fiancée), a bicycle, a bag of clothes, and a few boxes of paper that I thought represented something important stuffed below the window. And in retrospect they did, but not what I thought.

I'd only been in San Francisco a couple of days. I had run out of gas on the Oakland Bay Bridge on the way into town, and the emergency worker that showed up in a big padded truck asked if I had a death wish. I could barely hear him with the wind so loud and the cars racing over the bay. I had to yell to explain that the gas gauge was broken, that I usually got three hundred miles to the tank, but this tank had only gotten two hundred and fifty for some reason. He pushed me onto Treasure Island and injected my car with an electric pump, which forced a quart of gas straight through the hoses and into the engine. I'd been driving aimlessly

in the desert for weeks and hadn't had a conversation with someone in what seemed like a long time.

The San Francisco sky was beautiful and full of fog as the
ocean air drifted across the city. It was nearly summer. Tufts of
cloud hung on the edges of the peaks like cotton caught on a
drainpipe. The fog made the colors pop, and the rows of pink and
green pastel houses lining the hills had the quality of a painting,
like something too perfect to have happened by accident. Nothing
felt real, and I wondered if I would stay once I found a job and
made some money. I was running out of places to go.

I went to a poetry reading and met a poet there. Diana had
braided black hair, dyed in streaks of orange and pink. She was
taller than me by four inches and had a broad, strong back. Her
poems were the angry screeds of a victim returning home with a
box of matches and a can of lighter fluid. Her anger was ravenous,
and her words mixed with a sadness and self-loathing that ran
straight to the bone. In her combat boots, motorcycle jacket and
tar-stained jeans, she was beautiful.

It was late on a Sunday, and there weren't many people in the
sharply lit windows of the buses and trolleys clattering down Market Street. After the reading we found our way to a punk rock bar
with several rows of hardwood tabletops and a solid jukebox full of
Pixies and Ramones. There were five or six people bellying up at
the rail, which is where we sat. The bar was not well lit, but there
was enough light to see by.

Diana told me she was living with her girlfriend and would be
for a long time. She presented this to me defiantly, like it would
change my mind about something. But I didn't care. It had been
six months since I'd left my fiancée. Diana said she had been an
editor for a big magazine but now was unemployed and taking
pills. I told her I had won a poetry slam back in Chicago. We were
both dissatisfied with our current predicaments, not because they
were bad, but because they were insulting. We were better than

the world was willing to admit. I asked her if she wanted to add a shot to her beer, and she said she did.

After a few drinks, I slid my hand between her legs. Not inside her jeans, outside, rubbing the denim seam with the bridge of my hand, forcing her zipper against her pelvis. "Oh, we're doing that," she said, and unzipped my pants and pulled my penis out and started stroking me below the bar. The bartender looked over at us once, then glanced away. Diana gripped me tightly and pulled, letting her thumbnail scratch the tip of my penis. I thought she was going to tear my skin. I was so lonely that I laid my head on her cold leather shoulder.

I thought, *Yes, this is San Francisco.* Before San Francisco I'd spent twelve hours on a Moab park bench, unable to move. Moab is in southern Utah, home of the slickrock bike trail and lots of Nike commercials. Before that I spent four months as a ski bum in the Rocky Mountains. Those giant outdoor athletic parks are places where the men outnumber the women seven to one. I was fresh out of a two-and-a-half-year relationship which had broken everything inside of me, and I was still running from that.

I kept a hand on my drink. Diana yanked my belt buckle and unbuttoned my pants, forced her large hand down farther around my balls and gave a quick, solid squeeze. I let out a cry and pressed my face into her hair, but nobody seemed to care. I zipped back up and left my empty glass as I followed her drunkenly, belt still undone, into the ladies' room.

What I loved most was her size. She was proportioned like an Amazon, thin but with enormous breasts, wide hips, and Marine shoulders. She was so much bigger than me it seemed she could fit me in her pocket.

Diana forced me up against the back of the stall, her forearm on my neck, her hand inside my shirt. She kissed me hard. "What do you want?" she asked, pulling away and yanking my shirt over my head.

"Hit me," I said. Or I might have said, "Hurt me" or something else. But whatever I said was lost in the fabric; she didn't hear me right. She thought I said "Choke me" and gripped my throat, squeezing my windpipe shut. My breath was gone and I saw stars as she pulled on me frantically. "Come on," she said. "C'mon. C'mon." I felt my legs go as the screws and beams rattled in their bearings and then I came all over the stall.

I was lying on the cool pink bathroom floor and she was sitting on the toilet, her pants bunched over her boots. I ran my fingers gently across her laces while she peed. The bathroom door opened and closed several times but nobody said anything. That's the kind of city San Francisco is.

"I want to see you again," I said. It was easy for me. I didn't know anyone, and I had nothing to lose.

Diana snatched sheets of toilet paper and rubbed them quickly between her legs. She looked down on me with something resembling guilt, but not quite, rather the realization of two ideas that don't exactly contradict but affect and enhance each other. She didn't like me anymore. I was desperate and lost, and she had problems of her own.

"Usually, I'm a lesbian," she said, looking away, flushing the toilet.

At that point, I didn't know that I would stay in San Francisco for seven years and see Diana many more times. We'd become friends but not lovers, and one winter day, on our way to catch some acquaintances at a party, she would ask me to wait with her outside the building, then force her entire fist into my mouth. At the time, on the bathroom floor, I was pretty sure I wouldn't meet her again; I didn't know where I'd be. I leaned toward the tip of her boot, sniffing the old leather of her shoe.

# The Clay Man

## Sera Gamble

The clay man is sitting against my front door, which is why I can't get it open. He is crying. I hear his wet, dirty sobs, and a growing wash of mud is sliding under the door toward my feet. I bang on the door. He bangs back, heavy clay thuds that sound sticky.

I made him from the recipe in the old story. I sat in the bookstore coffeehouse on my day off last week reading books other people had left lying on the floor. In one was "The Golem." I went to the art store and I bought two hundred pounds of pottery clay.

I spread sheets of *LA Weekly* on the wood floor of my living room and stabbed through the cardboard box of the first package with a pair of scissors. The phone rang.

"What the hell are you doing?" my sister hissed.

"Nothing."

"Liar."

Then I remembered that I had dropped out of school this

week and the news would have reached her in New York by now.

"I'm not into it," I said, unwrapping the wax paper from around the first musty block of clay.

"What about . . . everything? What are you thinking?"

"I have a job. I don't want a degree. Degrees are bullshit."

"You are such a child." She smushed her words around the cigarette I knew she'd jammed into her mouth. I heard the click of her vintage Zippo, then the exasperated jerk of her breathing.

"You know, I told Mom and Dad you quit smoking."

"This is not about quitting smoking. This is about quitting any chance you have of rising above the sad, tired, *dwindling* middle class. You have no excuse. You should have come here."

Victoria is an assistant professor in the law department at NYU, teaching a course in criminal psychology for lawyers. Victoria: *never* Vicki.

"Vicki, me no wanna be lawyer."

She hung up on me. I thrust the scissors into the second package, which oozed red wet clay through the gash in the paper.

When I was twelve years old, I decided I would become a witch. Not the Halloween kind, but the real deal, a member of the Wicca religion, making wands of twig and burning sage and worshipping the earth. I wasn't going to kill anything, or hex anybody; I was going to be a white witch, and harness the powers of good for such noble tasks as landing a cute boyfriend.

We're Jewish. I suppose I was rebelling against the bat mitzvah, the conservative synagogue dresses, the endless reminders that ours was a legacy of persecution, that I would always be a Jew and must embrace this or else all of my ancestors who died horribly would have suffered in vain for me. I had no idea then that Jews were some of the oldest witches.

The Golem is yet another tale of Jewish persecution. The rabbi created a Frankenstein monster man out of clay because his village had endured one too many pogroms. Two things stuck out to

me about the story: the fact that this Jewish holy man was basically
a witch, and that the bit about creating the Golem read like a
recipe.

I own about forty cookbooks. I don't cook much; but when I
do, the study shows. I can bake a seven-layer tiramisu that's not
too wet. I know exactly how many seconds to sauté garlic so that
the flavor explodes into marinara sauce. But I rarely have anyone
to cook for, and I hate cleaning up.

So I am sitting on my living room floor, my bare legs smeared
with newspaper ink, roughly fondling my new two hundred
pounds of clay. The phone rings again, my sister calling back. I ignore it for about ten minutes as I roll an oval thigh of clay.

Finally, I answer the phone. "Fucking *what*!" I yell.

"Leslie," my sister begins, her voice calm and syrupy, dripping
cigarette smoke, "I want to read you this article about our department. Okay? It's written by a former high school dropout who
went back to school in his late twenties. He discusses quite passionately how NYU is the best thing that happened to him since
methadone."

Because she is going to keep calling me unless I placate her,
and because if I take the phone off the hook she is going to actually get on a plane and fly here, and because if I don't let her in
she's going to get my father involved, I let her read me the entire
article. It's long.

As she reads, I start on the other thigh. I put them together
and examine the cleft, contemplating the space where the clay
cock will attach. Of course, there was no information about the
anatomical correctness of the Golem in the legend.

I wet down a thick cylinder of clay and mold, punctuating my
sister's dissertation with periodic *mmm-hmms* in the pauses. I've
mounted the cock on bulging clay testicles before she finishes. I
hear the Zippo snap as she lights a fresh cigarette.

"What do you think?" she demands.

"That really gives me something to think about."

"Don't you dare condescend to me. I'm trying to help you."

I realize for the first time that, at least in her own mind, she is. "I know. You just have to give me some time to . . . reevaluate my life."

"Did you hook up with some boy? Is that it?"

"No," I tell her, smacking the balls into place.

"Are you lying to me? Answer me, Leslie. I know what's-his-name, in Entertainment, didn't work out, we only saw that coming five hundred miles away. So let me just say: you better not be throwing away your future in the law for some loser with a big dick."

He takes me a week to finish. I work in the evenings, surrounded by candles and takeout Chinese. First I create the basic form: lying on his back, about six feet tall, broad shoulders, lean frame. Then I begin the real work, adding detail, carving muscles, scratching in curls of hair with my fingernails. For this I steal reference books from the bookstore where I work as associate manager: *Gray's Anatomy*, da Vinci's sketches. Renaissance sculpture, which I look at till my eyes burn, trying to copy the face of one of the smooth church angels. By the weekend he looks positively pornographic.

Finally, on Saturday morning, I carve the magic word into his forehead.

It means Truth. And then I sit, leaning against his chest. And I wait.

The first thing I notice is that the clay grows warmer. At first I think I am imagining it, but soon it's unmistakable. Something is happening.

Then vibration: first at the toes and fingers, moving inward. It's working. I don't know why, but I'm not surprised. I sit and watch as the figure begins to flex, to move. Shortly after sunset, he sits up and opens his eyes.

"I'm Leslie," I tell him. "I made you."

I play my own version of He Loves Me He Loves Me Not. It's how I make many of my major decisions: computer solitaire. If I win in under three games, then the answer to my question is yes.

Because I have no idea what to do with the clay man I just created, I settle in for a few rounds of computer solitaire. If I win in under three hands, I have to talk to him.

I lose three times, but as usual feel compelled to keep playing. He finds his feet and tracks mud footprints all over my apartment as he explores, looking out every window, touching everything.

"Keep your hands to yourself," I tell him. "You're making everything dirty."

His head jerks to me, hungry for my voice. He clears his throat, which sounds like wet towels filled with gravel.

"Leslie," he says.

I lose my hand of solitaire, click on "deal again."

He kneels in front of me. Part of me wants to slap him. I'm used to slapping him, in a way, pounding all that clay over the past week to pop the air bubbles. "Leslie," he says again, sounding bewildered, his baritone strangely clear from deep in his clay chest.

"There's guy's clothes in the closet," I tell him, "if you're cold."

He walks in the direction of my bedroom.

Three things you should know:

1. My boyfriend of three years, Tom, got me pregnant.
2. I got an abortion.
3. He didn't take me.

I suppose it is my own fault. After all, I was sleeping with his cousin, Robert the public defender; who is so passionate about the law that I wanted to absorb some of it, and sex seemed the obvious way. Though I'm sure Tom doesn't know about Robert the public defender, on some level it serves me right. Besides, I knew better than to tell him I was pregnant on his voicemail. It was too easy for him not to call me back. What message?

All of this was last month, when I was still a student and future lawyer. This is how it happened: We were short three people at the monster chain bookstore, so I actually shelved a few books in the name of teamwork. *The Collected Works of Gertrude Stein*, hardcover edition, fell from the oversized-book top shelf onto my left foot. The big toenail turned deep, inky blue. The next day the whole thing was so swollen and meaty I had to limp to the phone to call my insurance company to find a doctor in my area.

The doctor prescribed me Keflex, a particularly turbo-charged antibiotic. Which gave me hives, a stomachache, diarrhea, and the worst yeast infection of my life. Which brought me to the gynecologist, who offered to throw in a complete pelvic exam since I hadn't had one since my freshman year.

Which is how we discovered that I was two and a half months pregnant. With twins.

Getting an abortion would have felt much more automatic if he hadn't told me it was twins. Something about the two of them floating in there together, holding hands. An old discount store jingle kept popping into my head: *Two for the price of one, two for the price of one.* But anyway, fuck it. I was planning by then to drop out and that's just what they would have needed, a career bookstore-scheduler for a mother, and a distant, ambitious entertainment lawyer for a father. Or his poor, excitable public defender cousin.

I call the clay man back into the living room. When I touch him, he embraces me immediately, as if he's been waiting and waiting for me. He begins to quake, unable to gulp enough air into his lungs.

"Relax," I tell him. "Let go of me."

He backs away reluctantly. I see that he is still naked, that the cock I'd worked on for most of Sunday and half of Monday night is erect and pulsing. "You couldn't find the clothes?"

"I didn't want to touch anything. You told me not to." His voice like the growl of a big cat, like a souped-up engine.

"Never mind," I say.

The phone starts ringing again when I kiss him: his mouth a few degrees warmer than mine, not smearing as much as I'd expected. I wonder if he is still forming, if he's solidifying, becoming less like clay and more like flesh. He tastes of fresh river water and trapped air and my own fingers. He doesn't touch me until I put his hands on me and move them, starting them on the course I want them to travel. A quick study, he has to unlock his mouth from mine to breathe, his eyes clouded with concentration, dizzy with new knowledge.

I do believe in God now. I think I proved His existence in making this man. I could be wrong. This man touching me could just as easily be proof of something else. But he feels much closer to proof than I ever expected to see, like following a rainbow for a couple of blocks and discovering a big pot of gold guarded by a little green man drinking ale by the side of the freeway.

He moans.

The phone seems to be ringing louder, if that's possible. I break away from the clay man and answer it. At first all I hear on the other end is crying. "Who is this?" I wait what feels like a reasonable amount of time for the crier to calm down. Then I ask again, less patiently.

"Robert," he chokes out.

"Why are you crying?" Robert the public defender: passionate; overwhelmed at the sight of a beggar in front of the grocery store; in bed, the endless giver, apt to wrestle me down rather than remain in the recipient position for more than a moment

("No, this is for you, this is for *you*"). Robert who begged me to
break it off with his cousin so we could marry and be poor, passionate public defenders together. Who cried when I said no way,
who told me he could only hope, then, that he would never, ever
see me again.

He takes a few deep breaths and then launches into his explanation with the focus of a seasoned lawyer, emotion tightening his
voice. "I'm house-sitting over here for Thomas, as you may or may
not know. I was perusing his datebook for the return flight information, and here under the fifteenth it says 'Leslie's abortion.' I
can only assume that this means you had an abortion on the fifteenth, Leslie, and I want to know (a) if this is true and (b) if it is,
what possible reason you could have had for not calling me, having
every reason to infer that it was our baby you had chosen to abort
on the fifteenth."

He sniffles, waiting for my response. My first impulse is to correct him: bab*ies*, not baby. Instead, I say, "I'm kind of busy right
now, could you call me back in about an hour?"

"*No,* I can't call you back in an hour. Did you have an abortion
or didn't you? This is something you should be able to answer in
one word, busy or not busy."

"Yes," I answer, and hang up. Predictably, he calls right back. I
stare at the phone, marveling at how it brings me only unwanted
conversation.

"You pick it up," I tell the clay man. He does so without hesitation.

"Hello," he says, then listens for a long moment. "I'm not certain," he says. A moment later he holds the phone out to me.
"He'd like to speak to you."

"What," I demand.

" 'I'm not *certain*'? Who is it that you have over there who,
when asked his name, replies 'I'm not certain'? Will you kindly tell
me what's going on?"

Poor Robert. Poor, upright, honest Robert, fallen into my life like tripping over chicken wire into a sinkhole.

"It doesn't matter whose fucking kid it was."

"How can you *say* that?" I hear him banging his fist on something. "Should I call Tom? I should call him. We have to have this out. Help me here. I don't understand this."

"If I hang up now, are you going to call me back?"

He's silent for a moment. "No," he says finally, his voice hollow.

I remember lying next to him after we fucked, my forehead pressed against his back, trying to absorb some of his energy. Thinking: this is a person who cares about things. Aware that this made his life—shitty car, moldy office, Top Ramen, and all—simpler and more fulfilling than mine has ever been. Robert the public defender was the lucky one.

I met Robert the night Tom bailed him out of jail. Robert had been found in contempt of court that day for throwing his briefcase at a judge in the heat of argument. On the way to the jailhouse Tom described Robert to me as "hopeless. An idealist."

"I wish I was an idealist," I remember saying. "I wanna be hopeless."

"Oh, you are," Tom had said, and we'd laughed, and kissed at the red light. We pulled into the jailhouse parking lot with his hand in my panties, but I already knew that if Robert the public defender was even passably attractive, I was going to construct the proper excuse, have him over to my place, fuck him and fuck him till my head filled up with purpose.

The clay man is kneeling before me again, his hands hovering above my thighs, waiting for me to tell him it's okay to touch me. I made a man, and he does exactly as I say. I start to laugh. I laugh until whatever spiked thing is lodged between my lungs snaps open and then I do it, I slap him as hard as I can. I slap him so hard I leave a perfect imprint of my hand across his face. He flinches. I close my fist and hit him. He grunts in pain but doesn't back away. If he had a will, he might; but I made him, and he has to sit there and take it. I stand up, letting the phone drop to the floor. Then I kick him.

We go on like that for three days. I take my anger out on him until I've drained it. He follows me around. I eat whatever's in the fridge, sleep in my clothes with his arms around me. Dropping the phone broke it, so no one calls to berate me for my poor choices. I smooth the dents I've made in the clay man's body and kiss them, then let him touch me, study me, figure my body out.

His top layer moves over the structure underneath, pinkened like skin. When I touch him his cheeks grow darker. He doesn't leave fingerprints and smears anymore, just a fine clay dust that floats away on its own. When I put my ear to him I hear things: breathing, a heartbeat like a whisper. I didn't mold internal organs, I made him out of solid clay, but I understand that he is changing.

He sits on the toilet watching me in the shower, riveted to the sponge in my hand as it coats my body with soap. He holds a towel open for me. He dries me, and carries me to the bed. He says "Please," and I tell him "Okay," and he parts my legs with his warm brown hands and examines me softly.

My sweat and my spit make us muddy. We come together on the bed like swimming. I'm filled with the smell of earth, the taste of it; I'm coated inside and out. It even fills my ears, till his groans and cries become distant and all I can hear is the pounding.

It isn't until later, when he's sleeping and I notice the teeth marks I've left in his shoulder, that I realize: when I bit him he tasted metal, like blood. The thought that races in is: he's getting away from me. I don't know where this will end, what will happen, what I could be responsible for. In the story the Golem kills people.

Even if it doesn't come to that, it's wrong. The fact that it happened, that he came to life and continues to grow more and more alive, proves that it's wrong. I've fucked with something I shouldn't have. I shower the dried clay off, trying to convince myself to do it.

But I don't want to. I want to stay here in my apartment with this man who is devoted and cares what I want and in three days has learned me better than anyone in my life.

Finally, as I slip off to sleep, I decide: tomorrow night. I can do whatever I want to him all day long. But tomorrow night, that's it. Unsure of whether or not I really mean to do it, I slip off to sleep, the clay man's chest against my back.

The clay man is on the other side of the door. He is crying, which reminds me of Robert on the phone three days ago. The mud is creeping toward my feet. I only went to get the mail.

I don't know how he figured it out. Maybe he can read my mind. That would make sense, since he seems to know exactly what I want almost immediately. Maybe it is only that I left him alone.

"Let me in," I tell him, kicking the door. He kicks back.

"I can't let you in," he moans. "I can't let you in, Leslie."

It only took him three days. Now I'm locked out, standing barefoot in the hall in my dirty pajamas. Somehow it feels familiar, it feels typical; it feels inevitable. I kick the door again, cracking a toe—or not a toe, though it does hurt—cracking the door. If he weren't sitting against the door, I could get it open. It's a cheap door.

"Leslie," he sobs.

"Shut up," I tell him. The noise stops. "Oh, are you doing what I say now?"

"I can't."

"You have to. You have to."

I suppose I can sit here all night. My apartment is on the far side of the laundry room; no one is going to walk by. I settle into the doorway and begin to sort through my mail.

The door opens a sliver. "If I let you in," he whispers, "you'll kill me."

"How do you know?"

"I read the story."

"Listen," I tell him, as soothingly as I can, "I'm not going to hurt you."

"Why did you make me then?"

Because . . . because fuck him, nobody ever sat *me* down and explained, I'm in charge, and I'm not up for the big existential questions; so instead I back quietly away from the door and then rush at it. He's caught off guard, and in the moment that he loses his balance, I get the door open enough to squeeze back in.

He's a mess, his face half melted by the tears. Though I was furious a moment ago, now I'm surprised to find myself sad for him. His face: it's actually quite beautiful. I did an amazing job, especially considering I'm no sculptor. Making him brought out a perfectionist I didn't know was in me. I realize again that I don't want to kill him. I go to the computer and pull up the solitaire window.

He kneels in front of me, crying silently, awaiting execution. And I do it. I cup his slick face in my hands, then swiftly rub out the first letter of the magic word. The word *truth* becomes the word *death*. He doesn't collapse, nothing dramatic; he just stops.

The cleanup is going to take days. I can't face it. I can't face anything. Or I won't—same thing. "I miss you," I tell him. Then I gently mold his face out of existence, and pry it off his body. I carry it under my arm to the kitchen where I hunt for trash bags.

# The Sound

## Maxine Chernoff

—I hate it when we have sex and you make that sound.

—What sound?

—The sound you make when you're about to have orgasm.

—What sound do you mean?

—I can't describe it. It sounds like no other sound you ever make.

—But why do you hate it?

—It scares me.

—Why would it scare you?

—I guess it's because we're at an intimate moment, and you make an unfamiliar sound.

—It must be my intimate-moment sound.

—But it doesn't sound intimate. It sounds . . . well . . . brutal.

—I make a brutal sound?

—Yes, I think that's how I'd describe it.

—Make the sound for me.

—I can't.

—Of course you can. You remember it, don't you?

—I'm embarrassed to make it.

—You're not embarrassed to tell me, but you're embarrassed to make it?

—Right.

—Just try.

—All right. It's something like "Yowwwww-oh-woe-woe."

—And that sounds brutal to you?

—It does.

—It sounds to me like I'm very happy.

—It doesn't sound happy to me.

—What sound would you like me to make?

—I don't have an alternative in mind. I just thought I'd tell you that the sound you make, well, it brings me out of the moment. Sex ends for me when I hear that sound.

—That's good, isn't it?

—Why is it good?

—Because you know I've had an orgasm when you hear it.

—But what if I want to do something more to you?

—More? We've both finished by then. What more would we do?

—What if I still want to kiss you and you're making that sound?

—Well, I guess you could try and see.

—Should I try now?

—Why do you think I want you to kiss me when you can't stand the sound I make at my most vulnerable moment?

—I didn't mean I couldn't stand it. I just meant it's distracting.

—Maybe you should gag me.

—Then you'd make the sound but it would be even worse.

—Why would it be worse?

—It would sound all muffled and sad, like the voice of someone locked inside of a car trunk.

—So you'd rather I sound brutal than all muffled and sad?

—I guess so.

—You must really love me then.

# Paradise City

## Bianca James

I left Karla when her bad taste in music and worse fashion sense reached a breaking point in my life. I was embarrassed to be seen in public with a mullet dyke in an Iron Maiden T-shirt; I refused to be finger-fucked to Mötley Crüe's "Shout at the Devil." I still miss her though. It's been six months since we broke up and I still think about her all the time. Sometimes I wonder if I made a mistake by breaking up with her, though really it was Karla who dumped me in the end. Perhaps I should have overlooked Karla's lack of college education and her unique predilection for having me wear Payless hooker pumps when we fucked. I should have overlooked these things because Karla was not only the best fuck of my life, she was also the best cook I've ever dated. And what's more important in life than food and sex?

My short-lived tryst with Janet had been starved of both things. At the point I met Karla, it had been three months since I'd stopped calling Janet, four since we'd had sex, thanks to premature lesbian bed death. Janet had seemed like a good catch when I first spied her at the Thursday Night Lesbian Support Group. She was a twenty-two-year-old with a shaved head, lean and tan with tufts of brown hair peeping out of the edges of her braless tie-dyed tank tops. I fantasized about being the older femme who would teach Janet the finer points of dyke sex, the sort of lover that she would have fond memories of as years went by. But I was wrong. Very wrong.

Janet insisted on dental dams and finger cots for every tryst, the plastic trappings of lesbian safer sex that seemed as useless a safety measure to me as confiscating nail clippers from carry-on luggage in airports. Moreover, Janet refused to be penetrated by my dildos or more than one finger, she wouldn't kiss me if I'd bathed with any kind of scented soap or eaten meat, and she wouldn't do any of the things I needed to get off. Janet's cunt seemed like an impenetrable fortress: I'd eat her plastic-wrapped pussy until my jaw was sore, and she still hadn't come. She'd roll off of me without returning the favor, then cook me vegan tofu stir-fry for dinner. Janet refused to eat at my house, knowing that dirty animal flesh had once touched the pots in my kitchen. Her cunt looked like hairy meat under the slick latex square, and I'd fantasize that I was eating steak instead of her hirsute cleft.

The road to hell is paved with good intentions, and Janet was living proof. The proverbial mercy fuck from hell wound up being my masochistic punishment for picking up women at self-help groups. I promised myself I would never go back to the Dakini Center any night of the week—from now on, it would be strictly bars.

Months of involuntary celibacy finally wore me down, though, and I was so desperate to be fucked that I was willing to endure hours of whining if need be. Luck was with me. I stumbled into a woman's 12-step meeting by accident and decided to stay. Narcotics Anonymous beat the crap out of the regular lesbian support groups: tales of blow jobs for heroin, cocaine binges, marriages torn asunder by perversity. The scruffy and dejected women of NA exuded a raw, predatory sexuality I found oddly appealing. Karla was the token butch in the group, clad in parachute pants, combat boots, and a camouflage crop-top muscle shirt that exposed a tasty pair of blown biceps. She had a shaggy black rock star mullet that hung down over searing blue eyes and a hard, mannish face. I got wet listening to tales of dishonorable discharge from the military for lesbian sex and methamphetamine possession, stories recounted in a voice like a rusty razor blade. She had been clean and sober for two years now, and she drove a forklift in the receiving department of Home Depot. Karla wasn't anything like the other girls I'd dated, but I knew I wanted her from the moment I saw her. It took me three meetings to work up the courage to ask her to be my sponsor.

I went to Karla's apartment the next night. I wore my white-trash finest in the hopes of a tawdry hookup: mounds of cleavage courtesy of a push-up bra, gaudy crucifix jewelry bobbing on aforementioned cleavage, and fishnet tights under a little black dress. Karla served me dinner from Burger King. The savory animal grease wiped the taste of Janet's latex-covered cunt clean from my memory. Karla insisted we listen to a Metallica tape while we talked about our recovery. I'd fabricated a story about being a divorcée three months clean from a Valium addiction. Once we had exorcised our personal demons, Karla had slipped off my fuck-me pumps and tied me to her bed with my own fishnet stockings. She was very particular that I leave my dress on while we fucked but removed my panties and pushed my bra down to expose my nipples. I suppressed a giggle as Karla began squirting K-Y jelly all over a huge strap-on cock she'd been hiding under her baggy pants. The whole scene seemed unbearably absurd, but I stopped laughing once she eased the slippery dildo deep into my cunt and proceeded to fuck me. I moaned and growled as I felt months of sexual frustration released every time Karla's thick cock pushed against my G-spot. I slammed my hips against hers, starved for dyke cock, my wrists straining against their fishnet bonds as Karla rubbed her wet thumb on my clit while pinching and twisting my nipples above their dainty little bra shelves. The sensation was so intense that I came within a few minutes—I couldn't control it, the orgasm that ripped through my body left me feeling completely drained. Karla wasn't content to finish so quickly, though—she fucked me deep and slow for an hour straight until my pussy was swollen and sore. She had positioned her cock so it bumped against her clit with every thrust, and I felt her come against me time and time again as she fucked me.

This sort of behavior is known colloquially amongst friends of Bill W. as "The 13th Step," as in "Step 13: Fuck Another 12-Stepper." Karla pulled her drenched cock out of my cunt, untied my wrists, and gave me a quick kiss before reaching for her cigarettes. I had collapsed on the bed, feeling utterly ravaged and good. We didn't talk, Karla just laid beside me smoking cigarettes and absentmindedly flexing her abs, finally drifting into a deep sleep punctuated by loud snoring. I rested my head on Karla's buffed arm and pulled the covers over us before falling asleep.

I felt utterly, perfectly content in the company of this intimate stranger, despite a sense of inexplicable danger. I had crossed the line with Karla in more aspects that I could count: She wasn't my type, for starters. I had lied about my past, violated the trust of the 12-step group in the wettest possible way with an ex-junkie Army girl. But after forty hours a week of my bullshit office job, drowning my sexual frustration in late-night trips to the gym and sci-fi novels, Karla was the unpredictable variable I had been craving. I not only wanted to spend the night at her place, but maybe the next day too.

The next morning Karla cooked me a greasy southern breakfast with two fried eggs, a tangle of crispy bacon, hash browns, toast, and black coffee. She played a Jackyl tape while she cooked, cater-wauling along to "She Loves My Cock." Her house smelled like cigarette smoke and dog, even though she didn't have a dog. When I left for work, she grabbed my face with her strong hand and tongue fucked my mouth, burrowing two fingers into my panties to feel my cunt juicing from the kiss. She smacked my butt when I walked out the door and said, "I'll see you at the meeting." I was utterly infatuated and couldn't stop looking forward to see-ing her again.

I think one of the reasons I liked Karla was because she reminded me of my high school boyfriend, Dave Randell. Dave wore a leather jacket (that he let me borrow when it got cold, his muscled arms prickling with goose bumps) and carried a switchblade knife (for protection, natch). He smoked hash out of a Coke bottle, and called me "baby doll" and "angel face" without any sense of irony. My mom always hated him, and she forced me to break up with him when she caught him going down on me on our couch on a day that we'd ditched school to get stoned and fool around. Dave was admittedly a loser; he made out with other girls at parties, flunked all of his classes, didn't bathe often enough, and showed up to school with a black eye on a semi-regular basis, but I was completely in love with him. He had the sort of body that comes from skateboarding and hopping fences, and he kissed better than any boy I've met since. He insisted on going down on me every time we had sex, and he would offer to beat up anyone who messed with me, including teachers. He was dumb as a post, but beautiful and vital, appealingly dangerous and insane. Karla was

the kind of girlfriend I'd been secretly waiting for all these years—
a sober, older, dyke version of Dave Randell.

We met up at the meeting the next night, and Karla sat next to me
and held my hand the whole time. I felt vaguely uncomfortable
when I saw some of the housewife types staring and whispering,
but the hetero biker chick posse winked and gave me thumbs-up.
After the meeting, we got ice cream at Baskin-Robbins and saw a
late night movie. The movie was Karla's suggestion—my cunt was
so wet, all I could think about was going back to her place and
fucking again. It was clear that what I had intended to be a one-
night stand was taking an entirely different direction, and I didn't
mind. I was completely smitten.

We saw some inane Hollywood crapfest at the two-dollar theater,
the floor sticky like a porn house. The film was some action block-
buster that Karla loved. I ignored the movie for the most part,
concentrating instead on Karla's hand. Her fingers played circles
on my knee, my thigh, creeping ever closer to my panties, then
shying away. I squirmed in my seat, frustrated, trying to arch my
hips to meet her hand. She wouldn't give me what I wanted. I
reached over into her lap. I was curious to see if she was packing. I
suspected she was. She grabbed my hand, like a teenager caught
shoplifting, and pushed it deeper into her crotch, so I could feel
the throbbing length of her dick, the heat rising from her pussy.

Karla leaned over and breathed on my ear just a little, so the
fine hairs on the back of my neck stood up and sent an electric
current from my spine to my pussy. I was hoping she'd say something along the lines of "Let's blow this pop stand and fuck at my
place," but instead:

"I want you to suck me."

I was taken aback. It wasn't so much that I was averse to sucking dyke cock, but the thought of kneeling on the greasy floor of a

two-dollar theater with *Armageddon* showing in the background to deep-throat a rubber dick seemed sort of ridiculous and unsexy. And yet, it was totally like Karla.

Karla unzipped her pants and pulled her dick out, stroking it gently, making me hold it in my hand. "If you want to get fucked later, you got to suck now," she growled in her cigarette voice, rolling a cheap, unlubed rubber over her cock. I leaned over the theater seat for a tentative lick. Karla grabbed a handful of my hair, easing my head down, and I felt her shudder. She seemed more in touch with her dick than some men I'd known. When I felt her thick cock hit the back of my throat, my eyes watered, and I felt my pussy flood. *She'd better make good on her promise,* I thought to myself. Karla gradually eased me out of my seat so I knelt before her, the length of her dick buried deep in my throat, my nose to her pubes. She came when I sucked her—really came, tensing her buffed thighs beneath my palms, which impressed the fuck out of me. She was positively glowing when we left the theater, me feeling vaguely sheepish yet horny as she gripped my hand tightly.

Walking home, she pulled me into an alley and pinned me to the wall. I squirmed beneath her. "Come on, Karla, we're just a few blocks from your house. It's not safe here."

She kissed me hard, pinching and twisting my nipples through my dress. "Don't worry, baby," she said. "I've got a knife and I know how to use it." She really was the dyke incarnation of Dave Randell.

I gave up control. Karla told me to face the wall, with my dress pulled down over my tits and up over my ass. My palms flat against brick, legs spread, ass out, she pulled aside my panties, and her cock entered me like a knife into butter. I was so fucking wet, my panties chafed against my labia while she fucked me. Karla squeezed my tits from behind, her sharp teeth buried into my shoulder as she stroked inside me. I had purple bruises on my neck the next day. I was so spaced out at work, too distracted by the afterglow of fucking to pay attention to my various menial tasks. I'd be standing at the copy machine, imagining Karla had me bent over it, pulling my hair and fucking me up the ass, and my hands would start shaking. During my lunch break I wasn't hungry, so I smoked an entire package of cigarettes instead of eating—Karla's brand, trying to recapture her sex smell, ruled by my desire, wondering when I'd get to see her again.

I was laid off my job a week later, with no severance (turned out my boss had been reading the e-mails where I called him a "micromanaging cocksucker"). I had no savings, I didn't know how I was going to pay my eight-hundred-dollar rent. I went to the NA meeting and cried for the entire fucking hour, hysterical and spastic while sitting on Karla's lap. I felt like an asshole, taking up everyone's time when I wasn't even an addict in recovery.

After that night, Karla and I became inexplicably entwined. I was so fucking vulnerable after losing my job and my apartment, and Karla was incredibly generous with me. I moved into her place, vacuumed and burned incense so it didn't smell like dog anymore. Karla went to her forklift job every morning, and I stayed at home, halfheartedly looking for work and writing my novel on my laptop computer, which looked very expensive and out of place on Karla's kitchen table. Karla would come home and cook dinner, we'd eat, go to a meeting, come home, fuck, sleep, and start over again. It was a strangely stable, tremendously comfortable existence.

One of the best parts of living with Karla was eating the dinners she cooked for me, shaking the pan with one muscled arm while a cigarette dangled from her lip. Karla's excellent southern cooking lingers as a shimmering grease spot on my memory: oily waffles with melted butter and brown sugar syrup, delicately crispy fried chicken and beer-battered prawns smothered in tartar sauce, pork chops with caramel baked apples, biscuits and mashed potatoes drowning in sausage gravy. I quickly forgot about Janet's dry humping and vegan guilt trips. Dinner at Karla's was orgasmic bliss, the surfacing of all my repressed food fantasies.

Karla had kicked meth and heroin but refused to give up cigarettes, black coffee, and saturated fat. She could bench press her own body weight and had arms like a sailor, so it didn't matter that she ate six thousand calories every day. I preferred to spend my days reading books and writing on the computer and consequently gained thirty pounds in a short six months. The extra pounds went straight to my ass, thighs, and tits, and Karla would grab a handful of my puffy flesh, delighting in my new curves. When I bitched about my clothes being too small to fit anymore, Karla took me to Stormy Leather and blew her meager paycheck on a form-fitting leather dress, size "Extra Lusty." I begged her to return it but wound up getting it sweaty while having doggy style sex on Karla's couch to "Paradise City," my bobbing tits hanging out of the low-cut top.

(How you can tell a loved one was raised on redneck liquor-store porn: They prefer strategically placed bits of naughty flesh peeping out of trampy clothes to actual nudity. Karla liked it when I didn't wear panties, but she liked it better when I wore skimpy thongs that she could hold to one side while she fucked me.)

Life with Karla was good. But there was only one problem: the meetings. I only cruised self-help meetings for sex, never love or emotional support. Self-helpers, despite many well-intentioned hours of processing and sharing, tend to be completely emotionally unstable as a result of wallowing in their neurosis on a regular basis. There are those 12-step junkies you see at every meeting, so addicted to the drama that fills the hole that drugs or booze left behind. These people are alternately clingy and cold and are terrible at relationships. Karla was a rare exception. The program actually seemed to make her stronger. But it drove me insane. I told her after I moved in that I thought we should start going to separate meetings, and that I needed a sponsor I wasn't sleeping with. She agreed. To tell the truth, I would have been happy if I never had to attend another meeting ever, but I had to maintain the facade for her sake. I told her I attended a fictional Thursday night meeting in a neighboring city and that I had a sponsor named Janet. After becoming so deeply involved with Karla so quickly, I liked having time alone, time I didn't have to account for.

I began to look forward to Thursday nights. After dinner I'd kiss Karla goodbye and promise to be home by nine. I spent all week plotting how I'd spend those stolen few hours. I did all the things that Karla wouldn't have been interested in: foreign films at the art house movie theater, poetry slams at the local cultural center, live jazz, cocktails with friends at trendy bars (I always carried mouthwash and cologne to mask the scent of booze so Karla wouldn't be suspicious). I even went to the vegetarian restaurant I'd gone to with Janet once, almost daring myself to bump into her. As much as I loved Karla, part of me missed being able to talk art and politics with other people with college educations, people who listened to public radio instead of Black Sabbath.

Hoping to scratch my itch for increased intellectual stimulation, I got a job at a woman's bookstore in town. It didn't pay much, but it was a step toward reclaiming my independence. Even though Karla barely made enough to support both of us with her forklift job, she became jealous when she found out I'd be going to work again. She demanded I change my outfit on my first day of work—a plain skirt and a low-cut top.

"Handsome bulldaggers go into that store all the time," Karla had hissed. "How do I know one of them isn't going to steal you away from me? I may not read a lot of books, but I'm in love with you, and if anything were to happen . . ."

Karla's possessiveness irritated me. I started dressing sluttier on purpose, flirting with customers every chance I got. Sometimes I even went out with customers on Thursday nights, but I never slept with any of them—I owed at least that much to Karla.

I thought I had it all figured out, but my watertight plan got busted. Karla found out that I'd been slacking on my sobriety. She'd shown up at the Thursday night meeting to surprise me on our six-month anniversary, only to discover me missing in action. Not only was there an actual Thursday night meeting, but Janet attended it; and when Karla asked about me, Janet had told her everything. I hadn't known that Janet was a 12-stepper, but it made sense. She'd use any opportunity to whine and process and obsess that she could get her fucking hands on. Part of me resented her for contributing to my breakup with Karla, but in a weird way I was relieved.

Karla had come home that night and caught me drinking a beer. I still had the occasional drink when Karla wasn't around— after all, I wasn't the one with the problem. Karla was so pissed at me that she screamed and threatened to lock me out, saying she couldn't trust me. I couldn't bring myself to tell her the truth, so instead I apologized. Finally, she burst into tears and forgave me. We didn't have sex that night, but she fell asleep with her entire body so tightly wrapped around mine that I could barely breathe. I wanted to squirm free. The next day I started looking for a new job and an apartment of my own.

Karla had gone from being my lifeline to a guilty pleasure, a dozen Krispy Kremes with a use-by date stamped on the side of the box. I was addicted to the home-cooked meals and scorching sex, but I couldn't deal with any other aspect of our peculiar relationship. I knew it was time to call it quits when I kept getting yeast infections from her cheap dildos and the polyester lingerie she liked me to wear, refrains from Bon Jovi songs were constantly stuck in my head, and I couldn't see my feet from all the fried food I'd enjoyed. Something had to break.

The incident with the beer had given me a way out of the relationship. I took up drinking and was sloppy about it, leaving vodka bottles for her to find in the trash. I even considered leaving some syringes and burnt pieces of tin foil lying around the bathroom but decided that was too cruel. So I drank instead. I took up drinking not because I wanted to become an alcoholic, but because I knew Karla would so abhor my rejection of sobriety that she wouldn't be able to take it. Karla attempted to drag me back on the wagon, kicking and screaming, but I refused. So she dumped me and kicked me out of her place, and I moved into the apartment I had signed the lease on a week earlier. I couldn't help that my feelings for her had died. We had irreconcilable differences in class and morality. I hated that I had to hurt her feelings, but I didn't know any other way out.

I respect Karla's integrity. She gave 100 percent in our relationship, and I treated her like crap. I know I was the bastard in this situation, but I had to get out. I know she's probably at a meeting right now, bitching about her dysfunctional ex-girlfriend.

But she changed my life, and I can't stop thinking about her. I think about her when I drink Pabst Blue Ribbons to unwind after work. I think of her every time "You Give Love a Bad Name" comes on the radio. I think about her when I eat bland salads for lunch instead of bacon cheeseburgers, trying to lose the weight I gained from her cooking. But most of all, I think of her when I'm jerking off to issues of *Hustler* purchased from the gas station down the street, trying to resist calling her up for one last booty call at one A.M.

# The Nasty Kind
# Always Are

## Steve Almond

He was high in the air, Slade was, very high, the twenty-first floor, on a wraparound balcony overlooking the coast of Southern California. The people down below were quite small, lying around the pool in their sickly tans, soaking up the golden hour, and he was here, on the balcony, standing behind a woman named Gretchen. He had just spanked her on her round little ass.

Rather than wheeling about and smacking his face, though, rather than tearing up or fleeing, all she'd done, this little Gretchen, with her slender shoulders and her yoga posture, all she'd done was stiffen a bit in the calves and laugh huskily into her cell phone. "I've got to go," she murmured, then she laughed again.

They were going to have sex, probably more than once. Slade felt a surge of something close to elation. He hoped it, the sex, would be a little violent. Afterward, depending on the hour, he would call his ex-wife and his daughter and say the things he said to them and lie on his bed and let the comforting misery of the road reabsorb him.

He gazed down at the shore, the stalls of stoner merchants hawking their awful hemp hammocks, the waves heaving swirls of foam across the sand, the dripping red sun of August.

Gretchen flipped her phone shut.

"Was I naughty?" she said.

Slade smiled. "It's always good to set goals."

Gretchen smiled back at him. Her teeth were exceptional. He saw himself coming onto them, in powerful spurts, her lips webbed and smiling. It was a tawdry image, but it contained a measure of tenderness, a consent to bear the mess inside of him. Was she the sort who sought such things? They'd need more liquor to find out.

"I'm sorry," Slade said. "I have a problem with discipline."

Gretchen gave her ass a theatrical rub. "*You've* got a problem?"

He reached for the scotch on the table and poured them each another glass. She'd brought him the bottle, and he'd known from this alone she wanted more than conversation. It was such a lovely, horny thing to do, something you did at a certain age, when you knew the obstacles that stood in the way of a good rutting, all the lousy wisdom.

Gretchen took a sip and turned to show him her profile, against the low railing of the balcony. She was a classic L.A. type; the camera was never far from her mind. Slade wanted to ask her to turn around, so he could see her from behind again. She was wearing a pale cotton skirt and the sort of underwear that disappeared into the crack of her ass. He liked this idea: the crack of her ass. He liked how the words sounded, the soft, dirty music of them. He wanted to say them aloud.

Gretchen was talking about a new film, or property values, she kept switching and Slade couldn't keep it straight. He finished his drink and poured a bit more. He needed to ready himself for this transaction, to loosen up, to venture (with the help of drink) into the Country of Happiness.

He thought of happiness this way sometimes, as a place, with babbling brooks and honeysuckle, whatever that might be. This is what the Jews had done, after all. They had converted their desires into a distinct geography, a land of milk and honey, to be found and settled. The conceit was a useful one, given his line of work, which involved speaking to small groups of executives about the grave necessity of their own happiness.

Slade called himself a Mood Consultant. His ex called him the High Priest Headshrinker to the Neurotic Autocrat, which wasn't very nice at all. This was one of the few things he liked about his ex—she was refreshingly direct with her animus. She called him what he was: a bored sadist, a corporate Svengali. And so forth.

They had a daughter as well, Charlize, a storky fourteen-year-old who spent her waking hours trolling the Internet for celebrity gossip. He'd wanted to name her something else, something less gimmicky, but his wife had insisted and now they were stuck with it. Slade flashed, as he often did, to an image of Charlize Theron, the actress. He'd seen her tits once, sad starving little things. He hated his mind in a deep, permanent way.

Gretchen had turned back to him. Her speech was loopy and abrupt, with too many question marks. He couldn't make her age, though he supposed she was older than her body, beneath the scarf and sunglasses.

"It must be exciting?" Gretchen was saying. "Your job?"

"Not really."

"How does it work? What do you do, you know, exactly?"

"I take these CEOs," Slade said, "and I line them up against a wall and give them all cigarettes and blindfolds. Then I shoot them full of mercy."

"Bang-bang," Gretchen said.

Slade held up his drink. "Precisely."

He hoped she might leave it at that, but she really did want to know, or she wanted to appear someone who really wanted to know.

"These big money apes, they get themselves into a few set patterns, psychologically speaking: the Assumption of Grievance, the Idealization of Discontent, a few others. It's a way for them to perpetuate their suffering. All I do is make them aware of these patterns and offer some suggestions for defusing them."

"Why do they want to suffer?"

"That's really none of my business. It's a relationship they have with their past. I'm more concerned with their future."

Slade sighed. The conversation, the dispensation of his rap, was boring both him and his penis. He could feel the liquor warming to its task. He wanted to lick her right up the crack of her ass.

Gretchen asked about his fee.

"There's a great deal of dumb money out there," Slade said, "and all of it is looking for a home. Shall I get us more ice? I think we need more ice."

When he returned, Gretchen had stretched herself out on a chaise longue. She had a hand across her forehead, Grace Kelly style, and there were her breasts, all pushed against her freckled chest. He hoped they'd been surgically enhanced. He loved a good, fake tit, the obvious, inorganic heft of them, the abject distortion of the maternal.

"Would you like another drink, my dear?"

"*My dear,*" Gretchen said. "What are you, an aristocrat?"

"That's right," Slade said, pouring. "I am."

"Do you have a coat of arms?"

Slade could smell her body lotion. It made him think of her as a fruit with skin.

"I do indeed," he said.

Gretchen licked at a piece of ice. "What's it look like?"

"It has ravens on it, pecking at a corpse."

"Classy," Gretchen said. "Mine has a bottle of Percocet and a vibrator."

Slade laughed. It wasn't clear to him yet whether she was bluffing, or whether she had that strange knack for pleasure, the ability to withhold judgment on behalf of her physical needs. It was this possibility that he had dreamed of for most of his life. The very word—*nymphomaniac*—was still enough to stiffen him.

The sun was gone now; the purple smog of dusk was upon them. This was a summer evening in L.A., just the way they drew it up all those years ago. A breeze came rolling in and the street-lights began to come lit. The very thought of the city beyond his hotel exhausted him: the knotted freeways, the vast, flat valleys of porn, the hot distance of everything from everything else.

Gretchen shivered a little.

"Are you cold?"

She shrugged.

"We should go inside," he said. "We can get you something to eat. The raven here is supposed to be quite good. No? How about a burger?"

"I'm a vegetarian," Gretchen said.

"Well then, we can skip right to the big, juicy vibrator."

Inside, Gretchen sat on the loveseat, facing the flat-screen TV. She was on drink four now, to Slade's three. Her gestures were becoming expansive; her story was emerging. She had spent some years in Germany, dating a series of glamorous academics. She'd hoped to write a book with one of them, her mentor, but he'd gone back to his wife, so she returned to the States and took up with a born-again Christian. He wouldn't have sex with her until they married.

"You didn't take this as a bad sign?" Slade said.

"Just the opposite," Gretchen said. "I admired his commitment. It was hot, you know, this big hunk all committed to the

Lord. I developed this whole set of ideas. *Spiritual excuses,* my therapist called them. The problem was he didn't want to have sex after we were married, either."

"Not at all?"

"A few times."

"How long were you married?"

"Two years."

"Christ."

"That's what he used to say." Gretchen shook her head and stared at the sunset. She looked sad and lovely. Slade wanted to touch her throat.

"I used to get so fucking horny," she said wistfully.

"Of course," Slade said. "That must have been pretty disappointing."

"Try humiliating. Having to beg for it like that. Having to beg for that measly Christian cock of his. And all those pathetic church services. Have you ever read the book of Revelation? I swear to God, it's so fucking Dungeons and Dragons. What a bunch of goddamn phonies." She turned and glared at Slade. "I was promised a vibrator."

"That you were," Slade said. "But what I'd like to do, actually, I'd like to get you out of those clothes. Would you like that, my dear?"

"Quit saying that. It gives me the creeps. It's like you're my uncle or something."

"You don't like your uncle?"

"You're one sick fuck," Gretchen said slowly. She stood and gazed at him with a sudden glassy intensity. It was as if she were about to announce to him the depth of her sadness, the manner in which her life had become a series of failed encounters. Then her lips set themselves in a posture more like petulance. Slade watched the breeze toss strands of hair across her face, a plain face, which was descending into the shadows of darkness, and he thought, unpleasantly, of his daughter and the expression she had come to assume in his presence, which went beyond regret, into some harder category of truth. He didn't want his daughter here, in this room, with all the things they were about to do. It made him angry that she lived inside him, that she lay in wait, patiently, as he went about his mortifications. The liquor had done this to him, opened certain portals of distress. It was the risk one took.

Gretchen's eyes slipped from his, moved down his body (such as it was), and returned to the drunken flush of their circumstance. Then she unzipped her skirt and showed him what he'd been waiting for.

They all trimmed themselves down today, like the porn stars. In his youth, women hadn't thought to do more than a little pruning at the edges. To do more was considered suspect. The vagina remained, even in nakedness, something mysterious, veiled, pleasingly inconvenient: the coarse hairs that tickled the throat, the rash that pebbled the groin, the powerful funk of genuine muff. It was all gone today, shaved or waxed or singed off with chemicals, leaving the labial folds exposed, a kind of glistening origami. It still embarrassed Slade.

Not that this kept him from Gretchen. No. He recognized her nakedness as a volatile invitation. There was an awkward moment, as she stood trying to decide what to do next, and he came to her and placed his hand on the small of her back, as if they might dance. He murmured some words into her ear, about what he wanted to do.

"Really?" she said. "Is that so?"

"It is," he said.

"And you think that's safe?"

"Yes."

"You don't think anyone will get hurt?"

"No."

His hand had drifted down, and he let it settle between the

cheeks of her ass. The skin was warm and smooth. He could feel a mist of sweat begin to rise.

She was standing quite still, with her sturdy pale legs and her thin torso. Her eyes were closed. Slade wanted to taste the liquor on her tongue, but to do so called for an intimacy they hadn't yet established, so he began to kiss her neck instead.

"Take off that absurd contraption," he said, meaning her bra. She unclipped the thing and let it fall away. Her breasts began high on her chest, but they had fallen; there were red crescents beneath, left by the underwire. He wet his fingertips and played her nipples between them. Gretchen braced her legs and smiled shyly.

Slade stared at the streetlights below and thought about what his daughter would ask him, when they spoke later. She would call him *Daddy-o*, the term she used to soften him up. She knew he was in L.A., and she knew also that some of his clients were in the movie business. He had managed to secure, for her last birthday, a poster signed by the boy who played Harry Potter, and she had nearly wept upon receipt of this gift, though she had since sold it on eBay for a mid-three-figure sum because she now considered the actor, in her words, "a dweeb." She had moved on to one of the young men who starred in the Hobbit films—Slade had his name written down somewhere—and she had made it clear to him that she would die of shame if he failed to bring her something from this actor, preferably a limb, for her next birthday. This was how Charlize expressed herself. There was nothing upon which her life did not depend.

"The common term," his ex explained, "is adolescence."

Gretchen had set about undressing Slade.

Despite the drink, he would have liked more time to adjust himself to nudity. His body shamed him. Sure. Why not? He was forty-six, long done with the minor jockdom and muscle restoration projects of his thirties. Shaw, who handled his PR and exhib-

ited the polite social fascism of the modern faggot, called him
*skinny-fat*. It was a new term to Slade (they were all new terms),
and it meant that he looked thin enough, until he turned around,
at which point the small, stubborn mound of his belly appeared.
There was the body hair to consider, which Slade now, as
Gretchen knelt before him, declined to do.

She began to fuss with his belt. He took note of the dark roots
just starting to show along her part. The world and its relentless
artifice. What was he supposed to do? He closed his eyes. Silence
filled the room. He could hear the tinkling of the bracelet
Gretchen wore around her left ankle, and it made him think of
Isaiah, those women of unclean lips who wore timbrels on their
ankles. Long ago, Slade had considered a career in theology. He
couldn't convince himself on the question of God, though, and so
the books became merely the poetry of human struggle, a set of
powerful fables whose only convincing moral was that men were
driven by lust and anger, always had been, and required an invisible authority to manage the resulting chaos.

He shrugged out of his shirt and there were his shoulders: two
furry softballs. The hair on his chest had begun to go gray.

"You're just an old bear, aren't you?" Gretchen said.

He pawed at her face and she took hold of him, through his
slacks.

"The harder they come," she said.

"Let's hope so."

Now Slade was down below, doing his level best. The drink left
him a little dizzy. He could see the girl's chin, trembling a little,
and one of her hands kneading at her breasts, which he rather
liked. She had the taste of sex: sweat, salt, that fruity lotion, yeast,
his own spit, the sweet, bacterial tang of a well-soaped ass. He
wanted to establish her pleasure before he touched her there, so
he slipped his fingers inside. He had long ago ceased trying to di-

vine the mysterious insides of a woman. There were *spots* that felt good, warm, fleshy knobs, sudden pockets of air—he had no idea. He took his cues from the responses he drew, though most women refused to speak plainly about what pleased them, and when, and how. It was part of something larger, an inhibition about naming the acts of pleasure. They wanted an instinctual understanding.

He could see the same pattern in his daughter, a tendency to shy from outright declarations. She seemed to seek, from each interaction, the opportunity for complaint. The last time he visited, she spent most of dinner running to her computer to check e-mail. When Slade objected, Charlize was gleeful with indignation.

"I guess you don't care if my friend Sophie is practically suicidal!" she said.

"I care about having dinner with you."

"You don't care that some *slut* just gave her boyfriend head— on a bus!"

"That's enough," his ex said.

"What did you just say?" Slade turned to his ex: "Is this the way she talks now?"

"What?" Charlize said. "She *is* a slut."

"That's it," his ex said. "Your dinner is officially over."

"*Fine,*" Charlize said. She spread her napkin neatly across her plate. "I don't even like chicken anyway. It's full of hormones."

Slade had seen the next few hours rising before him, the fruitless talk, the silences, the hot cloud of grievance descending over the town house for which, at the behest of a lawyer he hoped to someday read about as the victim of a slow, gang-related decapitation, he paid 31 percent of his taxable income.

And now, in a hotel suite comfortably far from the loathsome valley of San Fernando, with the hot breath of summer curling in from the balcony, with his fingers squinching about deep inside a semi-employed tart of indeterminate age, his frustration got the best of him. He jabbed Gretchen sharply, such that the knuckle of

his middle finger came against her flesh with a damp thud. She
bucked a little and let out a sigh—a pleased sigh.

Slade did it again, then again. The girl was squeezing her nipple between two lacquered nails and biting her lower lip. He
curled his hand and wet his ring finger with spit and reached
down and tunneled into the warmth of her ass.

Gretchen growled. "Good! You fucking pervert. Like that!"

He did as he was told. He enjoyed the feel of the flesh between his fingers, the rubbery back-and-forth motion.

"And lick, you pervert. Lick!"

Which he did, also, with a quick, suctiony vehemence, right on
her swollen little bud, repeating to himself, in a childish, mental
chant: *See Dick lick.* Gretchen grabbed the back of his head and
pushed him down and he went at his business harder, his fingers
cramping with the effort, until felt her pussy begin to clinch and
her ass begin to loosen, and her breathing was deep and hysterical.

Her cheeks, against the mound of pillows, had the red sheen of
exertion. She sat up, a little woozy, and brought her face against
his.

"You want that cock sucked?"

"Relax," he said. "Take a nap."

"Say it," she said. "Say: suck my cock."

"There's no rush, my dear."

Gretchen snorted. "He's back again. Uncle Pervy."

Then she was moving down his body, her mouth nipping at the
rolls of flesh around his belly. Oh, that shameful belly! The woeful
bloat of those flavorless airport calories. He would die fat and un-
happy and confused, like Elvis. Gretchen circled around his cock.
It was soft, a bit frightened perhaps. Then she began to lick at him
and when this didn't have the desired effect, she sucked him right
off his belly and into her mouth. He could see her cheeks expand-
ing, as if she were taking a giant gulp of pasta. Down she went, all

the way down and back up again. She jiggled his balls. She sucked at the head so hard there was a pop when she released. She was breathing furiously, through her nose. Slade felt like a machine whose essential part had gone floppy. He thought of the phrase his ex had used the last time they'd tussled: *Viagra bait.*

He began to worry that Gretchen would write him off. But she had her own stake in the matter. She got up to fetch her purse and withdrew a small bottle of what he supposed was lotion. She applied a generous amount to her hands and began to stroke him. The smell of coconut filled the room and this combined with the scotch and the sex excited Slade. She licked just below the tip, where the skin gathered in a tender spot. Her tongue went from wide to thin as it curled around. She began to work in earnest, twisting one hand and swallowing absurdly, her lips glistening onto him.

He was just at the edge of that great, involuntary joy when Gretchen stopped. She dug into her purse and withdrew a small object—it looked like a tiny rubber pear—and squirted oil onto it. Then she began to suck him again and dragged the object down, then pressed it up, inside him. Slade let out a soft yelp. It was a lovely, vicious, unexpected act. She looked up at him, hair falling across her eyes. "You better *relax,*" she said, "or this is going to hurt." He did his best, but he could feel his muscles tightening.

"You're missing all the fun."

He didn't know what to do. He felt ashamed and excited. Then as she went deeper, he felt a twinge of something he could only describe as blinding. She read it in his body and pressed again and now both her hands and her mouth were establishing a fierce rhythm. Every time she touched that spot, he felt himself spasm. His face was covered in sweat and he was thrusting into her and she into him and all seemed right with the world: him, his life, his little fractured family (all of them trying so hard), and the girl, this lovely sucking girl and the summer night as it spread across L.A., out across the peaceful ocean, everything right, everything lovely, hopeful, forgiven, ecstatic, over and over and forever, the suck and the stroke and the girl's shiny mouth, which, as he opened his eyes, opened to receive him until the feeling was so exquisite his body jackknifed.

Her face appeared in front of his; she was dripping from her chin. "See now? I know you weren't just another uptight corporate asshole."

He laughed and thanked her.

For a few minutes they lay caressing each other. It was a strange thing, the chemistry of intimacy.

"What's this?" she said, touching at a yellowed bruise on his shin.

Slade grunted.

"A war injury? Did you shoot an Iraqi?"

"Racketball, actually."

"Against an Iraqi?"

"No, a lawyer."

"What happened?"

"I swung for his head and whacked myself instead. Self-inflicted."

"The nasty kind always are."


They could have gone to dinner, but he didn't want to go to dinner. He didn't want to order room service, either. He wanted to take an Ambien and sleep for ten hours. He felt wrung out, pleasantly so, tired of the pressures put upon him by his own bad conduct, and his bum was a little sore. But Gretchen was restless. The sex had revved her up. She flung her legs over his belly and began telling the story of her wedding, the ridiculous vows she'd had to repeat and the dress, which included a bodice. It was supposed to be absurd and funny, but there was too much bitterness in her tone. She seemed to be asking, beneath her declamations, how she had wound up there, what alloy of optimism and loneliness had landed her in the presence of a mother-in-law who spoke in tongues. Slade thought: *It is the job of the world to make its sorrow known.*

He pretended to doze off, but Gretchen began to mess with his cock again.

"Come on now," she whispered. "Let's make a little history." Her breath smelled of old scotch. He could feel the small hot weight of her across his thighs.

He got up on his elbows and nudged her off, a little roughly.

"Hey," she said.

"I've got to go to the bathroom."

"You don't have to be an asshole about it."

Slade slipped into the bathroom. The place was clean and expansive. The fixtures were first-rate. But Slade couldn't relax. He wasn't alone. He stood before the mirror and considered his mean bald fat self. He'd caught Charlize doing the same thing recently, staring at herself with indulgent contempt.

He flushed and walked back into the room. Gretchen was out on the balcony, staring over the railing, smoking a menthol cigarette. She was naked and a soft light from above emphasized the roundness of her from behind, the dimples just where her ass divided, the backs of her knees. Slade moved toward her, with his dumb sausage of a cock swinging gently. He pressed against her.

"Well, well," she said.

"What are you looking at?" he said.

"The streets," she said. "They look so orderly from up here."

"That's the idea."

There they were—Sunset, Rodeo, Wilshire—the city's official personality, trimmed in taillights.

Gretchen flicked her cigarette over the railing and began rubbing herself against him and took a sip of the tumbler she'd fixed herself. She drank with the casual determination of a well-managed alcoholic.

Slade wet his fingers and began touching her ass.

"You going to make something happen?" she said slowly. "You got enough left? Because I really don't think you can hurt me, old man."

She told him to get the oil and he did so and she used that to make sure he was hard again and slippery and then she turned around and braced herself against the railing and he slipped inside. He wanted to go slowly, to make the thing last, but she was pushing back against him.

"Slow," he said.

"No, go! Harder!"

He did as he was told, with a gleeful malice, until the damp smacks echoed. He looked down and the sight was perfect, just perfect. Happiness was filling him again, pushing out all the rest of the noise. Gretchen was breathing hard, taking him inside with her little XXX grunts, her back starting to glow with sweat. He leaned down to whisper into her ear. It was this way for several minutes, until Slade felt himself getting sore and slowed down.

Gretchen looked at him over her shoulder.

"Well?" she said.

"Well what?"

"Ginny said you were all done sexually. Don't you want to prove her wrong?"

"Ginny?" he said.

Slade remembered, with a start, that Gretchen knew his ex-wife. They had worked at the same ad agency years ago. Gretchen had been her assistant, a coked-up little sophomore on sabbatical from USC. He'd assumed she contacted him because he'd done some work with her old company. But he could see now that it was his wife who had engineered the rendezvous. This made her, the girl, what—an offering, some kind of spy? It was typical of his ex, a way to keep his erotic life linked to the failures of his past.

"What?" Gretchen said. "I'm not going to say anything to her."

A summer storm was nudging over the Hollywood Hills, releasing threads of heat lightning along the ridges.

"Too bad," Gretchen said. She could feel him softening. "You're not going to hurt me after all." Her tone was full of pity.

Slade was outraged. He slammed into her and she let out a shriek. He did it again. He took a handful of her hair and yanked at it, for good measure, and she reached back and sunk her nails into his thigh. "Is that as hard as you can go?"

Slade continued to pound into her. His thighs were burning with the effort. But she seemed merely amused by his punishments, smirking, which made him even angrier.

"You think that hurts?" Gretchen was gritting her teeth. "You think that little ass hurts, Daddy-o?"

"Don't call me that," Slade said.

"Why not? You don't like that? You don't like that, Daddy-o?"

Slade took hold of her throat and squeezed.

Gretchen sputtered out a laugh. Her voice was thin and choked, like an old man. "You think that's going to do anything, Daddy-o? You can't hurt me."

He was looking down at Gretchen, watching her cheeks begin to flush, and he had the most terrible thought then, of his child being born, her face a tiny contortion of anguish. He wanted not to think of her, not as a baby, not as a budding teenager, who was no doubt half naked on this summer night, coiled in some room, waiting for the world of men, their vanity, their brief needs, their cocks and rough hands.

Gretchen managed to twist away from his grip and she bit down on the tip of his thumb. He felt her teeth come sharply against the bone. Then blood was dripping onto her chin and onto the balcony tile, and he didn't know whose it was—his, hers—but he knew he was going to come, hard enough to kill her he hoped, and this allowed him to ignore the hot, raw feeling down below, the sounds of the girl gulping and crying, her forehead banging now against the edge of the railing. He continued to slam into her, murmuring, "Is that *hard* enough? Is that *hard* enough?" until he reached that undeniable state, helpless with the sensation, and she, the girl, wriggled free of him at last, let her weight go dead and dropped away. Slade was still thrusting, bracing his feet, launching himself forward in a blind rage, such that he hit the railing and tumbled over instantly, falling through the warm night air of Los Angeles, naked, alone, a man coming, going, about to be dead and howling for his daughter.

# Contributors

**Steve Almond** is the author of *My Life in Heavy Metal, Candy-freak,* and *The Evil B.B. Chow and Other Stories.* For an executive summary of his other perversions, check out www .stevenalmond.com.

**L. Elise Bland** is a southern dominatrix living in Texas. Formerly a French and Italian instructor, she now teaches classes on erotic topics, including stripping, BDSM basics, and role play. In her spare time, she practices the art of Middle Eastern dance and indulges in exotic European cheeses and wines.

**Rachel Kramer Bussel** is senior editor at *Penthouse Variations,* a contributing editor at *Penthouse,* and a *Village Voice* sex columnist. Her books include *Up All Night: Adventures in Lesbian Sex* and *Naughty Spanking Stories from A to Z.* Rachel's erotica is published in more than sixty anthologies, including *Best American*

*Erotica 2004* and *Best Lesbian Erotica.* Her passions include sex, comedy, and cupcakes. Visit her at www.rachelkramerbussel.com.

**Maxine Chernoff** is the author of seven books of poetry and six books of fiction. One of her short-story collections, *Signs of Devotion,* was a *New York Times* Notable Book of 1993. Chair of the Creative Writing Program at San Francisco State University, she coedits the literary journal *NewAmerican Writing* with her husband, the poet Paul Hoover. They have three children and live in Northern California.

**Sidney Durham** lives in the high desert of northern Arizona, where he intends to stay. His work has been published in a number of places, including *Clean Sheets, Blue Food,* Maxim Jakubowski's *Mammoth* series, and *Moist,* a Canadian erotic quarterly. His website is www.sidneydurham.com.

**Stephen Elliott** is the author of *Happy Baby, Looking Forward to It, A Life Without Consequences, Jones Inn,* and *What It Means to Love You,* as well as the editor of an anthology of thirty original stories, called *Politically Inspired.* He attended the University of Illinois and Northwestern University, and received a Stegner Fellowship at Stanford University. Stephen regularly writes a Poker Report for McSweeney's.com. He lives in San Francisco, and is working on *Politically Inspired 2.*

**Lynn Freed** is the author of five novels and the inaugural recipient of the Katherine Anne Porter Award from the American Academy of Arts and Letters. She lives in Northern California.

**Sera Gamble** is a screen and television writer living in Los Angeles. Her work has been featured in *Washington Square, Suitcase: A Journal of Transcultural Traffic, Westwinds,* and *Caffeine.* She was a writer finalist on HBO's *Project Greenlight*. She enjoys singing in traffic and dancing her ass off.

**Will Heinrich** is a New York–born poet and novelist who won a PEN/Robert Bingham Fellowship in 2004. His most recent novel is *The King's Evil*.

**Bianca James** is a femme faguette caught halfway between San Francisco and Japan. Her stories have appeared in numerous anthologies and magazines and on numerous websites. Her first novel, *Star of Persia: A Post-Queer Love Story*, was a finalist in the 2004 Project QueerLit Competition. She can be reached at starof persia@gmail.com.

**Gwen Masters** has written hundreds of erotic tales for dozens of publications, including *Foreign Affairs: Erotic Travel Tales* and *Naughty Stories from A to Z*. Her latest novel, *Better Judgment*, met with wide critical acclaim. A guitar lover and classic car enthusiast, Gwen works and plays in the shadow of Nashville's Music Row. To learn more, visit her website at www.gwen masters.net.

**Peggy Munson**'s first novel, *Origami Striptease*, is the winner of the Project QueerLit contest this year. She is the most-published writer in *The Best Lesbian Erotica* series, and her work has also appeared in *Best American Poetry 2003, On Our Backs, Best Bisexual Erotica II, Genderqueer, Tough Girls, Blithe House Quarterly, Lodestar Quarterly*, and *Margin*. To learn more, visit www.peggymunson.com.

**Carol Queen** is a writer, speaker, educator, and activist with a doctorate in sexology. She founded one of the first gay youth groups in the United States, and became active in the emerging international bisexual community, as a sex worker and a practitioner of alternative sexualities. She is the author of the award-winning *The Leather Daddy and the Femme, Real Live Nude Girl: Chronicles of Sex-Positive Culture,* and *Exhibitionism for the Shy.* Queen is also the editor of *Five Minute Erotica,* and coeditor of *Best Bisexual Erotica Volume 2, Best Bisexual Erotica, Sex Spoken Here, PoMoSexuals: Challenging Assumptions About Gender and Sexuality,* and *Switch Hitters: Lesbians Write Gay Male Erotica and Gay Men Write Lesbian Erotica.* Her newest book is called *Sex Index,* and you can find out more at www.carolqueen.com.

**Tom Perrotta** is the author of several works of fiction, including *Joe College* and *Election,* which was made into the acclaimed movie starring Reese Witherspoon and Matthew Broderick. He lives with his wife and two children in Belmont, Massachusetts.

**David Sedaris** is one of NPR's most popular and humorous commentators whose original radio pieces can often be heard on *This American Life.* He is the author of the bestsellers *Barrel Fever, Holidays on Ice, Naked, Me Talk Pretty One Day,* and *Dress Your Family in Corduroy and Denim.* He is a recipient of the Thurber Prize for American Humor, has been nominated for two Grammy Awards, and was named by *Time* as "Humorist of the Year." He most recently edited *Children Playing Before a Statue of Hercules: An Anthology of Outstanding Stories.*

**Mr. Sleep** is the working name of Mr. Vinnie Rose, panjandrum of Mack Avenue Skullgame, www.skullgame.com, and a damned handsome guy to boot.

**Donna George Storey** has taught English in Japan and Japanese in the United States. Her fiction has appeared in *The Gettysburg Re-*

*view,* AGNI.com, *Clean Sheets, Scarlet Letters, Taboo: Forbidden Fantasies for Couples, Best Women's Erotica 2005,* and *Mammoth Book of Best New Erotica 4.* A story published in *Prairie Schooner* received special mention in *Pushcart Prize Stories 2004.* Visit her at www.DonnaGeorgeStorey.com.

**John Updike** was born in 1932, in Shillington, Pennsylvania. From 1955 to 1957 he was a staff member of *The New Yorker,* and since 1957 has lived in Massachusetts. He is the father of four children and the author of more than fifty books, including collections of short stories, poems, and criticism. His novels have won the Pulitzer Prize, the National Book Award, the American Book Award, the National Book Critics' Circle Award, the Rosenthal Award, and the Howells Medal.

**Bob Vickery** has five short-story collections out, including *Play Buddies* and his recently released audiobook, *Manjack.* Bob is a regular contributor to *Men* and *Freshmen* magazines, and his stories have appeared over the years in numerous anthologies, magazines, and webzines. Bob lives in San Francisco, and can most often be found in his neighborhood Haight Ashbury café, pounding out the smut on his laptop. Anyone interested in finding out more about Bob's writings can visit his website at www.bobvickery.com.

**Kweli Walker** is the author of *Walkin' Pussy,* a collection of her erotic short stories. She is also a Journeywoman electrician who simply loves to read and write. Born and raised in South Central Los Angeles, Kweli attended California State University at Northridge, majoring in African-American studies and biology, and Loyola University, majoring in fine art. *At the End of Silence* is the next of her four upcoming erotic novels. Visit her at walkinpussy.com.

**Helen Walsh** was born in Warrington, England, in 1977 and moved to Barcelona at the age of sixteen. She works with socially excluded teenagers in north Liverpool and is writing her second novel.

**Salome Wilde** channels her midlife crisis into publishing erotica, including her series on the sex lives of inanimate objects and a forthcoming BDSM novel. She is cofounder of KLLIT (Kinky Literature Lovers in Tennessee), a writers' group she thanks for inspiring "Granny Pearls," especially cofounder Kate Kinsey. Visit her at www.salomewilde.com.

**James Williams** is the author of . . . *But I Know What You Want*. His fiction has appeared widely in print and online publications and anthologies, including *Best American Erotica of 1995, 2001, and 2003; Best Gay Erotica 2002, 2004,* and *2005;* and *Best SM Erotica* and *Best SM Erotica 2.* He made his nonfiction debut with "The Mother and Child Reunion" in *Walking Higher: Gay Men Write About the Deaths of Their Mothers.* He was the subject of profile interviews in *Different Loving* and *Sex: An Oral History,* by Harry Maurer. He can be found at www.jaswilliams.com.

**Gaea Yudron** is the author of the best-selling book *Growing and Using the Healing Herbs,* and of the chapbook *Words Themselves Are Medicine.* Her poetry appears in *Raising Our Voices: An Anthology of Oregon Poets Against the War,* and the journals *For Now, The Little Magazine, East West, North Country Star, Hanging Loose, Evergreen Review, Provincetown Review,* and *Kuksu.* She has a vivid interest in bringing the mythic and sacred dimension of sound, poetry, and language to life, and has lived in Ashland, Oregon, for the past thirty years.

# Credits

"Fifteen Minutes," by Gwen Masters, copyright © 2004 Gwen Masters, first appeared in Ruthie's Club, published by RuthiesClub.com, January 2005, and is reprinted by permission of the author.

"Fairgrounds," by Peggy Munson, copyright © 2004 Peggy Munson, first appeared in *Best Lesbian Erotica 2005,* edited by Tristan Taormino and Felice Newman, published by Cleis Press, 2004, and is reprinted by permission of the author.

An excerpt from *Little Children: A Novel,* by Tom Perrotta, copyright © 2004 Tom Perrotta, first appeared in *Little Children: A Novel,* published by St. Martin's Press, 2004, and is reprinted by permission of the publisher.

"Grifter," by Carol Queen, copyright © 2004 Carol Queen, first appeared in *Master/Slave,* edited by N. T. Morley, published by Venus Book Club, 2004, and is reprinted by permission of the author.

"Beatings R Me," by Mr. Sleep, copyright © 2004 Mr. Sleep, first appeared in *Paying for It,* edited by Greta Christina, published by Greenery Press, 2004, and is reprinted by permission of the author.

"Full House," by David Sedaris, copyright © 2004 David Sedaris, first appeared in *Dress Your Family in Corduroy and Denim,* published by Little, Brown, and Company, 2004, and is reprinted by permission of the publisher.

"Ukiyo," by Donna George Storey, copyright © 2004 Donna George Storey, first appeared in *Foreign Affairs: Erotic Travel*

# Reader Survey

*Please return this survey, or any other BAE correspondence, to: Susie Bright, BAE-Feedback, P.O. Box 8377, Santa Cruz, CA 95061. Or email your reply to: BAE@susiebright.com.*

1. What are your favorite stories in this year's collection?

2. Have you read previous years' editions of *The Best American Erotica*?

3. Do you have any favorite stories or authors from those previous collections?

4. Do you have any recommendations for next year's *The Best American Erotica 2007*? Nominated stories must have been published in North America, in any form—book, periodical, Internet—between March 1, 2005, and March 1, 2006.

5. How old are you?

6. Male or female?

7. Where do you live?

8. Any other suggestions for the series?

Thanks so much, your comments are truly appreciated. If you send me your e-mail address, I will reply to you when I receive your feedback.

# Read the entire collection of
## Susie Bright's groundbreaking
# EROTICA SERIES

0-7432-5850-9

0-7432-2262-8

0-7432-2261-X

0-684-86915-2

0-684-86914-4

0-684-84396-X

0-684-84395-1

0-684-81823-X

0-684-81830-2

0-684-80163-9

Look for these hot reads from
# SUSIE BRIGHT

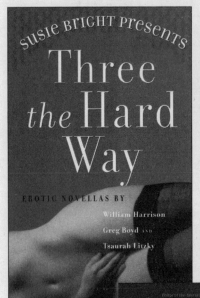

SUSIE BRIGHT presents
## Three
## *the* Hard
## Way

EROTIC NOVELLAS BY

William Harrison

Greg Boyd AND

Tsaurah Litzky

0-7432-4549-0

susie bright presents

## Three Kinds *of* Asking *for* It

Erotic Novellas by

Jill Soloway
Greta Christina
Eric Albert

0-7432-4550-4

SUSIE BRIGHT

## How to Write a Dirty Story

Reading, Writing, and Publishing erotica

"Every would-be and burgeoning author should read this." —Laura Miller, Salon

0-7432-2623-2

TOUCHSTONE
A Division of Simon & Schuster
A VIACOM COMPANY
www.simonsays.com